T0063472

BASUSU

An African's Quest of Hope, Courage, and Triumph

GEORGE S. PEART

iUniverse LLC
Bloomington

BASUSU
AN AFRICAN'S QUEST OF HOPE, COURAGE, AND TRIUMPH

iUniverse books may be ordered through booksellers or by contacting:

iUniverse LLC
1663 Liberty Drive
Bloomington, IN 47403
www.iuniverse.com
1-800-Authors (1-800-288-4677)

ISBN: 978-1-4917-0413-4 (sc)
ISBN: 978-1-4917-0414-1 (hc)
ISBN: 978-1-4917-0415-8 (e)

Library of Congress Control Number: 2013915164

Printed in the United States of America.

iUniverse rev. date: 11/8/2013

Dedication

This book is dedicated to my parents, Felix and Birdie Peart, who did not survive to see the publication but whose spirit has enabled me to continue during tough times.

Basusu is a celebration of the power of hope, faith, and a strong desire. He represents the hope and aspiration of all those who strive for a better future despite chains of every kind. The book *Basusu* is part of one of a series; in the near future, you may look forward to other volumes in the series.

There are many friends and associates without whom this book would doubtless never have come to publication.

I am deeply indebted to Dr. Trevor Grizzle, Dr. Leonard Lovett, Joe Luciano, Selena Owens, and many other friends who encouraged me to continue during the dry seasons.

Contents

Foreword

Most of us cherish a good story. Storytelling is an ancient art unbounded by culture, time, or geography. People of all ages are irresistibly enticed by its stylistic charm and held enthralled by its timeless simplicity, relevance, and mesmeric eloquence. There are many stories, but too few good storytellers. This is not the case with George Peart, who shares his gift of storytelling with the reader in his debut novel, Basusu. His use of language is the vehicle that lures the reader on a journey with him as he artfully sketches the moving panorama and vividly describes the terrain of the land of beginnings.

Born in Clarks Town, Trelawny, Jamaica, the author emigrated from his place of birth to England in 1960, where he attended Fircroft College in Selly Oak, Birmingham, where he studied the social sciences and Cliff College in Sheffield. Later, Lee University, Cleveland, Tennessee where did a BA in Sociology and later a MA in Sociology at Middle Tennessee State University. George Peart is a gifted communicator who has charmed audience in many countries of the world.

George Peart, who has lived in England, Canada, and the USA, and therefore brings a rich cross-cultural flavor to his work and has exhibited a mark of his genius in that along with his busy schedule he is able channel his mental and physical energies into a gripping and intriguing literary work of art such as Basusu.

The sun has slipped behind the distant horizon. Its last lingering rays have left a luminous spray of a gold and crimson glow laced with a solemn gray on the evening sky. Mother Nature slowly and gently unfurls her giant nightly tent across the landscape and safely tucks her children into bed. Though a superstitious people, the villagers seem to pay no attention to the vanishing asymmetrical profile of a tiger sketched in the sky—an evil omen of things to come. (George Peart's narrative descriptions are captivating as he weaves his story into a moving literary tapestry.)

A soft breeze whispers in the trees. Stars, recessed in the sockets of an ebony sky, shine gleefully like coruscating diamonds against a velvet backdrop. The primeval moonlight floods the earth with its silvery light, creating a romantic mood for a night that is alive with the sounds of nature's nocturnes. The intermittent shrill and ghostly baying of wolves in the surrounding hills strike a discordant, chilling, and ominous note that echoes throughout neighboring villages—a common nightly dramatic display.

It is close to midnight, March 20, 1841. The village is draped in darkness. The village is sound asleep—but not everyone! White men, who earlier in the day had staked out the village, pretending to be explorers, will now spring their deadly trap. Like a tiger from a thicket, they spring from behind the trees, where they were hiding, and pounce upon the village with savage fury. Ignoring the barking of neighborhood dogs and assisted by native Ghanians, they begin to torch the village, strategically starting at the circumference and working to the center.

Panicked, bewildered villagers hastily fumble toward an exit as bellowing flames leap from one thatched roof to the next. Shrieks of terror ripple throughout the village, rising in deafening and frenzied crescendo. Many, unable to escape, become human torches that blaze like tinderboxes. The scene is more than pandemonium; it is hell magnified a thousand times.

The conflagration, visible for miles around, sends animals, wild and domesticated, scurrying for safety. Dozens of young, strapping men—the cream and promise of the village—are kidnapped and manacled with chains, among them Basusu Mensua. Chains hanging from his hands and feet, Basusu, with terror-stricken eyes, gazes quizzically then pleadingly at his captors, then helplessly on the vast emptiness of a bleak and uncertain future. His fate is sealed. He feels it. Defiant though he is, he cannot throw off his chains, nor can he parry off his captors. Like many other of his countrymen, he must endure the humiliating blush of shame and wend his way through meandering forest paths till he reaches a waiting slave ship, where in the dark, disease-infected hold, he will spend months till (if fate is on his side) he lands on a plantation in the New World.

It was not the enticing beauty of the land or the pristine purity of its rivers; it was not its manganese or abundant rubber—but its gold—that initially enchanted them. As though attracted to a magnet, they were irresistibly drawn to the Gold Coast—German, Dutch, Danish, Swede, and English adventurers—all in search of gold. Tirelessly and incessantly, giant ships, like armadas poised for battle, plied angry seas from Europe to West Africa in search of wealth and fortune. Laden with the precious cargo—gold—they returned to enrich and enlarge the fortunes of their countries, kings, princes, and magnates.

But something of far greater value fueled the greed of these Europeans. As early as 1500, the Portuguese had found the slave trade to be profitable business. Many hungrier sharks soon weighed in for even more vicious attacks. By the time of the abolition in 1809, the slave trade had robbed the Gold Coast of over six million young men. Intense rivalry developed in the seventeenth century, and within a hundred years forts, like huge sentinels, dotted the coastline. Britain's mastery ultimately prevailed, and in 1874 the Gold Coast—which would be renamed Ghana in 1957—was firmly in its colonizing grip.

Fate smiles on Basusu. He lands on St. Simons Island in the New World with a fellow villager, Kwasi, and they will work together on the Jordan Plantation. Here he must cultivate the seed of a new future, create his own family, and forge a new destiny with the hand history has dealt him. How will it all turn out? Journey with Basusu and find out. Such is the genius of George Peart in the first of this groundbreaking series. There are many good stories in the world. In Basasu, this author stands equal to the task as a good storyteller. There is much more to come.

Trevor L. Grizzle, Ph.D.

PART 1

ODU, GHANA—1841

CHAPTER 1

The Village

At the base of the Ashanti region, about 160 miles from Accra, the small village of Odu could be sighted. Beginning at Elmina, Cape Coast, the winding dirt road passed through the central region, which was well known for its agriculture and gold mining and where gold was one of the region's most precious commodities. The golden path then snaked along to the Ashanti region, rich in history and legend.

Odu was similar to a variety of other small villages with their thatched-roof huts constructed of wood and straw, then hardened with clay. This method of building was strong enough to withstand the unstable weather that often came without warning.

From a distance, one would think the cluster of thatched-roof homes was a colony of makeshift pyramids; but up close, lush vegetation and fruit trees of many varieties could be spotted. A closer look revealed rich soil growing yams, plantains, cassava, maize, groundnuts, millet, corn, and other vegetables common to the region. In the distance, a fresh spring gently hummed—the source of water for everything there. The natural vegetation in the region depended mainly on the amount of rainfall and the length of the dry season.

A little farther in the distance, horses swung their tails gaily as they shared the field of grass with other livestock. Ears twitched warningly as a colony of cows and a number of donkeys lay in the cool shade of the brushes that were too high to reach, lazily chewing their cud. Bony-legged colts and bleating calves, which were no less spirited than the naked children playing in the field close by, joined in competitive play. Songs rose from the fields where parents were gathering food. A happier scene can hardly be imagined. It could only be equal to a painting of happy, smiling faces, bathed in joy and sunlight as they sang a song about the day of the week one was born.

Obiara a yewono Dwoada sore na sa
La la la la la la la la
La la la la la la la la
La la la la
Obiara a yewono Benada sore na sa
Obiara a yewono Wukuada sore na sa
Obiara a yewono Yawoada sore na sa
Obiara a yewono Efiada sore na sa
Obiara a yewono Memeneda sore na sa
Obiara a yewono Kwesiada sore na sa
Translation
Whoever is born on Monday, get up and dance
Whoever is born on Tuesday, get up and dance . . .
La la la

Children's laughter rose toward the heavens as they clasped hands and swung each other back and forth in a merry circle. A dark girl with beads tinkling from her hair ran around and around on the inside of the formed circle, laughing with playful fright and dodging the older girl who wove between the swinging arms after her. The chant finished, and the fleeing girl collapsed on the floor before separating two hands and joining the chant. Thus, on went the game.

Chatting in their native language, young mothers corporately planned the management of their family's daily supply of food, while streams of smoke lazily made their way up toward the sky before disappearing into oblivion. The smoke kept flies and insects at bay, and the meat that sat out was left unbothered by the irritating pests. Older women could be seen bent over a fire, some carefully stoking at the smoldering brush.

On the west end of this small remote village lived the Mensua (Men-sah) family. As members of Akan culture, the Mensua family had lived in this small village for several generations. Their ancestors, stemming from the heart of the Ashanti region, fought centuries ago to defeat the British.

Next to the Mensuas' hut lived the village priest and the medicine man. The village had many huts, but prominent among them was the large and long hay-framed buildings in which all the social activities and worship rituals took place. Late in the afternoon, in the shade of the buildings, a gentle murmur or occasional outburst of excitement arose from a group of men who were playing a game resembling Scrabble.

The elders of the village could be easily spotted, their white beards giving adequate evidence of their mature years and established position in the village. As was their custom, they gathered on a regular basis to dispute tribal issues, each arguing his own point of view with class and dignity, yet honoring the opinion of the others. It was not uncommon for them to debate some simple matter of common interest for hours nonstop. And listening from a distance, one might think from the tone of their voices that a civil war was about to begin.

Every now and then, inquisitive children purposely wandered into the common hall where the men were debating. Eventually, one of the elders would grab a long, thin stick and chase them off to ensure their privacy. But before long, these innocent little individuals would come creeping around the gazebo-like hall and peek their heads through holes in the thatch where each elder was situated on his rug in a circular fashion.

At the farthest end sat the chief, who listened more than spoke and kept the order. He was the one who gave the final word at every discussion. It wouldn't be long before the children would tire of their standing position and resort to the floor, where they would draw their knees to their chest, rest their chin in the crook of their elbows, and observe.

But this moment never ceased to be short-lived, for one of the elders would rise with the dreaded switch, and the children would flee.

There was one lean dark boy in particular who could be counted on to be present at every meeting—Basusu Mensua. His interest never ceased to be piqued by the elders' relentless debates, and at moments he wished to declare *his* solution but knew it was not to be so. He was the fastest runner and had yet to be switched.

"Basusu, if you come here again, you will know how this switch feels," his grandfather would threaten in his native language. Basusu would scramble up from the ground and take off laughing. Grandpa had told him that same line a thousand times. He knew that after catching him, he would receive no more than a playful swat on his backside or a sharp rebuke from his grandfather.

Basusu's grandfather, Chief Mensua, was a quiet but strong man, tall with broad shoulders and large hazel eyes hidden behind thick eyebrows. His eyes were clear and discerning. A salt-and-pepper goatee set him apart as one of great distinction. Since he was a quiet man, many times it was difficult to tell exactly what he was thinking. His eyes were hard to read, his words few, but when he spoke, there was no mistaking who he was. Possessing an authoritative air about him, denoted partly by his height but mostly by his wisdom, Chief Mensua was a conscientious leader of the Ashanti tribe, a tribe known for its strength and audacity. In battle, they were fearless; and of such a trademark they were proud.

Chief Mensua's hut flanked the village in such a way that in order to get into the village, one must enter through him and receive his blessings. No one dared to confront his authority or challenge his position. To be chief was something that must be earned, and Mensua proudly followed the tradition of his father and grandfather, proving himself worthy.

Mensua's position as chief granted him many wives, ranging in ages from early twenties to late fifties; and as a result, he fathered many children. Several years ago, his firstborn son and favorite wife had passed away. Many of his other sons who were eligible for the office of tribal leader had also died, some from disease, others in battle. This was a society in which men gained respect by bravery.

From his third wife was born a son. Birthed at sunrise on a Saturday morning, Chief Mensua decided on first sight "If this one survives, he shall stand in my place." Therefore, this son was named Addae Kwami, meaning "sunrise on Saturday." As he matured, Addae Kwami became tall and strong like his father and possessed a brave spirit. A single glance, and one could not deny the fact that a chief was in the making.

Addae, as everyone called him, was now thirty-five years old and had obtained all the training necessary to be chief should his father pass away. He too had many wives and fathered many children, among them young Basusu.

No more than a casual observation of Basusu would attest to the fact that Mensua blood ran in his veins. If one knew his father and grandfather but had not met Basusu himself, there was still no mistaking him for anyone else. He too was tall and broad shouldered with the same piercing hazel eyes Chief Mensua possessed; yet being only thirteen years old, he was still very slender.

Addae loved all of his many children, but he had a special love for Basusu, who displayed so many resemblances to himself. There was no doubt in Addae's mind that Basusu, exhibiting strength and courage surpassing that of most children in the village, was in line for the office of chief someday. But the reality was that Basusu, as well as all of the village boys, would be faced with a harsh society in which only the strong survive.

Addae Kwami's hut was situated not too far from that of his father. Although Chief Mensua had many grandchildren by now, Basusu was his favorite grandson, easily obtaining what he wanted from his grandfather for the simple asking. Many times, Addae quarreled with his father regarding the special treatment afforded Basusu. "This grandson of yours, Basusu, will never become chief; you have been too soft with him," he would say. "He gets things too easy."

"I have him close to me; and he learns a lot by listening, not by always working as hard as we did," Chief Mensua would patiently retort. "There's much to be said for a good listener."

He who would be chief must fight for everything. "Father, you must let the boy work for things like I did; that's the only way he will be ready to be chief one day," Addae responded. But no matter what Addae said or did, Basusu would go down the lane to his grandfather's hut because there he knew he would be treated with specialness.

Upon reaching age thirteen, the village boys could spend time in the main hall where the chief and the leaders had their regular meetings save for the times when precarious matters captured the time, as well as when even at day's end the elders would be enamored with the discussions. Yet Basusu, being the favorite grandson of the chief, occasionally remained in the chief's presence longer than his peers. This caused further friction between Basusu and his father because when Addae would demand that it was time for Basusu to leave, Chief Mensua, who was the final arbiter, did not always enforce the command.

"Don't you know that the boy will be chief someday?" Chief Mensua posed the question to Addae.

"Yes, Father, but not before me! I want my boy to understand my command," Addae replied in frustration.

"How short is your memory, Addae?" Chief Mensua asked, eyeing his son. "You were no different. No one could keep you from sneaking around." He bobbed his staff in Basusu's direction, "That boy is in line to be chief, and it is time he begins to know what the chief does, not only in the fields and in war, but also in the government of the village." The firelight cast a soft glow over Addae's face. A muscle clinched in his jaw before turning his attention back to the others present. True, he was not very pleased with his response, but who argues with the chief?

In Odu, from time to time, there were discussions about people leaving their village and not returning. Others told stories they had heard from tribesmen about a better life in other parts of the world, but no one seemed to have any facts to support the rumors. Most everyone in the village who heard about land far away took it to be no more than a fairy tale. The villagers of Odu had even heard of strange men coming around, who were different; but not seeing anyone but people of their own kind, the villagers thought it to be a folktale.

On one occasion, Basusu, lingering at the elders' meeting, overheard his grandfather and the elders conversing about people being taken away from their village and not returning. It was said that they went on big boats and crossed the sea to another land; but to the people of an interior village such as Odu, such hearsay sounded like no more than the idle tales old men talked about. Basusu agreed. He couldn't possibly imagine such a thing, because they lived in the interior and had to travel nearly four miles to get to the nearest river—the only place they would see a sailing vessel, which was often no more than a fisherman's dingy.

Basusu discreetly left the meeting and rejoined his friends at their familiar meeting place. The children talked and laughed, imagining being captured and taken to a foreign land. They devised a language and strange food and imagined life apart from the elders' meetings.

Later, when Basusu went home, he jokingly told his mother that he heard the elders talking about strange men who come and take men from other villages to some other land and give them a better life. His mother stopped seasoning the meal she was preparing and, turning to face Basusu, promptly quieted him. "Where did you hear such foolish talk?" she demanded. "Your father and I have told you to stay away from the elders' meetings."

Basusu laughed and looked at his mother. He sobered at the grim expression his mother gave him. "Everyone talks about it—about the floating house and about going to another land. Me? Going to another land? This is *my* land. My *grandfather* is chief, my *father* is going to be chief after grandfather, and then *I* will be chief."

"Well, don't let me hear you talking about that again." His mother looked intently at her son then turned her attention back to her meal.

As soon as Addae Kwami came home, his wife repeated to him what Basusu had relayed to her.

"Did you ever hear anything like that?" she asked.

Addae shrugged, pulled out a stool, and sat down. He did not speak.

"Did you hear me talking to you, Addae Kwami?" Addae was well aware of his wife's gravity. Not often did she refer to him by both of his names.

He glanced up. "Yes, Sroda, I heard you. I hear talk about such things, but you know how the elders are; they have many stories," he said with a light chuckle. Addae did not want to talk about the issue; he did not want to believe that it was happening.

Pacing the hut, Addae truthfully expressed his concern. "I told that boy to stay away from the elders' meetings, but he won't listen, and his grandfather is the cause of it all," he remarked to Sroda, speaking with a hiss. He paused, then continued, his voice raised: "Every time I tried to send him home, his grandfather kept saying, 'Leave the boy alone; one day, he too is going to be chief.'" Addae vented his exasperation at the situation. "But if Basusu doesn't stop interfering in adult matters, he won't live long enough to amount to anything!"

Addae frowned at Sroda's alarmed expression. He exhaled deeply and lowered his voice. Circling her chair, he placed his hands on her shoulders and calmly led her outdoors. He let the expanse of the region speak for itself.

"Look where we live. Can you imagine anyone leaving here to get to the sea?" he asked Sroda. With a wave of his hand and a nod of his head in unison he affirmed, "No! No! I do hear the elders talking about people going away, but I don't believe it. And you, my wife, should not be alarmed." He cradled her face and smiled assertively. "It's just tales, Sroda, just tales!"

Sroda smiled weakly. She wanted to believe it too, but she was uneasy. Addae clasped her hand. She glanced behind her once before following her husband back into their hut.

CHAPTER 2

The Raid

The sun, like a red ball of fire, began to lean over to kiss the western hills, forming a spectacular Ghanaian evening a few hours before night descended upon this small village. The year was 1841. It was simply another day in this small West African village several miles inland from the vast coastline.

As the beautiful sunset began to merge with the western hills, women could be seen preparing dinner for their hardworking husbands. These men had spent the day in a nearby wooded area, hunting for small game and fishing in a small lake that bordered the village. The aroma of deliciously seasoned food saturated the air as villagers found familiar relaxing spots for a lengthy night. Young adults sat around, engaging in small talk. They shared a common anticipation of completing their assigned chores before the entire village assembled to listen to the region griot. The griot was the oral historian who kept alive through stories the history of the village back through the centuries.

Basusu was playing games with other boys when he noticed several strangers approaching the village with strange tools in their hands. Normally, he would not be alarmed except that these strangers were white-skinned. This was a new experience for young Basusu, who had only been exposed to persons with dark skin like himself. He, running as fast as he could, alerted his grandfather who was taking a late-evening nap. "Grandfather! Grandfather! Wake up!" he yelled. "There are strange people coming to our village." Basusu impatiently shifted from one foot to the other, waiting for his grandfather to arise.

Chief Mensua slowly rose from his nap and grasped his shepherd staff that leaned against the wall. He knew it was not unusual for travelers to pass through the village, some even seeking shelter overnight. Basusu was persistent, insisting that his grandfather rush to give attention to this matter, for he was the village chief. He continually attempted to describe these strange visitors. He had never heard about black or white persons; everyone was the same in his village. His heart pounded a battle rhythm fueled by fear of the unknown. His knuckles tightened as he clutched Chief Mensua's hand.

By the time Basusu and Chief Mensua left their hut, the strangers were already in the village. Chief Mensua did not recoil but approached in a friendly manner.

Basusu's heartbeat pounded loudly in his ears, and he couldn't restrain his curiosity. His eyes fastened upon the strange tools in the hands of the white-skinned strangers. For a time, there was little communication because they did not understand each other's tongue. Believing these strange visitors would do no harm, Basusu's grandfather tried to make them understand that he would assist them in solving their apparent dilemma; however, one among the strange men knew a few words of the Odu dialect.

"There are two groups of us," he explained slowly, "and we cannot find the other. Did you see them?"

"No, no one like you passed here," Chief Mensua cautiously answered. Basusu was examining the strange creatures from behind his grandfather. Little did the chief know that these men had come to see if raiding the village of Odu would be worth their while.

The men saw just what they wanted, for all the people in the village came out to have their first look at foreigners on their land. The strange-colored men saw healthy young men, women, boys and girls. The chief, though leery, was more relaxed and asked the visitors if they needed water or food; but they insisted that they were not hungry, only anxious to find the rest of the group. Having ascertained the information they wanted, these visitors bade good-bye and left. There was an eerie silence in the air as the strangers made their departure.

There were indeed other strange men; but they were hiding out at a distance, waiting for their scouting party to return. Their experience in the business of slave-catching taught them not to travel in large groups so as not to alarm the villagers. Also, if the villagers attacked, the scouting party had reinforcement. Later, when the two groups met, they exchanged information and decided that the village was worth their while. Immediately, they set about to plan the strategy for attack and capture of the villagers of Odu.

Slave-catching was a tricky business, they knew, because Africans tend to live in clusters of villages located not too far from each other. Most slavers operated within a two-hundred-mile range of the coast, and they knew they must avoid alarming other villages near their target and those along the way toward the ship.

Back at the village, Basusu sat down and tried to occupy himself with child's play, but he could not get these strangers out of his mind. Most disturbing was their color and the clothing that covered their bodies. He noticed other things too. They had hats on their heads; and most carried strange sticks, which he had not seen before. He thought they were like the walking sticks his grandfather and other old men in the village had made. But these sticks were carried differently than the way villagers carried sticks and were hollow at the end. Unbeknownst to him, Basusu had gotten his first good look at a rifle.

Why are these men so different? he asked himself. There was no answer because no one in the village knew how to describe the differences of these men. The shadows of night fell, and Basusu's mother called him inside to get ready for bed. He was slow to get ready, his mind more on those strangers than getting to sleep. Sroda, checking on him before turning in for the night, noticed a disturbing demeanor about her son that evening. His face remained shadowed by a haunting expression. Suddenly, the evening became tranquil as acrid darkness descended upon the village of Odu. The time had come for rest, but it was far from Basusu who tossed and turned, the events of the day interfering with his sleep.

Deep in the night, just past midnight, several strangers approached the quiet village with torches in their hands. The fiery torches cast an eerie glow upon these white faces. With chains in hand they approached the first huts and signaled the half-asleep inhabitants to remain quiet. With tireless effort, the slave catchers placed a piece of cloth in their captives' mouths and meticulously placed chains around their feet, connecting each link, preventing any option of escape. It was the element of surprise that caught the sleepy villagers off guard.

Basusu heard the shouting. He bolted from his sleep and sat straight up. His people were yelling, "Fire! Fire! Get out of your huts! Our huts are on fire!" The crackle of the burning straw rang loud in Basusu's ears, and he saw the flickering of flames through the wall. Immediately, his mouth went dry and his heart beat as if it wanted out. Petrified, he ran outside. Though it was the middle of the night, Basusu could clearly see fear and terror etched on everyone's face—including his father's. Fire was everywhere!

Everyone hurried out of bed and into the open space. Unbeknownst to them, this was precisely the strategy of the slave catchers—the fire providing the necessary light to make their capture.

15

As the village burned, the slave catchers were busy taking advantage of the panic. Basusu was startled by sudden, loud noises and turned toward one of them. One of his people had fallen, and blood trickled from his face; black smoke bellowed into the sky, permeating the air and causing a suffocating atmosphere. Clouds of white smoke rose up around some of the sticks the strange men were now pointing at other villagers.

He backed into the shadows, fear gripping him. Suddenly from behind, a rough hand gripped his mouth, forcing it shut. A coarse cloth was tied over his eyes. Basusu felt panic rise inside him like a wave. He fought to stay focused, but the strength of his captor overwhelmed his own.

He felt his body being raised off the ground as his captor carried him to join the other captives. Opening his eyes against the darkness, Basusu felt the roughness of the cotton tearing into his skin. Gritting his teeth, he dug his fingers into the arm of the pale man. With a wild jerk, he felt himself being hurtled to the ground.

Basusu landed and ripped the cloth from his eyes. A large, pale man leered at him as he loaded his rifle. Basusu scooted backward. He glanced over his shoulder, his eyes widening with fear as a younger man of his village fell to the ground from the smoke of the large sticks the white men were carrying. He recognized with terror that it was the same stick being held in front of his face at the moment.

Addae watched with terror at the chaos before him. He had crouched below one of the burning huts in search of his son. His eyes watered from the smoke, and he struggled to keep them clear and alert. With swiftness he crept behind the pale man keeping watch over the captives, lunged onto him, and with a quick jerk to his neck sent him to the ground.

Adrenaline surged through him, and he ran into the middle of the space fighting all who came into his path. He searched around him for his son, unaware of the metal sticks being raised by the white men. The sight of all his people becoming captives and the smell of his home burning brought tears not caused by the smoke to flood his face. His strength suddenly fled him, and he glanced at the faces of those now dead.

"Father!" Basusu found the strength to scream. He heard a click from the stick in front of him.

Addae whirled and searched for a face. His stomach knotted in fear as he stumbled forward. Smoke blinded him but caused the faces of those men to glow with an eerie light. The burning wood echoed in his ears. *Where was Basusu?* Hadn't he heard his son's call moments ago?

Addae stumbled over a body lying in the dust and heard voices mumbling in a language unlike his own. He struggled to find his feet. Everything he loved was disappearing before his eyes. His hopes for becoming chieftain, his hopes for his son, and his hopes for the future disappeared in the smoke rising before him.

He felt a cold grip on his neck and with a jerk he was brought to his knees, the large metal stick hanging idle at the side of the man now in front of him. Then looking beyond, the smoke suddenly cleared and Addae saw his son. The fear etched on Basusu's face caused him to forget his own and with the last ounce of strength, Addae called out words of hope in their native tongue. He called out to his son until Basusu was dragged beyond the bend and out of sight. His voice dwindling to a whisper, Addae glanced up at the face of the men leering in front of him. All hope was gone.

He didn't feel the pain from the blow of the gun to his temple.

Together, the captives were carried away, uncertain of all that was happening around them. They had heard of people being taken from their villages before and carried to a big house on the sea. But now it was coming to pass in their village. Young Basusu was overwhelmed with confusion and grief. It rose up like a threatening wave, ready to crash over his sanity at any moment. Basusu willed himself to remain strong. He was the grandson of Chief Mensua. He would show courage. The knowledge that others from his village were with him roused a flame of hope in his spirit. *I will make it,* he said to himself.

CHAPTER 3

The Village in Disarray

Within hours, the small village of Odu was in complete disarray. Wails of grief and fear could be heard everywhere as the strangers led the village natives away in iron coffles. The captives submitted to their captors without any resistance. Hired natives who understood the language of the villagers convinced them that they were going to a better place. It was through this method that the captors mollified the fears and suspicions of the captured. They trudged for miles with only their clothing upon their back. After trudging for miles into what seemed like an abyss of darkness, the strangers gave the captured natives water. By early dawn, the trek from the village to the sea was nearly over. The slave catchers pressed the captives on, keeping a measured yet constant pace.

The following morning, the sunlight cracked through the clouds arousing everyone's spirits. Basusu glanced down at another captive and shook his head. "Where are my parents?" he attempted. He received only the same forlorn glance of sympathy in return. Turning to other villagers, ones who were older, Basusu asked in a strained whisper, "What are they going to do with us? Where are they taking us?" Basusu bit his bottom lip irately and pounded the ground with his fist in exasperation as all around him people groaned in anguish and fear. There was a unanimous air of confusion and perplexity—no one knew anything.

Youngsters of various ages looked at the adults, searching their faces for answers and receiving the same miserable shakes of heads in return. Some sobbed unceasingly, while others folded themselves up with stone-faced anger painted on their face. Flinching, Basusu turned to a lady from his village. "Why do they hurt us?" he asked. She only shook her head with a frown while tears slipped down her brown cheeks, clearing a path through the dust that clouded her skin. Upon seeing that, Basusu swallowed the lump that rose in his throat.

As the sun rose higher in the sky, the heat increased on the hilltop. Basusu was hungry and thirsty, but he was given no water to drink. Instead, the captor's men came with chains, which they fastened around his feet and hands. Then they chained Basusu to people from Odu as well as captives from other villages.

Once twenty villagers were chained together, they were pulled from the hill and made to go toward the water. The lady that Basusu had spoken to was chained to him. The leader of the line was rudely shoved. He began walking at a steady pace. "Faster!" A whip sizzled through the air and landed with a snap on the leader's back. He cried out in pain as he quickened the pace. The sudden speed caused several to stumble, but they scrambled to their feet and continued. Basusu heard the lady behind him heaving terribly.

"Basusu," she moaned. "I can't go that fast," she told him in their native tongue. She hopped in an attempt to catch up, but her knees gave in and she stumbled. Basusu jerked with the impact of the fall but held himself up. Vainly, he pulled at his manacles, hoping they would haul the lady up; but she was too weak to get up on her own, and the white men would not stop walking. The dust in the road muffled her cries, and Basusu cringed as she was dragged mercilessly.

Basusu did not know what to say to his people when they had fallen or were crying. He wanted to demonstrate courage. He wanted to show he could take his captors' punishment and cruelty, for he was the first son of his father; therefore, he had been trained from an early age not only to become the next chief but also to be strong in adverse situations. Suddenly, a thought hit him: *How can I be chief of my grandfather's people and my father's people if I am being taken away from my village?*

Anyone who cried out in fear or yelled from pain was beaten. Basusu pushed on, hot rage boiling inside of him. He clenched his teeth against the tears that threatened his will. He would not cry. His face flushed with anger as he passed two white men standing stationary with their arms crossed. He slowed enough to stare at one. The white man stared back. He appeared no older than seventeen years old; but his face, hardened with hatred, added years to his look. Basusu stared boldly. The young white man's eyes widened at the open display of disrespect and lunged forward with his whip raised.

"Leave him alone, Charles," the older man chuckled. "You'll meet plenty of them along the way." The insulted young man lowered the whip. Basusu glared at them until he was forced to turn away.

The captives were led to shanties near the water where they were given a bowl of hearty soup. Men and women were separated at the water's edge, and the weak were separated from the strong. A physician visually checked each native and decided who would board the ship. The day of final reckoning was near, and many decisions had to be made with this newly found load of human cargo.

Before, these invaders had traded only sugar, rum, and other commodities. Now they were interested in strong, burly males who could shoulder loads and work for hours at laborious tasks. They were shoved and pulled to a dock the white men had built on the beach. The size of the ship tied to the dock frightened and amazed them. *The legend about the floating house is true,* many of them thought. The captives were pushed, beaten, and dragged up splintered boards to get them on the ship; however, their final resting place was not on the top deck where there was air and light. Made to climb down ladders and cleat planks until they could go no lower in the hold of the ship, the captives were forcefully crushed together side by side, one behind the other and still in chains.

Basusu struggled to keep his balance once he was forced to stoop, not being able to stand because the ceiling was so low. He scrambled onto the bench and hastily yanked his feet up from the foul water below. With terror, he realized he'd have to endure the entire trip bound on the bench with his knees up. Grasping his knees tightly, Basusu held them close to his chest as the others boarded. The air reeked of nausea and polluted water, and his stomach churned in disgust.

As the ship rocked, the water below the slaves sloshed back and forth. The ceiling above their heads was the floor of the deck above. Above him, Basusu could hear people crying and screaming with fright. The dragging of chains made a loud scraping noise on top of his head. He cringed and ducked his head lower, wondering whether the people above him also had to uncomfortably crouch and sit like him.

Basusu closed his eyes against the commotion that whirled around him and thought of his home. He had yet to know what had befallen his parents. Had they made it? He had only seen his father once during the raid, but not his mother . . . or Chief Mensua. Basusu peered cautiously at the others on board for it was too dark to see clearly. Running his tongue over his mouth, he asked, "Is anyone here from the Ashanti region?" Several of the men rattled a yes, in the common Ashanti language. "Has anyone seen Chief Mensua?" Basusu ventured. "Or Addae, my father?" There was a low mumble. "No," they replied. Basusu grimaced angrily and turned himself straight. He gripped the board tighter as the boat jerked violently. His eyes bucked, and he struggled to keep himself balanced as the vessel rocked wildly. The voyage had begun; and the water underneath him sloshed heavily to one side and then to the other. He strained against the pull and steadied himself. *I will be strong,* he thought. *I will be strong.* He nodded in encouragement to himself. *I must.*

Captain Jennings, the owner of several slave cartels, fastened his eyes upon the young men from the village of Odu. With an eye for detail he instructed the physicians to treat their colds as they entered the ship. Basusu would not look into the eyes of his captor as he waited for the final instructions. The sounding of the gong served notice that the ship was about to leave harbor.

Night soon settled, and the captives were given their final meal of beans and rice. Basusu stared at the food before him before shoving it into his mouth and gulping it down hungrily. It was the blandest food he had ever tasted, but it quenched his ever-present hunger. That night was his first night away from his village.

The darkness that engulfed him was dense and stifling. Basusu tried to imagine where they were going. Would it be like his village—hot, dry, but sometimes rainy? No. He did not think so. There was no place like Odu. His father had said so. Basusu exhaled heavily and willed himself asleep. Despite the continual rocking and occasional moaning of the oppressed captives, the first night on board was calm, as the ship moved stealthily throughout the river. The slaves never said good-bye to their native land as they continued on their journey past the point of no return.

For several days the voyage was calm as slaves began to adjust to the routine of mandatory exercise twice a day. Once a day during the voyage, food was thrown to them. Though it had dreadful taste, they ate it for they were hungry. But it was never enough. Some of Basusu's people became sick from the food, even as they ate it. Even though he did not enjoy it, Basusu downed the rations. He was determined to stay alive, and with each day, he became more accustomed to the dreadful-tasting food.

Some of the captives died soon after the voyage began, the misery of their circumstances causing more to die. Others sickened because of the food and were unable to keep it down. Eventually, they were denied rations and left to starve—the captain not wanting to waste food on those who were dying anyway. And die many of them did—still in their chains. Thereafter, their bodies were thrown overboard.

The atmosphere on the ship was unbearable, particularly at night. The captives were so crowded together they held each other up with their knees at their chest while they slept. The air stank of nausea and human waste; and the odors of the bilgewater under the boards Basusu sat on sickened him to his stomach, causing him to barely manage a suitable breath. For Basusu, the voyage seemed to last forever. He wondered if the journey would ever end.

The lull of the splashing water underneath him bade him to sleep, but he shook himself awake. They had been on the waters for many miles now. It still felt unreal. Finally, Basusu allowed his eyes to close. The sooner the voyage was over, the better.

A loud creak startled Basusu, and he awoke. The water sloshed wildly where it had once lapped calmly against the sides. With a grunt, Basusu wiped the spray of water that squirted him. Above him, he could hear a loud commotion and words being yelled in an unknown tongue.

"We've encountered some blustery winds, Captain." A young seaman glanced at the helm of the ship where he could clearly see lightning flashing as it blazed through the mass of thickening clouds. The skies had suddenly darkened, and the black waters churned warningly.

"Steady . . . steady . . ." Captain Jennings stood by the helmsman as he rolled the wheel lightly in his hands. Jennings and the other ship crew had encountered severe weather before, but never had it darkened like this as early as nine in the morning. The sinister waters below him moved the ship in a shifting motion he had never before experienced.

The sails snapped sharply with the gusts of wind that blew, and the ship creaked eerily as it moved stealthily through the ocean. As the weather front moved near, the roar of ear-splitting thunder exploded from the skies, and with it, a mighty downpour of rain fell. The crashing sound of thunder sent a wave of panic through the multitudes of slave cargo. Captives groaned with seasickness as the rain fell and violent waves pounded the deck.

Basusu held his knees tightly to his chest not only to keep his feet from slipping off the wooden plank but also in an attempt to slow down his pounding heartbeat, which beat against his rib cage as if it wanted out. He closed his eyes against the thunder, but nothing would suffice to calm his fear as the thunderbolts struck with overwhelming fury.

Farther in the corner, an older man coughed fiercely and clutched at his heart. His eyes bucked wildly, and his face dimmed to a deathly tan. He wheezed before exhaling loudly and falling silent. His hand fell to his side, but his eyes retained their wild glaze. He was not the only one. Elders from numerous clans held their hearts and gasped their final breath as they died from terror and heart attacks.

Basusu longed to go to their aid, but his chains prevented him. His eyes blurred with angry tears. He went hot with rage and felt it boiling inside of him. Unable to contain himself any further, with a loud breath, Basusu screamed to the top of his lungs. He couldn't bear the thought of being less than a foot away from a rotting body.

The door burst open and a wide-eyed shipmate stood in the doorway. He glanced at Basusu who could only glance in the direction of the elders who had died of heart failure. Behind the lanky man, Basusu could spot the rain falling and lightning erupting from the sky. He clenched his teeth and laid his head against the shoulder of the man next to him. That night was the first time he allowed himself to weep.

The next morning when he was brought on deck with the other captives for morning exercise, Basusu was able to take a deep breath. Instead of foul air, he smelled a clean, salty, refreshing odor. The water lapped with a gentle current and sparkled with promise.

CHAPTER 4

The Arrival

Fortunately, the ship and its crew encountered no more storms during the last leg of the voyage. The clean air revived everyone's spirits, and away went the sight and smell of the deceased. But the oppression and fear of the future darkened the captives' spirits. Basusu couldn't imagine a place where everyone was as pale as the moon. Thoughts of the imminent future as a captive assaulted his imagination, but he brushed them away and focused on life, one day at a time.

Three days after the storm, Basusu was awakened with a rude shove from the man next to him.

"We've stopped moving," the man whispered, fear lacing his every word. Basusu's stomach dropped, and he slowly raised his head. The ship's forward motion had truly ceased, the water underneath them barely moving. Basusu sucked his breath in sharply when the ship bumped against a wooden dock.

Boom!

Basusu spun his head around at the sound of the barrier being opened.

"All right, everyone, get movin'." A stocky pale man hunkered down and slammed a plank against the wall so that it reached down into the hole where Basusu and the others anxiously waited.

The man climbed down and yanked the chain of the first captive. The captives weakly climbed up the plank—some stumbling, some struggling, straightening their backs and blinking at the bright sunlight that met them. Basusu winced, the sunlight blinding his eyes as he stood straight on the top deck. Wind! Air! Basusu inhaled deeply.

He grimaced as his joyous relief was suddenly cut short; he was yanked off the deck and led down the plank that led to the dock. The feeling of firm ground under his feet caused him to become dizzy, and he thought he would faint. Basusu, along with the survivors, were led to a long cabin where they were rubbed down with a burning salve and made to rinse. The salve burned their skin, but it was necessary to kill the lice and other germs. Basusu was given pants and a shirt to wear. The brown color, the buttons, and the cord around the waist, which he tied to keep the pants from falling, intrigued Basusu. His clothes were not new, for there were rips and stains throughout. His shirt, in particular, once had bright, colorful stripes but now had faded. He wondered who wore his clothing, not knowing that the fading resulted from exposure to the sun all day long.

Basusu stumbled out of the cabin after the others, tears stinging at his eyes. The reality of abandonment and the feeling of loneliness rushed upon him like an avalanche as he shook with heavy sobs. *How will I ever make it in this place of pale-skinned men? How will I survive?* He closed his eyes as the memory of the night of his capture flashed before him. The screams of the injured and frightened still rang fresh in his mind.

Collapsing to the ground, Basusu let out a scream of frustration when he realized that all of his hopes of ever becoming chieftain had been dashed away in a single night, as well as all of his hopes for a lifetime in his village. However, relief for survival of the journey momentarily flooded his being, but the uncertainty for what lay ahead caused the spark of hope to die.

Facing the ground on all fours, Basusu wept freely; yet in some ways he felt blessed to be alive because so many others had not survived the journey. He thought of Chief Mensua and Addae and struggled to stop the onrush of fresh tears. Raising his head, he looked out at the ocean he had been taken across against his will. It sparkled and shimmered so brightly he could not gaze at it for more than a moment. He wondered if the sea looked that way while he was crouched below in the darkness and stench in the hold of the ship.

Rising to his feet, Basusu closed his eyes to keep out the sand that a gust of wind from the north was now stirring up. He turned to face the wind, letting it sweep the sand across his face. When it ceased, he opened his eyes and saw far off in the distance a multitude of plants growing in rows—some perfectly straight, others curving gracefully up and down the low hills that rolled to the other end of the island. The more he stared, the more detail he saw. Now he could see Africans like himself hunched over the rows. There were men, women, and young boys and girls, all black, picking and cultivating the fields of what he would later come to know as Oglethorpe's farm and, next to it, the Hamilton Plantation.

With his back to the ocean, he looked across the little sandy islands to the expanse of marsh and hills beyond. Bridges had been built, connecting the mainland to the little islands and then to the island where he was confined. Today, like all the other days, white people would come, riding in wagons pulled by horses and accompanied by boys, women, children, and men who had black skin like Basusu. Soon, Basusu would learn that the people like him were slaves, and their fate would be his destiny too.

The crew had landed on St. Simons Island, where, one hundred years before, settlers bought smuggled slaves after the trustees of the Colony of Georgia had imposed a ban on slavery. But when the ban was lifted after a mere seven years—the landing and selling of slaves proceeded without interference from authorities.

Nothing looked like the land from their villages. White men with guns restricted Basusu and the other Africans to the southern end of the island, taking or making shelter wherever they decided.

Basusu saw many wagons. Some were driven by slaves and filled with bales of cotton, boxes of yarn, and rolls of another kind of cloth called "osnaburg," which was coarse and rough. Other wagons were filled with crates of fruits and vegetables, and sometimes Basusu would eat a sweet fruit that had fallen from a wagon to the ground, taking precaution to look around, however, to make sure no white man was looking his way.

Usually, Basusu would stand away from the island's activity, watching the slaves unload the wagons and carry goods on their heads and shoulders to the other ships that had arrived. On one occasion, he was made to help load the ships, and he did as the slaves had done by finding opportunities to secretly eat fresh fruit and vegetables when no one was looking. Sometimes, the white men would look inside the mouths of Basusu's people. The strange men spoke in words Basusu could not understand. They passed bits of papers around and took away men and women still in chains that now were rusted.

Many days passed, and no one took Basusu away. He wondered whether it was better to be passed over rather than to be taken away. *What will they do to those who are taken away?* he thought, remembering that sometimes people left his village and never returned, thought to have been eaten by strange people. *Will this be my fate?* Basusu wondered. His body heated at the thought. Brushing the thought aside, he glanced around. Over in a farther area of the island, he spotted one man from the Odu village identified as Kwasi. White men stood by, talking and looking at Basusu. One of them nodded and beckoned toward Basusu.

Basusu arose from his seat and headed for the group. His heart pounded loudly in his ears, but each step was firm.

Basusu was then cut free and tied to Kwasi, the man from his own village. Though he did not understand what was happening, a feeling of security overwhelmed him for the first time since his kidnapping. He was with someone from his own village.

Because he was so young, no one wanted to purchase Basusu alone, so he had been sold collectively with Kwasi for not much more money than the price of Kwasi. A while later, both were taken, tied to one of the horse-drawn wagons, and made to walk alongside the wagon while the white men sat inside and talked as they guided the horses.

Basusu's heart thumped with apprehension as he was led away from the island. His eyes widened with fear when the bridges groaned and creaked from the weight of the wagon, horses, and people. After the last shaky wooden bridge was crossed, their path took him and Kwasi over rocky dirt roads through tall marsh grass and then onto drier ground. Walking for many hours made them tired and faint. They wanted water but did not know how to ask for it. Many times, as they were led along, Basusu and Kwasi saw water flowing in abundance but could not have it, their bound hands preventing them from enjoying even a meager scoop. As the day passed on and nightfall descended, Basusu and Kwasi were still walking.

PART 2

THE JORDAN PLANTATION, BRUNSWICK, GEORGIA—1841

CHAPTER 5

The Plantation

Much later, when darkness made it difficult to see, the troop of enslaved captives and their captors turned off the road onto a smoother path. The horses stopped and waited a while. The captives were grateful for a time to rest although they had to stand, not sit. Basusu's feet ached and his back still dripped with sweat although the night air was chilly.

Soon they saw three people with lights in their hands coming toward them. As they approached, he noticed a man, a woman, and a young girl. To their surprise, they too were some of their people although dressed like the white men. Approaching, they released the horses first; then they released Basusu and Kwasi. For a moment, Basusu felt some relief, until the woman spoke to him with words like the white men used. Basusu's momentary relief sank into the darkness surrounding him.

Basusu and Kwasi were taken to a small house not far away, and the same woman brought them food. Though he and his companion were tired, thirsty, and too weak to enjoy it, they forced themselves to eat.

The woman looked sadly at the captives, particularly Basusu. Food was still in their mouths when they drifted off into a deep sleep.

Days turned into weeks, and Basusu and Kwasi slowly began to regain their strength. Some days were better than others both physically and emotionally. At times, neither captive was able to fully stomach the strange food made worse by their emotional turmoil. Having seen gestures between the black woman and the white man indicative of the fields, Basusu and Kwasi knew that their time of rest and recuperation would soon draw to a close and that they would head for the fields for heavy labor. Both men were placed into the care of this woman, a dark-skinned woman like the people of their village, until they were ready for the fields.

Finally, the day of reckoning came. Early one morning, Basusu and Kwasi were led to the fields by Sally, where they were placed in the care of the overseer from whom they received a crude crash course on picking cotton. Sacks were tossed to the new field hands as they were prodded to begin their task.

Neither Basusu nor Kwasi were properly trained to pick cotton and were slow workers, pausing often to correctly separate the cotton from the branch and, even more often, to stretch their backs. They were unaccustomed to continually bending over in the hot sun and longed for a break and water. A swift crack of the whip across their back by the overseer served to remind them that they were slaves in every sense of the word.

Working at a faster pace, Basusu and Kwasi evaded the overseer's whip although they routinely saw its evil performed on the backs and legs of other field hands. Fear so separated Basusu and Kwasi that even when they were together in the cotton fields, they behaved like total strangers, hesitant to converse.

Basusu's young mind raced with questions, and finally, he made up his mind to speak. He neared Kwasi and stooped beside him, still picking cotton.

"Where are we, Kwasi?" he asked. "Will we ever get back to our village someday?"

Kwasi did not answer right away, but the look on his face spoke louder than words. Finally, after a quick glance in the direction

36

of the overseer who was busy shouting to another slave quite a distance away, he replied, "You are wondering if we will ever get back to our village? I have not only left my village; I've left three wives, seven children, my entire family and possessions. If you think *you* want to go back to the village, me the more." Kwasi reminisced for a few moments then turned back to the cotton plants.

From that day on, Basusu often thought about how to escape and go back to his own people. Whenever Basusu was not talking, he was studying the landscape, trying to remember how he got there. The fear of his journey from the island caused him to forget most of it. He had seen nothing except other chained captives for weeks. As his time on the plantation lengthened, Basusu realized he had to learn how to survive as a slave. Kwasi reluctantly, though never fully, came to grips with his life in the New World.

As time passed, Basusu not only learned a few words of the white man's language as spoken by the slaves he worked with in the fields but also became accustomed to eating strange new foods. Nearly every day as he worked in the fields, there were moments when he stopped to look around, observing the landscape and wondering if there could be any opportunity for him to make a dash for freedom. He closed his eyes and thought about his father, mother, grandfather, and Akosua, his childhood friend and sweetheart. Akosua and Basusu had grown up with each other and had developed a slight fondness for each other.

Just a year ago, Basusu and Akosua were content to walk through their village, talking and eating treats that his mother generously bestowed upon them. But as puberty set in, their friendship began to take a turn and delve into more private matters. Akosua cherished Basusu and claimed him as her own, proud to be linked to the arm of the son of a tribal warrior as they went for walks; and Basusu was content to let her have her way. Akosua was the more outspoken and daring of the two and felt more comfortable with the change in their relationship. Because he had known her all his life, Basusu felt that his awkwardness at the changes he was experiencing would be less uncomfortable at the hands of Akosua. No matter his faults, shyness or clumsiness, Akosua was patient with him, never once chiding him. In reality, they were friends helping each other come to terms, as best they could, with their newfound adult stage.

Whenever Basusu reminisced like this, his fellow workers would whistle or shove him warningly. A look or glance toward Kwasi was enough to warn him to continue his work, lest the overseer whip him for daydreaming.

Buddy Johnson, the overseer, was a tall white man with dark beady eyes and a grating laugh. Nicknamed Bud for short, he always carried a whip and a gun as he rode around on his horse, overseeing the production of the fields. One look at him was a clear reminder that it would not take much for him to use either weapon.

Bud was the overseer of not just the cotton fields but also the rice fields. His expertise in caring for all the plants grown in the fields in the plantation's low, marshy places afforded him the dual responsibility, and he proudly flaunted it, even against the overseers of the smaller vegetable fields.

Basusu toiled in the higher fields. He bore the heat as long as he could before lowering the sack from his back and bending over. He gazed across the field for a sight of the water bearer, but the water bearer was not out. He swung the sack onto his back and returned to work. The pounding of his heart echoed louder and louder in his ears, and his chest rose and lowered with pants. The heat flooded his being, and sweat poured into his eyes. Suddenly, his knees caved in under him as he fainted. He was revived not by a drink from the water bucket but by the whip across his legs. Scrambling to his feet, Basusu looked up into Bud's glittery eyes.

"Get to your feet, boy," Bud hissed. Not understanding a word but realizing the implication as Bud's arm started to raise above his head, whip in hand, Basusu weakly backed away, returning to his cotton, listening as Bud marched off. Tears stung at his eyes as the thirst that consumed every part of his body formed a pit in his stomach. However, he worked on angrily, angry at himself for being reduced to a coward, angry at the white man for his loathing of human life, and angry at life for the circumstances that he now found himself in.

A rage churned in his being, and Basusu recognized it as the feeling of a suppressed warrior. On the verge of screaming, a breeze flew over the fields, calming him. Basusu felt a hand on his shoulder and turned cautiously. A canteen was thrust into his hands, full of ginger water. He drank hastily and returned the bottle. Only then did he look up. It was the overseer's helper, an African slave called the Driver. He was not as brutal—if Bud was looking the other way. Basusu managed a grateful nod before turning and resuming his work.

Eventually, Basusu adapted to his new world and learned how to cultivate the vast fields of cotton, which greatly outnumbered the much smaller fields of corn, potatoes, rice, peas, and wheat. Most of his days were spent laboring in the cotton fields because there was an immense need for cotton. Fifty years prior, the need for slaves had actually declined. But then the invention of the cotton gin paradoxically decreased the need for slave labor in the cotton mills but increased the demand for slaves in the fields to plant and pick cotton.

By now, there were four million slaves in America, and Basusu's plantation owners were enjoying the profits of the slave-based economy. Millions of pounds of cotton were being exported from nine hundred Georgia plantations every year. Thousands of slaves were utilized under harsh conditions to fulfill the large demand for cotton.

Picking cotton day in and day out proved to be backbreaking labor, and often Basusu didn't think he could endure another day. He worked by day and cried and slept fitfully by night. He poured out his complaint to Kwasi, who was not much help to him except that he was from the same village and spoke the same dialect, which was not always of emotional benefit. Sharing the same language made it easier for them to talk about life before they were kidnapped. Remembering their happy days, however, filled them with much sorrow.

CHAPTER 6

Basusu Meets Charlotte

Four years passed, and Basusu approached manhood. He was now eighteen years old. He knew that if he were back in his village, he would be going through the various initiations young men were given in becoming a man, after which he would be free to find a wife. Rites of passage in African society were common. But in this strange land, he was lost. *After all, you cannot become a man without the chief and the priest pronouncing manhood upon you, but here they don't do that. How am I going to become a man?* he asked himself. Basusu could not be content. He pondered over these things for days.

Finally, Basusu decided to talk to Kwasi, but there was one problem. He knew that until he became recognized as a man himself he would not be allowed to share the things he wanted to share with an older man of the village. In his village, all older men had authority over the boys in the village whether or not they were related. Basusu rose one morning and cautiously approached Kwasi as they headed for the fields. "Kwasi, how can I become a man here in this land?" he asked in their shared dialect.

Kwasi's jaw clinched as he yanked at the cotton harder, knowing he could not give Basusu an answer. He continued picking the cotton, saying nothing.

Basusu's heart dropped. "Kwasi," he said, turning away, "I'm sorry I asked."

Kwasi straightened and grasped Basusu's shoulder firmly. "Basusu," he said, "there are many things that will not be the same for us as slaves." He shook his head regretfully. "In this strange country, many things are different." Tears welled up in his eyes as he said, "You can *never* become a man in this land."

You can never become a man in this land. As he thought about it, the concept became more and more a reality. Basusu nodded grimly. He turned to face the horizon from where the sun was rising. Closing his eyes, he allowed the wind to blow across his face. Then he stooped next to Kwasi and joined him in work. They worked together in silence, both sharing a mutual feeling of great despair, and Kwasi's words continued to ring in his ears for a long time afterward.

Several days passed from the time Basusu and Kwasi talked. Basusu's mind was entirely consumed with Kwasi's words. The idea of survival in this very different world was still very vague, but Basusu was determined to make it one day at a time. Pushing his way out of the fields, Basusu headed for the depository where he would unload the cotton he had harvested. Removing his hat, he wiped the sweat from his brow as he waited because a long line had already formed. Basusu took his position at the end and landed his sack firmly on the ground. Glancing around at the other depositories where other slaves from other fields were bringing their harvest, he saw men and women and even children bearing heavy sacks. A gentle murmur rose up from a crowd as a young woman appeared at the front of the crowd and shoved her basket onto the counter.

"Massa Jordan needs mo' corn," she said out of breath. Gazing at her intently, Basusu saw a slender dark young lady no more than age seventeen.

"Runnin' again, miss?" the man at the counter asked as he filled her basket with corn.

The girl nodded. "Yes, suh'. Mo' guests."

"Hey!" The man on the other side of Basusu's counter snapped his fingers. Basusu shook his head and blushed, realizing that he had not stepped up. Yanking his bag of cotton, he swung it onto the counter. It was weighed, and Basusu was given his food rations before being dismissed. Walking toward his cabin, he realized that the young girl had captivated his mind. Shaking his head as he thought about her, he quickened his pace toward his cabin. Turning left at the corner ahead would guide him to the cabins. If he turned right, he would be directing himself toward the big house. Making a sharp left he ran into a straw basket. Then he heard a soft cry and saw corn rolling all over the ground. Apparently, a girl coming in the opposite direction inadvertently ran headlong into him. Basusu peered at her and gasped. It was the girl he saw at the counter. He gently touched her on the arm.

"Yo's okay?" he asked. She nodded yes as he helped her to her feet, placing the basket back onto her arm.

"Tank yo'," she said. Sensing her nervousness, Basusu swallowed, being at a loss for words. Looking up at him she said, "I'm Charlotte, but de calls me Chati." She gave a faint smile. "I should've obeyed Mama and not come down de back way tru da cabins," she said as her brown eyes met his.

"Yo' okay?" she asked him. Heat rushed into Basusu's face, and he shook himself.

"Yo' 'min' me like my motha," he heard himself say.

The girl's head tilted to one side. "Where she at?" she inquired innocently.

Basusu looked beyond the girl into the sunset. "Home . . . Africa," he managed. "I don' know wha' happen wid her . . . don' know . . ." He continued to stare at the sunset, blinking back tears.

Chati gave a small gasp. "I'm sorry." Her eyes moistened. "I was born here . . . I don' know da otha lan'." Her honest compassion warmed Basusu. He smiled and gestured toward the house.

"Yo' motha . . ." Basusu did not know how to communicate the thought that Chati's mother might be worried that she had not yet returned.

Chati laughed heartily. "I mus' go." She lifted the hem of her skirts and hurried away. Then she stopped. Turning back to Basusu, she tilted her head. "Waad yo' name?" she asked.

"Basusu! Basusu Mensua . . . dem call me Base." (pronounced bah-see)

"Basusu Mensua." She tested the words on her mouth. "I will rememba." Then she was gone.

It was the first time since arriving in America that Basusu delighted in something other than a few fond memories of home and an infrequent laugh with Kwasi. Chati was pleasant. She was, to some extent, cultivated in the ways of the white people yet still managed to retain an African-like dignity and pride in spite of being raised among white people. Basusu immediately thought of his mother, who would have approved of Chati.

It was washing day, and Chati was assigned the task of stripping the bed linens. Working quickly and thoroughly, she pulled the sheets off a bed and tossed them into a corner by the window. Once the linens were stripped and piled, she gathered them into her arms and took them downstairs to the washing room. There they were sorted and put into basins before being hauled down to the creek and scrubbed by hand.

Stepping out of the room and onto the balcony for a moment's rest, Chati, squinting, observed the field hands at work. From this height she could see the workers and had recognized which one was Basusu. Scanning the fields, her eyes came to rest on him. Tall and dark, he worked at a steady pace. She remembered that Basusu was called "Base," the name the white people called him because they had little patience, or respect, for learning how to say "Basusu."

Chati thought that he was handsome. Pausing every so often to straighten, he wove his way along the strip. She smiled as she watched him in the field.

Basusu also thought about Chati as he plucked the cotton and dropped it into the sack. She worked in the big house, and he worked in the field, a situation that posed a problem for them. Those who worked in the house did not mix with those who worked in the field.

First, I can't become a man in this land, he thought aloud in his native tongue. *And now I cannot cross the line between house and field. In my village, we are all one.* Even though he was expected not to cross over, Basusu continued to show his interest in Chati; and by talking to Kwasi, he found out that she was the girl that came with her mother to untie them from the wagon the night they arrived on the plantation. It had been dark that night; and being so weary from his ordeal, Basusu only vaguely remembered her. Although Sally had continued to nurse him and Kwasi back to health, Chati had remained in the big house, tending to her duties. He never crossed paths with her again until their recent encounter.

I am the first son of my father; I will show that I have the courage of a man. I will find a way to meet her, he resolved. Little did Basusu know that Chati too was desperately trying to find a way to connect with him. Several weeks passed, and it seemed like there was no way to cross the great divide. It was Chati who succeeded in making the first move.

On an unexpected rainy afternoon, certain that everyone was at work, Chati cooked Juba, a stew that was routinely made of leftovers and commonly shared with the field hands. After spooning a generous amount into a bowl, Chati reached for a pen. Swiftly, she glided a quill pen over a piece of parchment. "Basusu," she wrote, "dere is a place Massa Jordan does not min' people from da house and da field meeting: da chapel." Donning her shawl, she stepped outside. Walking carefully, she laid a small dish on the steps of his cabin, confident that the food would be welcomed.

Basusu came home late that evening after a long and tiring day in the cotton fields. Not only was he tired, but he was also wet, as it was raining profusely. Just as he was washing his hands to prepare something to eat, he noticed a covered dish and picked it up. Slowly he lifted the cover and recognized the meal of Juba. "Dis smell good! Dis lookin' good!" he said aloud. "Who did dis?" He saw the note but could not read it. He shook his head and sat down. "Who done dis for me?" he asked himself. He did not have to stretch his imagination too far. It must be Chati. Basusu smiled widely and sat down to the meal.

He savored each bite and enjoyed it like nothing he ever enjoyed before. Finishing his meal, Basusu turned his thoughts to the note. Examining it more closely, he fought to read and comprehend words that were alien to him. His delight at the fact that Chati wrote him a note was short lived, however; he was troubled because whatever the note meant for him, it would have to wait. Coming to the realization that someone else would have to read the note for him, Basusu discouragingly tossed the note aside. He wasn't at all sure that he wanted someone else knowing about his private affairs.

Whatever in dis note is fo' me; no one sho' know but me. Gingerly picking up the note, Basusu secured it under his pillow and lay down to rest. The prospect of asking someone to read it for him presented itself once more, and this time he considered it favorably. *Who to ask?* he thought, furrowing his brow as he tossed and turned helplessly. "Firs', one problem, now two," he uttered quietly to himself. He sat up and laid his head against the wall and closed his eyes, frustrated.

"Maybe I learn to read." Basusu laughed, then sobered. It would be very risky because any slave caught trying to read would be in severe trouble with Master Jordan. Upon further contemplation, Basusu realized that the enormity of the task outweighed the hope of even finding someone that could be trusted to read it to him.

The next evening amid a lazy breeze, Basusu sat in front of his cabin after a long and exhausting day, whittling away at a stick, hoping to catch a glimpse of Chati. His head lifted at the sound of people approaching. He didn't notice the younger boy, but he noticed the taller man, Norm, a house worker. He watched them subtly, still whittling.

"Base," Norm called, "dis Julius. Massa Jordan say dis boy stay 'ere wid yo'."

Norm left, and Basusu was alone with the new boy, Julius. They stared at each other for a while, neither of them knowing what to say.

How we all gonna live in dis small cabin? Basusu thought. There were several other men of differing ages already rooming with Basusu.

Finally, the silence broke. Basusu asked, "Why yo' here?" He gestured for the boy to follow him inside the cabin. Julius appeared to be no more than fourteen years old, lean, with a thin face, somber eyes, and a long body. He answered, "Ma massa sol' me 'cause he foun' out dat I was learnin' to read."

Basusu was about to ask what the meaning of "sold" was, but then remembered the note.

"Yo' read!" he exclaimed.

"A little," Julius replied with a light shrug.

"Den read dis fo' me." Basusu anxiously retrieved the note from under his pillow and handed it to Julius. He studied his face intently as Julius began to read. Chati's handwriting was not very good, nor was Julius's ability to read. Julius kept working at it until Basusu happily understood. Letting out a slow whistle, he leaned back in his chair and stared up at the ceiling. Now he knew that Chati would have him to go to the chapel. He smiled; it was something he could manage.

Understanding that the chapel would probably be the only place they would be allowed to meet, Basusu wondered what his first meeting there would be like. The rest of the week, he thought of nothing but the day of chapel. He wondered how Chati would react when she saw him and how he would feel when he saw her.

Upon arriving at the plantation, each slave had been given a pair of boots, but they were not used unless it was cold or they were traveling far. Realizing that it would be improper to be in the chapel without shoes on, Basusu pulled the heavy shoes from under his bed and slid his feet into them. He inhaled heavily and took a step, his ankles dragging as if they had lead wrapped around them. Shaking his head he tried again.

CLUMP. CLUMP. CLUMP.

Basusu turned around and marched back. He lifted his legs far in front of him and landed them firmly.

CLUMP. CLUMP. CLUMP.

Back and forth he marched until he became accustomed to the weight of the boot. His ankles throbbed that evening as he rested, but Chati's sweet face and laughter filled his dreams, making the pain more than bearable.

On Sunday morning, Basusu awakened and prepared eagerly for his first chapel service—the bells ringing across the field, announcing the beginning of service. Hastily pulling his boots on, Basusu stood tall, thrust his hat on his head, and headed out the door. Birds chirped, and Basusu smiled with eagerness; however, his good feelings trickled away once he realized his field companions were peeping out of their windows, watching him as he walked down to the chapel. Everyone was wondering what change had happened to him.

As Basusu approached the edge of the clearing, his stomach dropped, and he felt strangely out of place. After some hesitation, he saw a group of people led by a slave named Rod file into the building. He recognized Rod; he was the man who pumped the organ. Breathing deeply, Basusu marched forward and made his way up the steps and into the small building to watch the people to see what they did.

Rod went straight up to the front of the chapel and sat in one of the front benches so he could go to the organ in time. Basusu smiled, pleased that he had found where to go. He marched up to the front, his stride sure and confident—but inside, he felt scared as a kitten.

Basusu took a seat on the front bench and folded his hands in his lap. Everyone gawked at the odd action. The front bench was no place for a field hand, and his selection of seating caused him to look conspicuous.

With everyone staring, Rod whispered, "Whaad yo' doin' here?"

"I come to chapel," Basusu replied.

"You no sit here."

"It's okay, suh, 'cause yo' sat here," Basusu replied.

"I pump de organ," Rod replied. Basusu did not understand what Rod meant by pumping the organ, so he replied, "Dat's okay."

Rod replied, "You don' understan'. Go to de back of de chapel." Blood rushed into his face, and Basusu clenched his jaw firmly. As quickly as he possibly could, he made his way to the back of the chapel. He had almost made it when the back doors opened and in came Sally and Chati. Basusu's heart began to pound. He glanced shyly at Chati, unaware that everyone was still watching him. Sally marched forward and neared Basusu. She calmly lifted his hat off his head and placed it in his hands.

"Yo' look very nice, Basusu," she whispered in his ear. She then gestured for Chati to follow her, and together they found a seat.

Chati fluffed her skirts and took her seat next to Sally. She held her head high and quietly folded her hands in her lap. Her apparent quiet demeanor veiled the inner happiness that she felt. She could not believe her eyes. Basusu was in the chapel! He really came! For her! Of course, it was not terribly unusual for slaves to attend chapel, although it was usually reserved for the privileged few who worked in the big house. Basusu was a field hand so many wondered why he was there. However, no one would discourage him because there was a notion among many masters that those slaves who attended church were more obedient and cooperative. Chati smiled slightly and toyed with the strings from her bonnet. She knew in her heart that Basusu came to the chapel on her account.

Master Jordan was among those plantation masters who believed the presence of a chapel promoted cooperation. He trusted in the stabilizing effect of chapel services so much that he often arranged for visits by white pastors from nearby towns. Today's chapel service was no different. Master Jordan had asked Reverend Abe Zebedee Marshall, a white Baptist preacher from Savannah, to accompany the Reverend John Dwight Stockport, a black preacher from Augusta, to the Jordan Plantation.

After a few hymns, followed by a prayer, Reverend Marshall rose regally, tilted his spectacles and took his place at the podium. He gazed around the building and shifted his standing position before clearing his throat.

"I want to introduce to you," he said, "to the Reverend J. D. Stockport." He gestured toward a stocky black man sitting behind him. Stockport stood and made his way to the podium, where Reverend Marshall stood. He bowed slightly to the congregation and positioned himself by Reverend Marshall's side.

"Reverend Stockport," Reverend Marshall continued, "has traveled all the way here to your chapel from the Springfield Baptist Church, which is two days away from here in Augusta. You should also know that his church is probably the first independent church built for Negroes, which is what white folks are now calling you people brought here from Africa. Reverend Stockport is one of two preachers now serving Springfield Baptist Church, which is right next to the beautiful Savannah River. Someday, perhaps your Master Jordan may allow you to establish such a church right here on this plantation. A church for Negroes only!"

Turning to Reverend Stockport, Reverend Marshall said, "I place this service entirely in your capable hands, for I know your words will bless all who listen and pray with you. I must leave to conduct a Sunday prayer service for the Jordan family."

When the Reverend Stockport began the service, Basusu watched carefully because he didn't know what to do. He followed the crowd. He stood when they stood and sat when they sat, only becoming conspicuous when they were singing because he didn't know the words or the melodies. But some tunes were the same as those his fellow slaves sang in the fields. By now, he too could mumble some of them.

Reverend Stockport was a short, balding African whose skin was the deepest, most intense black Basusu had ever seen. His eyes smiled, the whites contrasting markedly with his skin. His words were like a song. Basusu was entranced; he listened to every melodious word.

"For with God, nothing shall be impossible," he perfectly quoted.

"Yo' are my chilun!" exclaimed the preacher, grasping the sides of the podium. "You are de Lawd's chilun! Chilun o' de Lawd yo' is! An' yo' know whad dat makes yo'? Dat makes yo' important. Even tho' yo' slaves here."

The congregation did not sit quietly during the sermon. So often did they respond to Reverend Stockport that he was limited to a few words at a time. Chati was as vocal as the others, exclaiming, "Dat's right!" or "Thank yo', Lawd!" or "Praise de Lawd!" Basusu got as excited as Chati did. Soon, he too was responding, although he did not understand all that was said nor all the words the preacher used.

"De Lawd's wid yo' all de times, my chilun! De Lawd helps yo' do everytin' no matta how hard. He's wit' you' when dey whips on yo' back. When yo' sweatin' over de cotton." And then he told them a story that encouraged them and fueled their hope in God.

"Just seventy years ago, a slave jus' likes yo', name Andrew Bryan, decided to lead his brothers an' sisters in prayer in a barn," he said softly, as if he were telling a secret. The congregation listened intently; no one made any noise or moved. "Andy Bryan's a slave jus' like yo' all 'ere! It was de Reveren' Marshall dat helped Andy start a Baptist Church in Savannah!"

"Praise de Lawd!" Sally shouted.

"Yes, ma'am!" answered the preacher. "Dat was 'bout sixty years ago. An' today, dey callin' dat church the First Amer'can Baptist Church," he said, standing proud as he reminisced of the goodness of God. Waving the Bible, Reverend Stockport's eyes glimmered with hope. He seemed to look past the people, the praises, and amens, totally enraptured with a faith and assurance that Basusu did not understand but longed to know. Although he had only heard it for the first time, the text that Reverend Stockport quoted sank deep in his consciousness. "Wid God, notin' is impossible," he repeated to himself many times.

CHAPTER 7

Base Wants Know God

As the service ended, everyone gathered outside for fellowship, shaking hands and talking about the sermon. Basusu stood just outside the door of the chapel, hoping that Chati would speak to him as she went by. To his surprise, Sally came up to him and said, "How is yo'? I rememba yo', but does yo' rememba me?" Basusu was distant. He was trying to memorize the sermon text.

"Yes, ma'am, I rememba yo' well, ma'am," Basusu replied, humbly remembering his first night on the Jordan plantation.

"Yo' lookin' fine now," said Sally. Basusu did not know what else to say, so he just smiled. Chati was standing by, and she too did not utter a word. Just as they were moving off, however, their eyes met for a few moments; and in that brief time, they communicated care for each other.

Both Basusu and Chati went their separate ways. Basusu not only showed he cared but got a chance to exhibit the spirit of an African chief, having bravely crossed the dividing line between the people in the big house and the field hands. For Basusu, this demonstrated the makings of a man. But nothing was as satisfying as the new idea—the text. *I mus' know dis God,* he pledged to himself.

As he walked back toward his cabin, Basusu's former worries and fears were replaced by new things to worry and wonder about. "Wha' goin' happen now?" he asked himself. "How to keep seein' Chati? How to become a man in dis land? Chati still in de big house, and I still be da fiel' han'."

After a bit of contemplation, he remembered that there was chapel every week. A thought hit him—he would continue going to chapel in order to see Chati.

For a brief moment, Basusu felt something beyond himself comforting his thoughts and giving him hope. Faith coursed through his spirit, and he felt warmed by a presence he did not know but that he felt knew him very well. He wondered if this was the presence of God that Reverend Stockport had preached about. Not sure of the presence he felt but feeling encouraged that he should inquire, he stopped walking and reverently asked, "Lawd, is dis yo'?" He listened intently. Nothing extraordinary happened, but he felt a continual peace. Satisfied, he headed for home.

Monday morning came, and Basusu had to face the drudgery of work in the fields. For him, Sunday became a taste of the heavenly—worship of the Lord and seeing Chati.

Basusu could hardly wait for Sundays to come. He intently listened to the preacher and committed to memory passages of Scripture that the preacher touched on. He learned simple prayers and uttered them before he went to sleep and upon rising in the morning. On more than one occasion, he found himself uttering "Lawd!" whenever he became frustrated or encountered a grueling day in the field. Before long, everyone accepted him as a regular at chapel, and they also observed that something was brewing between him and Chati.

By now, Sally knew that her daughter was in love. She had noticed the changes in her mood from time to time. One day, she decided to talk to Chati about what she was experiencing but, like most mothers, pretended not to know what was going on.

"Chati, yo' been actin' kinda diff'rent dese days. Honey, whad's wrong?" Sally asked as she scrubbed a stubborn stain on a chair cushion.

"Nothin', Mama. Nothin'," Chati replied, pretending to act casual. She gave too much effort to polishing silverware that didn't need polishing.

"Chile, I was not bawn dis big, yo' know. It's dat Basusu, ain't it?" Sally eyed Chati until she got her attention.

"How did yo' know, Mama?" Chati asked, exhaling as she laid down the polish and the rag.

"I tol' yo' dat I was not bawn dis big." Sally extended her arms for emphasis.

"Mama, what do yo' think 'bout it?" Chati asked as she sat on a stool, giving Sally her full attention.

"Well, it's okay, but yo' so young; yo's only seventeen," Sally answered.

"Yes, Mama. But yo' had me when yo' was jus' fifteen," Chati replied, clearly unaware of the possible repercussions of marrying too young.

"Yes, dear chile. But look whad happen to me." Sally attacked the stain more feverishly.

"Whad, Mama?" Chati innocently asked.

"I ain't neva saw yo' fatha again." Sally wiped the perspiration from her forehead and blankly stared at the cushion.

"Where is he, Mama?" Chati's voice was barely audible.

"Somewhere in de world, chile, somewhere in de world." Sally averted Chati's gaze. Finally, she dropped the rag, bit her lip, and met her daughter's stare.

Tears came to Sally's eyes as she embraced her daughter. After a few minutes, they loosened their hold on each other and looked each other in the eye as Sally said, "I don't know. Yo' see, yo' are de only one I have. If yo' marry an' leave, I'd be alone for de rest of my life." Sally felt as though she were the daughter and Chati were the mother.

Chati had never seen her mother so vulnerable. She hoped to ease some of her mother's pain and fears. She swallowed and, with assurance, said, "But, Mama, dere is nowhere fo' me to go."

"Well, girl, whatever yo' decide, just rememba dat I loves yo', and rememba you are all dat I have." Sally regained her composure and assessed the cleaning job she had performed on the cushion. The stain was gone.

"But, Mama, if we marry, where we gon' live?" Chati felt her heart sink.

Sally shook her head and said, "Chile, I don' know; I jus' don' know. But yo' rememba wha' de preacha say? Wid God, everytin' is possible!"

Strangely enough, the same question was bothering Basusu; but he had begun to take things in stride, praying and uttering to God whenever he needed help. His faith grew, and he began to deeply believe beyond a shadow of a doubt that the God of the Sunday chapel services was answering his prayers. His ancestors believed in supernatural powers and a divine being; and being somewhat familiar with these entities, Basusu relied exclusively on the God that was now a part of his life. He thought to himself, *I come so far. I'll fin' some way fo' dis to work.*

Basusu lived in a small cabin with several other men, while Chati lived in the big house occupied by the Jordan family. Not that she had use of the whole house, because house hands occupied only a few sparsely furnished rooms, but in comparison to the dilapidated cabins that the field hands lived in, it was luxury.

Chati wondered, *Could I live in Basusu's cabin or wou' Massa Jordan give us room in de married cabins?* Many things cluttered both Chati's and Basusu's minds, yet the week passed without incident.

Once again, it was Sunday morning. By now, Basusu was a familiar sight going down the narrow path coming from the row of small cabins that housed the field hands. This Sunday, when chapel ended, Basusu waited outside as usual. Chati stopped and spoke to him when she exited the small church. Approaching him with a radiant smile, she simply said, "Come." Basusu could not believe it! He was amazed, walking at a leisurely pace with Chati as Sally strode ahead to the big house. Peace and faith once again permeated his being, and he recognized the hand of God at work.

The enchanted couple walked along to the gate that separated the big house and the row of cabins, pausing for a moment to chat, among other things, about God. Basusu was excited to know that Chati shared his faith in God and believed that God was answering his prayers. Chati had gone to chapel all of her life and possessed some knowledge of God that she enthusiastically shared with him.

As they stood there talking, Sally stepped out onto the porch and said, "Invite him in, chile!" Chati, swallowing, asked, "Would yo' like to come in fo' a while?" Basusu looked intently at Chati and before he could reply, she nudged him and said, "Come on, don' be afraid."

Basusu had never been in the big house before and hesitantly followed Chati into the servants' quarters of the house. Once inside, his eyes opened wide in amazement, for everything there was luxurious compared to his cabin's furnishings.

"Sit down, Basusu, and make yo'self at home," Chati softly said.

Home. Basusu had mixed emotions at the mention of that word. Home was his village, his grandfather, his father, his mother, Akosua . . . anywhere but here in this land where he was treated inferior to people who had no idea that he was the son of a warrior, nor did they care.

Chati, not wanting to disrupt his thoughts, stood quietly in a corner, watching the object of her affection. She could tell that he was struggling with his past and hoped that she had not asked too much of him by extending the invitation into her world for an afternoon.

A breeze coming through an open window ruffled the curtains and interrupted his thoughts. Basusu breathed deeply before looking up and locking eyes on Chati. *She's beautiful,* he thought. Chati, sensing his feelings, blushed and absent-mindedly fingered the hem of her skirt. An uncomfortable silence passed between them before Sally emerged, announcing that dinner was ready.

In a little while, there was a lovely meal on the table. Basusu was not much of a talker in public, so he was glad Sally and Chati carried the conversation. Though he preferred to be a listener, and was hoping that was all they would expect of him at this time, he was asked some questions. He thought for several moments before giving answers, which consisted of the fewest of words as he was still grasping a very basic comprehension of the English language and strived to be accurate in his answers.

By the time the evening was over, Basusu knew for certain that he was in love with Chati, but he had no idea how to develop the relationship. Sally, sensing it, wanted to help as much as she could. While she did not want to appear pushy or meddling, she could not resist. As gently as she could, Sally asked, "Well, Mistah Jordan, whad yo' plans fo' my daughta?"

Basusu did not answer; after all, it seemed all too soon to be talking marriage. Besides, he was a little angry and confused by how she addressed him. He had never been called "mister" before, to say nothing about "Jordan." He was Basusu Mensua, not "Mr. Jordan."

Immediately, there was silence at the table. Basusu looked at Chati; she looked like she was waiting for an answer. He looked at Sally, who now leaned toward him to emphasize her interest in his answer. Obviously, both of them misunderstood why he was withdrawn—he was angry about being called anything but Basusu or Mensua.

"My name not Jordan. My name . . . Basusu. Basusu Mensua."

"No, not no mo'," Sally said, leaning back in her chair. "Now, I am Jordan. Chati is Jordan. We all has de massa's name."

Pushing his chair backward and standing up, Basusu exclaimed, "My name is Basusu Mensua. De massa is Jordan."

Realizing Basusu was seriously upset, the women turned their attention to finishing the meal. Their strategy worked; the silence allowed Basusu to calm down, and he resumed his seat.

"Miss Sally," he said, "I needs to tink 'bout yo' question. All I knows . . . all I wan' . . ." He saw Chati smile. "Well, I love Chati, but yo' and Chati is in dis big house. My cabin not de same. But I wan' Chati. Jus' gimme time to tink 'bout it." He reached for a glass of water, suddenly feeling parched. He continued to stare at the glass, turning it from side to side. He would ask God to help him with this situation that seemed to try his faith yet encourage it at the same time.

The women began to clear the table. Chati brought out a small basket filled with purple grapes and red-orange peaches from the Jordans' orchards and offered the fruit to Basusu.

Basusu plucked one grape, plopped it in his mouth, and began to think about his homeland, remembering especially the weddings celebrated in his village. His thoughts turned to Akosua and wondered if she would experience the wedding that she deserved. Almost instantly, evil thoughts swiftly bombarded his mind, thoughts of Akosua suffering on a slave ship, becoming ill, and being left for dead upon reaching shore. Never knowing what became of her, Basusu squeezed his eyes shut to rid his mind of the wicked scenario.

"Lawd, show mercy," he mumbled under his breath. Regaining his composure, he fondly remembered how the men of the village would get together and build a house for the couple preparing for marriage. Here, in this land, he had only a small cabin, now overcrowded since the arrival of young Julius coupled with the few older men who also lived with him. Here he had no village friends to build a house for Chati and him. What disturbed Basusu most of all was the absence of his father, his mother, his sisters, and his brothers. What had become of their lives? He felt vulnerable to the prospect of marriage, overwhelmed by the magnitude of it all. He loved Chati but wasn't sure that she could accept the ways of a tribal warrior. Everything changed since coming to this foreign land, and the women seemed to accept it as so, even to the point of changing their names to suit Master Jordan. Basusu found it hard to embrace these ways. He silently prayed for a sign from God that he was doing the right thing in considering Chati as his wife. Could she accept change to suit her husband?

Chati touched him, and Basusu jumped as though he had awakened from a deep sleep. "What's de matta?" she asked.

"Notin'. I'm okay," he replied, offering a genuine, albeit weak, smile.

Chati smiled back and helped herself to a few grapes. "Lookin' late ou' dere," she said, gesturing with a nod to the shadow of nightfall approaching.

Basusu nodded and sighed deeply, wishing he was going home to his hut in Odu. He bid Sally and Chati good night. Following him to the door, Chati thanked him for coming.

"Than' yo' fo' dinna' an' dis time wit' yo'. An' than' yo' for da stew dat time. Tast'd good," he replied.

"Oh, da Juba," Chati answered, recalling the meal that she had left with the note.

"Juba—dat's a name in Odu!" Basusu exclaimed. He tested his petition to God and asked in a hushed tone, "Chati, can I calls yo' Juba?" He searched her face. "Jus' fo' me?"

Pleased at the thought of an intimate name between them, Chati replied, "Yes, Basusu. Juba, jus' fo' yo'."

Basusu Mensua, pleased with himself at bestowing a Ghanaian name upon his bride-to-be, thanked God and headed for his cabin.

CHAPTER 8

Base Consulted With the Sage

Basusu pushed through the wooden doors and stepped into the night air. Insects swarmed around the light posts, and crickets chirped in the distance. He swatted at the bugs that fluttered around him, and stepped out of the light. Ambling down the worn dirt path, he headed for his cabin. The air was warm and muggy and thrived with mosquitoes, which suited his muddled mood perfectly. Yanking a stray grass absently, he swatted at the foliage that lined the path. He sighed and gazed at the starlit sky. His heart ached for his home. He thought of Chati. He loved her so much it ached. Her gentle ways and warm presence made his dreary life more bearable.

Basusu wandered sluggishly up the wooden steps that led into his cabin. They creaked under his weight and announced his arrival to the men seated on the porch. They watched him intently, but he avoided their eyes for fear that he would betray his own self and his inner turmoil. He bent over and sat on the stairs outside of the porch light and fiddled with the straw in his hands. The silence between the three friends was almost tangible.

"Whad's wrong wid you?" Kwasi finally asked. He eyed his old village friend intently. Basusu was unusually quiet. "Julius, bring de chair ou'side for him," Kwasi said without averting his gaze.

"Somethin' here is not right, an' we gotta find out whad happen to him." Basusu was foolish to think he could hide his frustration from his wise old friend, and it would be a worse attempt to try to hide the exasperation he felt. He joined them on the porch.

"Yo' ain't goin' to sleep till yo' tell," Kwasi commanded. Basusu eyed Julius blocking the doorway and frowned, wondering how much he would have to tell. He was sorely outnumbered physically, and the mixture of their wit and resolution left him with slim chances.

Turning his gaze to the darkened field in the distance, he felt their eyes boring into his head; and he felt they could just about read his mind. He sighed. "I loves Chati and wants to marry her," he finally mumbled. Julius strained closer to hear.

"Whad?" he asked.

"I loves Chati an' wants to marry her," he repeated louder.

Kwasi shook his head in disbelief. "Yo' goin' marry Miss Sally's dawta from de big house!" he exclaimed. "Where yo' goin' live? An' where yo' goin' keep her in dis cabin?" He waved his hands around for emphasis, his eyes wide with shock. The two of them laughed cynically at Basusu's fanatical proposition.

"Laugh all yo' wants," Basusu said wryly. "Whad worry me is how to do it."

Kwasi leaned back in his chair and folded his hands across his chest. "Whad yo' tink Massa Jordan gonna say?" he asked.

Basusu shrugged.

"Yo' know de house servants don't marry de fiel' hands, Basusu," Kwasi said.

"I know dat. But I love Chati." Basusu stood and leaned against the wooden frame. His chest heaved with a deep sigh.

"Well," Kwasi thought aloud. "Maybe Chati shoul' live in de big house and yo' lives wid her." He looked around the grimy cabin. It was practically falling apart. "Yo' can' bring dat chile to dis cabin; look at it. Look at dis place!"

It was true. The cabin was not a place Basusu wanted to bring his new bride. It leaked tremendously throughout the rainy season and offered diminutive comfort during the time of heat. A candle provided the only light they had. Basusu's African home had at least three separate rooms; but in this dwelling, there was barely enough space for the men to comfortably lodge, and they would be extremely cramped and uncomfortable with the addition of a new occupant, especially a woman.

The fact that marriage was not allowed between house slaves and field hands by itself seemed to scream defeat. Basusu clenched his fist in mild rage, fighting against the resentment that rose in him, causing his heart to beat a wild rhythm that pounded loudly in his ears. *I loves Chati . . . an' I goin' marry her.* He closed his eyes. *I will marry Chati.* He opened his eyes.

"I don' know how to do it," he declared, "but I love Chati an' will fin' de way."

The week was long and tedious. Basusu woke at dawn and shortly thereafter went to work in the fields. He and Kwasi worked intensely through the scorching heat. Up and down the rows they went. Their muscles cramped terribly, and their backs ached from the bending position in which they were forced to work. At evening, they returned to their cabins with barely enough stamina to scrub themselves with water and eat a rationed meal of field peas, yams, and okra—foods that brought them some comfort as they were foods from their native Africa.

Enduring this labor until Sunday was the ultimate test of Basusu's patience. He never had the blessing of catching a glimpse of Chati. Many nights he lay awake and thought of her. He suffered from torments of her possible refusal, or if Mr. Jordan refused to let them marry. He reflected on her feelings for him but often feared she might give up on him. He knew the proposal was impossible, but he had faith that her love for him was as strong as his was for her.

When at last Sunday came, Basusu arrived at the chapel early. His fatigue was soon replaced with an uneasiness and fear for the future. His stomach tightened at the sight of Chati. She didn't notice his entrance, and he watched her earnestly for any signs of rejection. Basusu observed her modest exploration of the room. Her eyes found his; and in an instant, he knew he had not been refused. Being warmed by the smile that danced across the room and filled him with joy, he thought, *She loves me*.

When they all gathered outside after the service, what Basusu had hoped and prayed for came true: Chati invited him again for Sunday dinner in the big house.

Throughout dinner, they conversed about their lives during the week. The discourse didn't solely concern the troubles they endured; each made an effort to balance the hard and demeaning times with the joyous moments of their new life—though those were few.

Basusu attempted to explain what it was like to work the fields for an entire day. In return, the women enlightened him on how early they had to rise and the many tasks that were laid before them. The stoves had to be heated so they could cook and serve hot breakfasts for Master Jordan and his family. They described the daily struggle with time, which they barely had enough of, and how they raced to clean all the rooms, change bed linens, and wash the family's clothing. Basusu had no doubt these women too worked very hard, although they were not in the fields.

There was a pause in the conversation. A mutual knowledge hung in the air, both parties knowing what was to be discussed. Chati glanced nervously at her mother, who subtly beckoned for silence. She lowered her head and bit furiously at her bottom lip. Her heart pounded, and her hands fumbled nervously for something to grasp. They found the solace of her cotton smock and worked at it fervently. When Basusu finally spoke, only then did she find the courage to look up.

Basusu searched the room in desperate need of the right words. His memory for the speech he had long ago practiced for this moment suddenly escaped him, leaving him vulnerable and nervous. He finally planted his gaze on Sally and spoke what he knew.

"Miss Sally, I wants to marry Chati . . . but dere's sometin' dat's botherin' me," he sputtered. Chati's head slowly rose, and he felt the heat rise to his face.

Sally smiled at his frankness. "Tell me, son; tell me," she coaxed gently. *Son* was a word as sweet as honey on her lips. She loved every minute of the short word and planned to utter it as much as possible.

Basusu found confidence in Chati's eyes. He inhaled. "I jus' know Chati can't live in my cabin wid me. Too small," he replied. Chati's eyes reminded Basusu of dancing stars. They twinkled and shone with merriment and expectation.

He continued, "Why, de walls got cracks in dem too. Yo' an' Chati already gots dis big house . . . beautiful an' nice."

Basusu silenced himself before continuing any further. What he was about to propose was a solution that he realized was unlikely to be received enthusiastically. His jaw clenched firmly. He had come this far and wasn't going to resign. If the proposal met opposition, they would simply have to battle through it. He had faced harder situations than this and conquered them. Therefore, he had no doubt that the result of this situation would vary.

"Miss Sally," he continued slowly, "if yo' don' mind . . . when we marry, Chati could keep livin' here, an' I will stay in de cabin." His head lifted, and his eyes met theirs with a steady gaze.

The silence in the room was almost audible. Chati closed her eyes meekly and squeezed her hands together furiously. Had she been alone, she would've screamed in declaration of her fury and impatience at such a life-wasting quandary. Surely something better could be the solution. She couldn't imagine being away from Basusu! No, there had to be a better way. Her mind searched in vain for a trustworthy response.

She knew there was none. The fate of their married life was solely in the hands of Master Jordan—if they were to have a life of marriage together. Tears stung at her eyes, and she fought anguish. There simply had to be a better approach.

"Basusu, whad kind of marriage will dat be?" Sally finally managed. Her throat was as tight as ropes, and she felt she would give in at any moment to the frustration that built up inside of her.

"Well," Basusu replied slowly. "We could visit each otha," he said dejectedly. "We have to do it dat way 'cause she jus' *can't* live in dat cabin o' mine."

Sally and Chati realized Basusu was not jesting with them. He was determined. They both were at an equal loss for words.

"Mama," Chati said, her voice lined with emotion. "We are de slaves here, an' it does not matta whad we want." The truth of these words instantly neutralized everyone's thoughts and ideas, including her own.

A tear slipped down Sally's face, and she dashed it away. "My chile"—she sighed—yo' right; it's all up to Massa Jordan." Sally put her elbows on the table and rested her face in her hands.

A pang of guilt stabbed at Basusu. "I'm sorry, Sally," he offered.

"It's not yo' fault, Basusu," Sally assured him. She pressed against the emotion that rose up within her.

"Don' worry," she continued. "We'll figure dis out, but yo' betta go now 'cause Chati and me gots much work to do tonight. Massa Jordan's got lots of guests."

Basusu nodded and glanced at Chati. She smiled weakly in return. Her eyes shone with tears but pleaded with him to stay strong.

Sally shook Chati gently, rousing her from her sleep. The sun had not yet risen, a purple glow hanging over the atmosphere. Sally slid into her smock and apron, moving quickly. She frowned at Chati who had grasped the blankets further under her chin. Sally grabbed a handful of the quilt and gave it a quick jerk.

"Get out de bed, Chati," she said in a hushed whisper, tilting her head toward the door. "We got to get goin'." She wrapped her head in a black cloth and knotted it in the back.

"Meet me in de kitchen," she whispered. Chati stumbled out the bed and nodded.

Sally laid the logs into the furnace and wiped her hands clean of the wooden shavings. She poked the flames to a decent measure and stepped back from the sparks that flew in all directions. The orange and blue flames danced around, casting their glow upon the sides of the furnace. Sally sighed, wishing she could feel as alive. She reached for a wooden bowl from the shelf above her. In it, she mixed the ingredients for the hot water cornbread.

Sally's brow furrowed, and she bit at her lip anxiously—the remembrance of last night's discussion still fresh in her mind. *Would Massa Jordan know da love dat Basusu has fo' Chati?* she thought. Never had a marriage been conducted between slave hands and house hands. Sally shook her head. No, not in all of her thirty-four years as a slave had she seen such a thing; and she doubted that she ever would.

She selected a large whisk and rapidly mixed the cornbread. The muscles in her arm pulsed with the work. Sally had slaved for the Jordans all of her life. They trusted her with just about anything. Sally abruptly stopped stirring the cornbread as a thought hit her. Mrs. Jordan often told her that if she needed anything she should feel free to ask. No other slave had received that privilege, and Sally would never take it lightly. She was devoted to the Jordans and knew herself to be blessed. *Suppose I ask de Jordans to let Basusu work in de yard?* she thought. *Den he would live in dis house, in de servants' quarters.* Sally felt relieved at the prospect of a solution, although it still seemed far-fetched. She would have to approach Mrs. Jordan at the right time. The entire situation *was* somewhat disquieting, and Sally had no idea how Mrs. Jordan would take it. She was a kind woman but did not show it easily. Resuming mixing the cornbread, Sally wondered if she would be reproached for encouraging the relationship across the established boundaries.

Approaching the conservatory carrying the customary tray of coffee, Sally inhaled deeply and assumed a facial expression that portrayed worry and concern. Pulling the doors open, she stepped inside and slowly made her way to where Mrs. Jordan was seated at her desk, absorbed in writing a list. Joan Jordan was a short, portly woman with a headful of curls and small piercing eyes. She was not beautiful but possessed a kindness that created a sense of loveliness about her and sparked a fondness in many people. Joan Jordan glanced up and searched Sally's face and frowned. Sally's face was drawn in and her eyes lacked their usual spark. "What's wrong, Sally?" she asked. "You don't look good this morning,"

"Oh, no, I'm okay, Missus Jordan," Sally replied hastily.

Joan searched Sally's face intently, then returned to her list. She began to describe what the household would need during the week. "Now, you need to remember to tell Grace to purchase fresh linens from town," her Southern drawl paused, "and make sure they have lace on them because I don't like them without it . . ." Joan looked up and frowned. Sally was fully absorbed with the activity going on beyond the window. Noticing the puffiness under Sally's eyes and the brow that was furrowed deeply, she exhaled and pushed herself from the desk.

"You are not all right, Sally," she said firmly. Sally shook herself and turned her gaze back to Mrs. Jordan. She felt the piercing inspection and hoped her masquerade was working. Instinctively, she bit her lip.

Joan gestured toward a chair. "Sit down and tell me what is wrong with you. Is Chati okay?"

"Yes, ma'am, Chati is fine," Sally answered. She accepted the seat and folded her hands calmly in her lap.

"Then what's the matter?" Joan searched Sally's face for signs of illness.

"Well, Missus Jordan, I does have a problem, an' I don't know whad to do."

"How can I help you, Sally?"

Sally's inability or reluctance to talk increased Mrs. Jordan's concern. She searched for the right thing to say but lost the opportunity to speak as Mr. Jordan entered into the room. Instinctively, Sally rose to her feet. The tension between the two women sparked his attention, and he noticed that something was amiss.

"Joan, what's the matter?" he asked.

"Well, something is wrong with Sally, and I was just trying to find out what it is. But she won't say."

Mr. Jordan turned toward Sally. "Come on, Sally," he encouraged, "tell us what it is, and maybe we will be able to help you."

"Well, Mr. Jordan, you see, my Chati . . ." Sally began.

"What's wrong with Chati?" he queried.

"Notin' bad," Sally squeezed her hands nervously, "but Chati is wantin' to marry." She took a deep breath and looked around anxiously, understanding full well that what she was requesting was out of the ordinary. Exhaling, she continued, "Well, yo' know dat boy, Base, de fiel' han'?" Sally was careful to refer to Basusu by his field name. Neither of the Jordans replied, so Sally felt obliged to go on. "He wantin' to marry Chati, an' Chati loves him too . . . very much. But . . . ," she continued, her voice barely a whisper, her throat tight, "where she . . . gonna . . . live?" Sally felt the weight of her request fall off her at the mention of those words.

CHAPTER 9

Base Seeks Permission to Be Married

It seemed as though an eternity passed, and yet time seemed to stand still.

Finally, Mr. Jordan looked at Joan, and then back at Sally. "So how can we help?" he asked, his voice booming, which shook Sally.

"Well, in de first place, sir, I don' know dat you min' dem to get married." Sally quickly glanced at Mr. Jordan.

"Well, Bill, what do you think?" Mrs. Jordan glanced at her husband.

"I don't know," Mr. Jordan replied tersely. He paced around impatiently. "Our field hands must not be busy enough if they're thinking about marriage." He glanced back at Sally. "Look, I don't want to have a big problem here. You know how complications upset me." He went over to the window and glanced down below. "I have to leave soon to look over the slave cargo that's expected to land tonight at Jekyll Island." He waved his hand and shook his head as if to dismiss the matter entirely.

Sally's heart sank, her "worried look" no longer forged. She wondered whether or not she had said the right thing.

Joan joined her husband at the window. "Don't be like that, Bill," she retorted. "They are humans too, you know. And besides, Base is a very good worker and a good boy."

Mr. Jordan turned to face Sally who dreaded having to meet his eyes. "Listen, Sally. I'm not in the business of making slaves' lives comfortable. I've got a plantation to run and this marriage nonsense is taking time away from *your* job right now."

Bill turned his attention to his wife and asked sarcastically, "Got any ideas, Joan?"

Ignoring his sarcasm, Mrs. Jordan approached Sally. "Sally, have you given this any thought? Base is a field hand." She searched Sally's face, coaxing her with her eyes to respond.

Sally felt the lump rising in her throat but forged ahead with her bold request. She faced her master. "Well, suh, I was wondrin' if'n yo' could make Base a yard han' so my Chati would not be havin' to live in dat cabin."

Bill Jordan looked gravely at Sally who simply stared at the floor.

"I'll have to think about that Sally," Mr. Jordan tersely replied. He had never been entirely convinced that giving slaves what they asked for worked in his favor.

The delay of response caused Sally to worry more now, for she was taking the risk of having her daughter sent away—or having Basusu sold or traded for one of the new slaves Mr. Jordan might see tonight. Joan too was troubled for she knew that when Bill became upset, he could be very unkind and irrational.

"Don't worry, Sally," Mrs. Jordan advised. "I'll talk to him as soon as I get a chance." Sally nodded and returned to the daily activity they had begun.

Mr. Jordan went out and didn't return until later that evening, which had both Sally and Mrs. Jordan worried. When he did come home, Joan called Sally to set Mr. Jordan's supper. The atmosphere was very tense. Mr. Jordan was not saying much to anyone. After supper, Mrs. Jordan went to sit with him in the conservatory. He was not talkative. A few minutes of silence passed between them.

Feeling compelled to raise the subject, Joan finally spoke up. "Bill, what do you think of Sally's request?" she asked.

"Well, I don't know." Bill lowered his newspaper and removed his eyeglasses. "I don't know what things are coming to these days—slaves wanting to get married." He shrugged and continued, "Maybe they don't know their place. What are they going to ask for next?"

He turned a few pages of the paper then continued, "The girl is very young anyway. What is she, fourteen?" He closed his eyes halfway. It had been a long day, and he was tired. Joan knew that her time was limited. Not long—and he would make an irrational decision and stick to his guns.

"Bill, you know that Chati is nearly eighteen now," Joan replied patiently. She hoped to convince her husband to see the lighter side of the situation.

"Why doesn't she marry someone from the house?"

Joan sighed. "Bill, they're not unemotional . . . she loves Base." Impatience rose inside her, but she pressed it down. Sally was depending on her. "She can't love just anyone."

Bill eyed his wife. "Are you defending them?" he asked.

Joan's eyes widened. "No . . . no," she stuttered. She neared him and rested her hand on his arm.

"Bill, Sally has worked hard for us for a long time . . . and I think it would be nice to let her see her daughter happily married. Base is a hard worker, and Chati is gentle."

Shaking her head, she said, "I don't foresee any trouble coming from their union." Turning Bill's head and forcing him to look at her she asked, "Please, Bill."

Bill's chest rose and lowered, and he exhaled loudly. "Okay," he relented. "Just this one time I am going to let it happen."

"Do you mean Base can work in the yards, or that they can get married?" Joan pressed.

"I wasn't talking about the work, Joan, I was talking about their getting married." Bill resituated his spectacles and returned to his reading.

"But that's only part of what she asked," Joan persisted, not caring that she displayed her affection for the slave family so openly. She pressed down his paper and searched his face. "It can't be that difficult, Bill. You can replace him in the field with the new workers you purchased." Her eyes moistened.

Bill softened. "All right," he said. He tipped Joan's chin and gazed into her eyes. "But I hope things are going to turn out well, and if they don't, just remember you pushed me on this." Joan nodded, stood, and allowed her husband to pass as he headed for the door.

"Oh, don't be fresh, Bill," she chirped. "Everything will work out just fine."

A smile washed over Mrs. Jordan's face as she watched her husband exit the room. Her heart was joyful for Sally and Chati's good fortune. Although she was happy about the decision, social position made Mrs. Jordan believe telling Sally this good news right away would be inappropriate. She would wait until morning.

Sally awakened and began her chores much before dawn, her worry for both Chati and Basusu continuing until she heard Mrs. Jordan's footsteps. She knew Mrs. Jordan would sit in the living room for a while, reading Scriptures or writing a letter. She would read or write nearly every weekday morning and looked forward to the cup of hot coffee that Sally customarily brought to her.

Sally brought the coffee and, afraid to ask what was really on her mind, greeted her with a neutral "good morning" and turned to leave the room. Mrs. Jordan restrained herself until Sally was nearly at the doorway and then called out to her.

"Sally! Wait. Don't leave just yet. Come back; I want to tell you something." She took a few sips of coffee and continued in an even tone of voice. "Don't you want to know what Mr. Jordan had to say?" Her eyes twinkled with merriment.

"Well, yes, ma'am." Sally was hesitant, but she had to know where things stood for Basusu and Chati.

"Your request is granted." Mrs. Jordan resumed sipping her coffee, which both concealed her own excitement and restrained her hands from grasping Sally's.

Sally brought her hand to her cheek and exclaimed, "Really?" She leaped up and ran over to Mrs. Jordan to hug her, almost lifting her out of her chair. Immediately she realized that she had crossed her limit. She apologized profusely. "Oh, Missus Jordan, I'm so sorry. I jus' couldn't help m'self."

Sally clasped her hands together and walked backward out of the room. "Oh, tank yo', Missus Jordan!"

Mrs. Jordan enjoyed Sally's happiness but could not afford to let it show.

Until now, Sally hadn't told Chati or Basusu what she was planning to do, because she was uncertain of the outcome and didn't want to raise their hopes in case it didn't work out. For now, she floated into the kitchen and began to prepare the morning meal.

When Chati returned from her chores, one glance at her mother's face told her all she needed to know.

"Chile, you won' believe whad happen today," Sally said. "You know how Basusu has been worryin' 'bout where yo' goin' to live if yo' got married?"

"Yes, Mama." Chati's voice coaxed for more.

"Well, I ask Missus Jordan to let Basusu work in de yard, so he can live in de servant rooms. Would yo' believe she said yes?"

"Yo' are jokin', Mama." Chati could hardly believe her ears.

"No, chile, I ain't jokin'," Sally replied.

"Yo' did dat fo' us?" Chati felt such gratefulness toward her mother for being so bold as to risk so much for her and Basusu. She purposed right then and there that her mother would not regret this day.

"What do yo' mean, did I do dat fo' yo? Of course, I did it fo' yo'."

Chati laughed and threw her arms around her mother. They hugged, dancing around the kitchen, crying and kissing each other.

"Mama, when are we goin' to tell Basusu? I'll go tell him now." Chati bolted for the door.

"No, yo' had betta not. Yo' know Massa Jordan don' let ladies go to de men's cabins!" Sally was determined not to cross Master Jordan no matter what liberty he had granted her.

"But, Mama, we are goin' get married. Why can't I go see him?" Chati insisted, stomping her foot lightly in agitation.

"Chile, yo' know yo' can't," Sally chided. "Yo' have to wait 'til Sunday, and dat's all dere is to it." Chati sat down, feeling a bit sad but overall very happy. Both mother and daughter could scarcely wait for Sunday to come.

It seemed an eternity before Sunday morning came, but it finally arrived, and with it the joy and bliss of Sally's and Chati's hearts. They were among the first to arrive at the chapel, but Basusu didn't arrive until the chapel was half filled. For Sally and Chati, the service dragged; they were anxious to tell the good news but could not—not during nor after the service as they wanted to be out of everyone else's earshot. Mother and daughter just had to wait until they had Basusu in their kitchen, following their customary dinner preparations and service to the Jordan household.

So anxious and excited were they to get from kitchen duty to actual time with Basusu that Sally and Chati looked like two horses proudly cantering with a reluctant mule in tow. "Come on, Basusu! Mama has got good news fo' us," Chati encouraged. "Why you draggin' along?"

Sally opened the kitchen door. "Get in here, man. Sit yo'self at dis table. Chati, let's you and me put dinna on de table so we can have a nice talk," Sally suggested. The two women scurried here and there to bring out the dinner, already cooked and kept warm in the oven. They had even set the table before leaving for chapel.

Finally, they all were seated. No one spoke right away. Basusu felt shy in front of Chati's mother, more so than when he was alone with Chati, which was not often. And Chati, certain that her mother would know what to say and when to say it, remained mum.

The meal was nearly half finished, yet no one had spoken about anything of substance; there was only small talk about what was growing in the fields and about the meals the Jordans and their friends ate in the big house. Finally, Sally spoke, with no lead-in to the touchy subject.

"Basusu, I asked Missus Jordan if yo' could work in de yard so's yo' could live in de big house servants' quarters. She sho thought dat was good. She even asked Massa Jordan. And he said yo' could do dat right away!"

Basusu just stared at Sally. His face did not portray either happiness or relief. He was wide-eyed and stunned, not knowing whether he should be joyful or scared. Basusu had grown accustomed to the daily chores in the field, however exhausting they were. Now he was troubled that he had to get used to something else, becoming a yard hand.

What was even more troubling was that he would have to dress up fancy each day; he also would have to be ready at any time to give special personal services for the master, his family, and their guests. He would even have to drive the master to town whenever necessary. Furthermore, he would be substantially more visible to all his bosses, all the way up to Mr. Jordan.

Basusu was not sure whether he could deal with all of that. As a field hand he knew what he had to do, and, as long as he did it, everything was fine. With this new role, he would be called upon to do many different things each day. Every detail of his performance would be under scrutiny.

Basusu was definitely upset, and Chati and Sally found that quite odd. In private, Sally asked Chati, "What is it about deese men dat make dem so diff'rent?" Sally mumbled to herself. "I thought Basusu would be glad. Wad's de matta wid him?"

As the evening wore on, Basusu became more relaxed about the forthcoming change. However, he wanted to know what was involved in this job. Chati had not said much all evening. In fact, she was a little confused herself. Finally she said to Basusu, "I thought yo' wanted to get away so we could live togetha."

"I do," he replied, "but dis is happ'nin fast. If I knew all dis was comin', maybe I would o' had time to think 'bout it. How do yo' feel 'bout it anyway?" Basusu asked Chati.

"Well, I think it's a good idea, but what mattas is what yo' think, Basusu."

"I guess it will be all right, but I neva been 'roun' deese folks from de big house. I'm jus' frightened," Basusu fearfully admitted.

"Was I pushin', Basusu?" Sally interjected. "I was jus' tryin' to help."

"Dat's all right, Miss Sally. I know yo' jus' wants me an' Chati to be happy."

Nevertheless, Sally did not understand Basusu's independent spirit. She thought the impact of slavery had broken him completely. She was unable to understand the feelings of the son of a warrior.

Chati laid her hand on his shoulder to comfort him. "Don't worry, Basusu. We'll be all right. Won' we, Mama?"

Sally nodded her head reassuringly, her eyes darting from Chati to Basusu.

Though they all talked into the evening, wedding plans were not discussed. Basusu did not bring up the topic, and Sally thought she had pushed enough. Indeed, she had arranged a significant job change for him—without getting his approval first—and his marriage would take place soon enough. She would give the boy a rest.

Before the evening was over, however, Basusu reluctantly accepted the idea of his new job, realizing it would pave the way for his marriage to Chati.

CHAPTER 10

Base's New Job

About two weeks later, Basusu nervously started to work as a yard hand, but he quickly got used to his new role and lack of routine. He realized that he was more relaxed as a yard hand because there was one less bully to threaten or hurt him. In the fields, there was a black man who always worried him. The others called him the Driver, whose job it was to make sure the slaves were always busy, always moving, always working. The driver sometimes brutally whipped slaves for petty reasons, just to impress Bud, Mr. Jordan's overseer.

But in the yard, there was no driver to worry him. The yard was more refined; work inside the house, where mostly girls and a few men worked, was the most refined of all. As a yard hand, Basusu now took orders from Mr. Jordan or from a different overseer.

Basusu learned that Mr. Jordan and the overseer were easily pleased whenever he showed gratitude and interest in new assignments, regardless of their nature. Yes, he was made to dress differently than the field hands, but that made him feel more important. When the overseer told Basusu that he was expected to improve his speaking, he began to pay closer attention to new words and their pronunciation by the white people. He practiced to himself throughout the day, and Chati was a great help, having been raised on the plantation her entire life. His effort proved to be worthwhile; he gained more respect from Mr. and Mrs. Jordan, the overseer, and even the other yard hands.

On Saturday, the twelfth of October, Basusu and Chati became husband and wife. Their mutual feelings for each other were evident by the glow on their faces and the nervousness they displayed. Sally couldn't contain her joyous tears for two reasons: one, her daughter was happily married; and two, she had gained a wonderful son. Her own heart simultaneously grieved and rejoiced. She never experienced a wedding herself, yet she knew the longing to be loved and to be desired by a man.

Squinting her eyes to alleviate the tears, Sally silently uttered a prayer and resolved not to worry about Chati's well-being. A few minutes passed before Sally gained the courage to look at Chati. One glance at her daughter dispelled her fears and quelled her grief. Her daughter was blessed today, favored by God.

The wedding preparation was simple and plain. Everyone looked forward to it, however, for celebrations of weddings between slaves were very rare. In the afternoon, when the sun warmed the autumn coolness, slaves emerged from their cabins everywhere to witness one of the few weddings to ever take place on the Jordan Plantation, although there were a few disappointments for the couple. For one thing, they wanted to get married in the chapel as they had seen some poor whites and field masters do from time to time, but Mr. Jordan would not grant their request. They had also wanted to be married by the Reverend Stockport, but that request too was not granted. They had to get married the slaves' way, which was "jumping the broomstick."

Basusu dressed himself as formally as he could, and so did Charlotte looking as beautiful as possible, arrayed in a simple cotton dress that Sally managed to sew from remnants of material with a large white satin ribbon sewn on the back at her waist.

Mrs. Jordan discreetly supplied the ribbon to Sally one morning during her customary morning service to her. Joan offered it as nonchalantly as possible, but Sally knew that she wished for Chati to have some measure of elegance on her wedding day.

In a few moments, the crowd of onlookers cheered as loudly as they could. The brief ceremony was over; next to come were eating, singing, and dancing. This was the grandest festive occasion slaves could have.

By nightfall, the festivities had to stop—an order from Mr. Jordan. He was afraid of what might happen with so many slaves together. Basusu and Chati had served many dinners to the Jordans' guests, which became occasions for overhearing many conversations. They knew Mr. Jordan still worried about the slave uprisings that occurred every now and then. The guests continued to talk fearfully about a slave rebellion led over twenty years ago in Charleston by Denmark Vesey, who fought to free his people from slavery and who was held in high esteem by slaves.

As the night settled down on them, the slaves returned to their cabins, while Basusu and Chati went off on their honeymoon in yard-hand quarters, which was plush compared to the cabins of the field hands. The honeymoon would be over by dawn of Monday morning when he would resume yard work and she, housework.

Sally was very happy with the outcome, just as she thought she would be. Chati still worked with her in the big house, and both women saw Basusu several times throughout the day.

For Basusu and Chati, Monday came all too soon. However, although they had to return to the mundane, their ecstasy continued. They were madly in love and cherished each other in spite of the lack of freedom.

About two months after her wedding, Chati became sick to her stomach one morning as she began a special task for Mrs.

Jordan. Standing on the unsteady kitchen stool to reach and dust the highest part of Mrs. Jordan's favorite mirror, Chati suddenly felt dizzy. She decided to step down off the stool before she fell down. That measure wasn't good enough: Chati headed for the floor and sat down rather clumsily, which caught Mrs. Jordan's attention.

"Chati," Mrs. Jordan called out in alarm, "what's the matter?" Holding Chati by her shoulders so she would fall no further, she yelled toward the kitchen. "Sally! Sally! Come here right away! Chati doesn't look well at all." She reached for a cloth napkin to wipe the sweat that beaded on Chati's brow.

With Mrs. Jordan's permission, Sally helped Chati get to her room. Both women were certain Chati had become pregnant. Sally promised to keep the pregnancy a secret from Basusu, whom Chati said she would tell after she was certain that she was pregnant.

"Basusu, yo's goin' to be a fatha," Chati said about three weeks later. "Ain't dat wondaful news?"

Basusu was so elated he couldn't contain his joy. He picked Chati up and swung her around as if she were a doll, then caught himself and steadied her feet on the floor, afraid that he would jolt her. For several hours, he giggled like a child in a candy store.

Eventually, Basusu calmed down and discovered, as he was prone to do, a reality that saddened him so much he suddenly sat down with his hands over his face.

"Whad's de matta, Basusu?" Chati inquired when they were alone.

Basusu was unresponsive, clearly deep in thought. Chati patiently continued asking until he told her about his fears and worries. His child was going to be a slave. It brought tears to his eyes and great fear to his heart. He remembered seeing children being taken away from their parents and sent away to other plantations, or to other fields at very young ages and made to work very long hours. All this pierced his heart and left him in tears.

As they talked, Chati too acknowledged this awful possibility but not to the same degree as her husband. After all, she had been a slave all her life. She had never known the freedom of a village of her own, let alone a family of her own. She silently prayed for guidance.

Each day, Basusu's mood would change; and the more Chati's abdomen swelled, the more anxious he became. Although their plantation was quite stable, there were stories of slave children being sold to other plantations that came to their knowledge. This caused Basusu tremendous distress even though he knew they were privileged to be so close to the Jordan family. When he was captured and sold into slavery, Basusu was a boy of hope. Now he was a man of hope and prayer, asking and even begging God to prevent Mr. Jordan from ever taking his child away from him.

Early one morning before the household was awakened, Chati's labor began. Basusu immediately went to find out what he could do. He summoned Sally who had prepared herself for this moment; but beyond that, there was nothing more he could do except pray and wait. As the custom was, he was prevented from seeing Chati while she was in labor, which made him very anxious. But that's just the way it was; he had to wait until the announcement came.

It was only about three hours later, but for Basusu it seemed like an eternity. When Sally came out of the room and announced, "Basusu, yo's a fatha," Basusu did not quite know what to say. Bubbling over with joy and a question etched on his face, he mumbled something that was not quite audible.

"Yo' can come in now," Sally said. As he climbed up the few steps that led to the servants' quarters, Sally could see that he wanted to ask a question. He was almost stammering.

"Whad yo' sayin'?" Sally asked."

"Ah, ah, is it a boy or girl, Miss Sally?" he asked.

"It's a boy—Chati had a boy!" she exclaimed.

Basusu was so happy he picked up Sally and twirled her around. Little did she know that his happiness came not only because he was a father, but more so because he had fathered a son. In the African tradition, for a man's first child to be a son is reason for celebration beyond just being a father. It means that that man has a son to carry on the family name and tradition; and indeed, as it were, a chief was born.

Finally, Basusu was allowed to see his newborn son and his wife. But Sally noticed later, that all was well with everyone except Basusu. He ate the evening meal silently with Sally, who had been jubilant all day, but her joy now was not enough to restore his.

"Basusu, yo' don' look like a bran'-new fatha," she pointed out. Basusu was crippled by a fear that he could not easily explain.

"Miss Sally, I be worryin' 'bout my son." He stopped eating altogether.

"Whad's wrong wid yo', son?" Sally asked, mopping her gravy with a piece of bread.

"I hear 'bout chilun bein' sold to otha plantations. Dat's whad is botherin' me."

"Don' worry, Basusu. I don' think Massa Jordan would do anythin' like dat to us," Sally confided, finishing her meal. Basusu wasn't so sure.

Sally was surprised when Basusu confided the most private of his thoughts to her. "Ya know, Sally, I been hearin' 'bout slaves runnin' 'way to de North, but I neva thought 'bout it. But if'n da white man try an' take my son, I wou' run too."

Sally stared intently at her new "son" and realized that Basusu was dead serious. These past years of slavery had not diminished the yearning for freedom in Basusu; rather they had intensified it. Freedom for his son meant more to him than anything right now, and he was determined to see that he had it, no matter the cost.

Basusu had heard frightening stories of slaves who did not make it because they were killed by slave catchers who chased them down with dogs. In spite of that fear, he was contemplating more and more the possibility of escaping. He often listened to stories of those who escaped and obtained their freedom. He resolved that if anyone ever tried to take away his son, he would kill to keep his son, or at least try to escape with him. Presently, however, more routine matters demanded his attention.

For example, Basusu and Chati had several disputes over the name for their son. Basusu wanted to name him "Addae Kwami," after his father, while Chati wanted to give him an American name.

"Addae Kwa . . . Addae whad?" she curiously asked. "Whad do dat mean? Who gon' say dat name? Basusu, honey, whad de matta wid yo'?" Basusu felt the sting of her comment in his heart although he knew Chati meant no harm. Basusu was the son of an African chief; there was no denying it, and for him to relate to his son as anything but a descendant of such tribal honor that was transferred to him was inconceivable.

No one seemed to understand how deeply Basusu felt about his tribal African heritage. His face registered deep pain. He wanted nothing more than to have someone who would just understand what it meant to him to hold on to some vestige of his homeland. And one sure way of holding on to something is to perpetuate his father's name. Basusu even consulted with Kwasi, hoping that he could get help in the matter, but Kwasi did not want to get involved.

After a near feud and several bouts of hopelessness, Basusu and Chati were able to select a name that satisfied both of them. Actually, they settled on one version. They gave their son the African name "Swamasa," which meant Samuel in English. Soon, they and their friends were calling him by his nickname, "Sam."

When Swamasa reached the tender age of one month, Basusu recalled that back in his country they would have celebrated the birth of a child, especially when the firstborn is a boy.

"Chati, whad we do to cel'brate de birt' of dis chile?" he asked.

"Whad do yo' mean, Basusu?" she replied.

"Well," he said, "back in Odu, my fatha kill de pig, goat, an' cow to cel'brate de birt' of de firs' son. Ever'body come to de celebration wid us. But in dis place, nobody cares."

Chati did not quite know what to say. Besides, she was afraid to say the wrong thing. She knew that it did not take much to send him plunging into a melancholy state.

"Basusu, yo' know dat we ain't in no Africa," she softly said to him.

"I know dat, but I wish we was," he replied in a deep guttural voice that sounded like it would break anytime.

"My fatha, my gran'fatha . . . all my people wou' come see dis here chile." Basusu looked helplessly at Sam who was asleep at Chati's breast.

Chati thought quickly. "Well," she began, carefully positioning herself so as not to wake Sam, "maybe we cou' ask Mistah Jordan if we cou' have a celebration like de one he had fo' his chilun in de chapel." Chati was referring to the dedication of the Jordan's children. That suggestion made Basusu feel a bit better, but he knew that asking for such a privilege was risky business.

"I don' know," he said. "Whad if de massa don' like dat an' get mad? You know how de massa is."

"He let yo' work in de yard so we cou' be married; maybe he won't min'," she responded.

Grateful for Chati's optimism but saddened all the same, Basusu replied, "It won' be de same; my people's not here."

Chati had to come to grips with the fact that her husband would never cease to long for his family in Africa—not that she wanted him to, but at times, it was difficult to deal with the disappointments he experienced, which she couldn't relate to. On happy occasions, he was sad. When changes were necessary, he mulled over having to adjust. Chati wondered, from time to time, if her husband would ever accept his life in America. She carefully unlatched Sam from her breast and laid him on the bed, eyeing her young husband, a warrior who courageously fought back tears.

Chati knew all too well when Basusu was not happy, and by now his melancholy state of being was affecting her too. Immediately, she set about to see if she could come up with a solution. Finding Sally and having told her all that Basusu had said, Chati asked, "Do yo' tink de massa, Mistah Jordan, wou' min' dat we do like he did fo' his chilun when dey was bawn, Mama?"

"I don' know chile'. Dem 'tings ain't fo' us. Yo' ain't neva seen no slave doin' 'tings like dat wid they chilun," she said, scratching her chin in deep contemplation. Scurrying away to do her chore, she left Chati with no answer and no promise.

Sally would always sleep on things before she would attempt to do anything. She always trusted her gut feeling. But she too was wondering what the master's reaction would be if it turned out that he did not like their request. Many days had passed, and Basusu had said nothing more about the celebration for Sam, nor did Sally. By now she had decided that she would, as usual, take the pulse of Mrs. Jordan before she went any further. She also knew that approaching her for any favor was as sensitive as putting a tender plant into the garden. Timing was everything.

CHAPTER 11

Base Wants Celebration for his First Born

The weekend was slated for a quarterly social gathering that plantation owners participate in during which time they discussed the goings on in the North as well as local matters affecting their plantations. This time, it was the Jordans' turn to host the gathering.

Sally set about to do the best job she could. She knew that if she made the Jordans happy, it might give her an opportunity to request a favor. From Friday morning, no one could distract her from her chores. She was as busy as a honeybee gathering nectar on a summer day.

By ten Saturday morning, the carriages started rolling down the long tree-lined gravel road. Under the large shade trees and on the porch were tables with every delectable food imaginable. To see it one would conclude that it was a world culinary show. On such occasions, each plantation owner would strive to outdo the other; and Bill Jordan was the kind of man that would not be outdone by anyone. But trust Sally, she knew how the Jordans felt about these gatherings. They would have to outperform the others by all means, and it was up to her to see that it happened. She set her mind to the task at hand, working with motive. Basusu and Chati were equally busy, but with no notion of what was driving Sally.

The gathering lasted until one on Sunday morning, by which time only the servants and the horses hadn't imbibed. Sally, Chati, Basusu, and the other house hands worked until the wee hours of the morning, trying to get everything in order. Even though Sally had not gotten to bed until four in the morning, in three hours she was up. It was about nine when Mrs. Jordan stumbled into the conservatory, desperately needing her morning coffee. "Sally, don't you ever get tired, my dear? I can't believe you made it up," she said, unintentionally, still rubbing her eyes.

"Yes, ma'am, I sho 'nuff tired, but I want yo' an' Massa Jordan to look good 'fore all de people dat come," Sally responded.

Mrs. Jordan replied, "I was not talking about that; you didn't have to get up this early to make all this breakfast. Who's going to eat it anyway? Nobody is hungry right now."

"It's my duty, ma'am," Sally replied.

Mrs. Jordan, having gulped down a cup of coffee, disappeared, heading straight back to bed. It was almost midday when the guests came stumbling into the dining room in a stupor. When they had finished eating, drinking, or simply finished waking up, the topic of discussion turned to the party. Everyone had something to say.

Finally, when Mrs. Jordan thought it appropriate she said, "By the way, Sally, you did a very good job for us last night. Thank you very much."

"Das okay, Missus Jordan. Dere is non' a dem' folks dat gonna outdo yo' an' Mistah Jordan. No, sir, not as long dat I hav' anyting' to do wid it. No, sir—neva," Sally proudly replied, turning her attention back to the seated guests who overheard every bit of the praise for her. Some turned their nose up at the thought of such open admiration for a slave while others hungrily devoured the feast that Sally prepared. Mrs. Jordan looked at Bill. Bill looked back as they both smiled and said, "Thank you, Sally."

The day was a long one; and when it was finally over, everyone was tired. It was hardly 8:00 p.m., and silence fell on the house like a thick cloud—the guests returning to their chambers and the slaves to their quarters to pass the night away. But like every other Monday morning, everybody was up with the sun. Customarily, at 7:00 a.m., Mrs. Jordan came to the conservatory, coffee and book in hand. She thanked Sally once again for working so hard to make the party a success.

Sally sensed that it was a good time for her request. She ventured, "Mrs. Jordan, I been wantin' to ask yo' a favah, ma'am, I hope yo' don' mind'," she started, careful not to take Mrs. Jordan's kindness for granted.

"Well, Sally, you know I can't read your mind. I would never know unless you ask," she said, savoring a warm sip of coffee. She placed her cup on the saucer and gave Sally her full attention.

"Well, ma'am, ah, yo' know dat Chati an' Basusu done hav' de baby," Sally said.

"Yes . . . I'm aware of that Sally," Mrs. Jordan replied flatly.

"Well, yo' kno' dat dis Basusu say, when dey was back in Africa dem have celebration fo' de first chile. I try to tell 'im dat dis is no Africa, but he still wan' to hav' sometin' fo' his firs' chile," she said, stammering. Mrs. Jordan could see that she was visibly nervous about this conversation. She had to admire Sally; this was the second time she had risked asking something for Basusu and Chati in the light of falling out of favor with her master and his wife. But she also had to think of her household, her societal position and, above all else, her husband.

It was a few moments before Mrs. Jordan responded. She was mulling over the request and the possible consequences. When she finally spoke, she was curt and to the point.

"Must I understand that you are asking for us to allow Basusu to have a special celebration for y'all's baby? Don't you think you've asked enough already? I mean, you should know my husband by now; you've been in this house almost all your life.

Why would you even bother to ask anything like that?" Mrs. Jordan quipped.

Suddenly, Sally felt sick in the stomach. *Did I go too far,* she asked herself. She knew she had to offer a reply. She regained her composure and gingerly said, "Ma'am, it's 'em young folk dat be talkin' 'bout celebration; it ain't no problem wid me, Missus Jordan."

"I don't think I'm going to approach my husband with this one," Joan continued, not about to face the wrath of her husband again. She remembered how close she came to experiencing it when she sought his favor to allow Basusu to work as a yard hand. Mrs. Jordan showed no anger when she left the room, but Sally was left with a very uncomfortable feeling.

After Mrs. Jordan departed, she thought about what Sally has said to her and felt a little bad about the way she responded. She knew that Sally would do anything to make the family a success among their influential friends and socialites. With that in mind, Mrs. Jordan decided that she would approach her husband if she could catch him at a good time. In the meantime, Sally said nothing to Chati or to Basusu. She knew that they would worry themselves to death if they knew the reaction of their master's wife.

Nearly a week passed, and Mrs. Jordan could not seem to find an auspicious moment; but that evening, it was raining so hard everyone, masters and servants alike, had to come in. While the Jordans were sitting on the porch, taking cover from the rain, they could see Basusu in the servants' quarters playing with little Sam.

"Look at them two," Mrs. Jordan said to Bill.

Bill looked and nodded his head in acknowledgement. "He sure loves that boy," he replied, with a pleasant look on his face. Mrs. Jordan thought it was a good time to broach the subject.

"By the way, I heard Sally talking about having some kind of party for the baby, if they could." She stood perfectly still, awaiting his reply.

"I don't mind long as there is no big gathering and nobody take time off work," her husband replied, still studying Basusu and Sam frolicking.

This was one time Bill responded before he thought about it. He wished he had not answered that quickly. He wanted to take his word back, but it was too late. So he hastily added, "What did you mean by that anyway, Joan?"

"I suppose they want to bless the child and have some kind of party for him," she answered as calmly as possible.

Bill got up from his seat, as he often did when troubled about something. Joan interrupted whatever he was thinking, "Bill, these people are so faithful to us." Bill held up a finger, which meant "Where are you going with this?" Joan interrupted, "I know, I know . . . they are slaves. I understand, but they are human beings, and surely we can give and take sometimes." Her eyes locked into his, and compassion was deeply etched into them.

Bill sat down again, his anger subsiding a bit. "One of these days, you are going to ask me to leave this house that I work so hard for to your slaves," he said sarcastically.

"That's ridiculous, Bill, and you know it." Joan wasn't offended at his statement. She understood that he had to have the final say even if it was a foolish idea.

Bill got up to leave when Joan uncharacteristically shouted out, "William Jordan, you did not answer me." Bill Jordan was clearly taken aback. He tilted his head, rubbed his chin, and with a slight curve in his smile that Joan caught, answered, "Do whatever you wish, Joan. Just be sure no one loses any time from work." Admiring his wife's grit, Bill headed to their private chamber.

It was a torturous couple of weeks for Sally. She was forced to quietly suffer in silence. But one morning, after Mrs. Jordan had finished her coffee, she said to Sally, "By the way, Sally, what did you and your family want to do for your grandson?"

Sally, still apprehensive, said, "Dey wan' to hav' some kin' a celebration; dey say dat he is da first son. Das all I know, ma'am," Sally answered dejectedly.

"I talked to Mr. Jordan, and he gave his permission, but you be sure you and the others don't lose any time from work," Mrs. Jordan said.

Sally did not quite know what to do. She wanted to jump and shout, but she knew that would not be appropriate in the presence of Mrs. Jordan. No sooner had she been informed of this than she left the room and went to find Chati. Scurrying down the narrow hallway, she ran headlong into Chati, who was coming out from one of her morning chores. Sally picked her up like she was a rag doll. "Chile, yo' ain't gonna believe dis. De missus said, y'all can hav' some celebration fo' y'all baby!'"

Chati stood there looking as though she hadn't heard what her mother had said. It was Sally alone celebrating. After all, Chati was not aware that Sally approached the Jordans. But finally, like someone coming out of a deep sleep, she started to celebrate as well. They muffled their giggles and laughter and crouched together like two girls sharing a secret.

Later that evening, Basusu barely entered the house when Chati broke the news to him. Like her mother earlier in the morning, she was the only one jumping for joy. Basusu did not know that his mother-in-law sought approval for a celebration. When he got the message, he tried to celebrate like his wife and mother-in-law, but he could not. After all, his parents were not there to complete what he needed to celebrate.

Once more, Basusu's thought took flight back to his village. *I only wish I was back in Odu wid my people.*

Sally and Chati did not waste any time planning the celebration. But all of a sudden, everything came to a screeching halt when they remembered that they had to wait until Reverend

Stockport was coming to the plantation again in order to perform the ceremony and administer a blessing on little Sam. After much inquiry, they found out that he was due to be back on the plantation in two weeks. They resumed their plans.

Two weeks later, Reverend Stockport arrived to the scene of slaves sitting on the rustic benches. The better seats were reserved for the few whites who attended from time to time, including the master and his family. However, whenever the black preacher came, the whites did not attend chapel. Everyone sat in anticipation. Most had never seen a baby dedication before. The reverend held his slave congregation spellbound for the next hour with responding shouts of "Yassuh. De Lawd is sho 'nuff good."

At the end of the service, there was food enough for everyone, including a cake that Mrs. Jordan had clandestinely given to Sally, charging her never to let anyone know that she had provided it. It seemed to the celebrants like time passed on swift wings. As soon as the sun began to go down, they knew that the celebration was over, and they did not wait to be told. Basusu knew he was especially privileged to have these favors, and he was not about to abuse them. The reluctant celebrants went down the narrow dirt roads that led to the small wooden cabins. Basusu and his family turned into the servants' quarters where they quietly continued the celebration.

Sam brought very special joy to Basusu. He was his pride and joy, so much so that Chati thought he was ignoring her. Many days, Basusu would spend the entire evening on the back porch with his son. When Chati argued about it, Basusu simply assured her that he loved her, but that a man must spend time with his first son.

By now, little Swamasa was growing nicely, and Basusu regretted that he could not spend more time with his son as he would have done back in Africa. Sam was only fourteen months old when Chati told him she believed she was having another baby. Again, Basusu became alarmed. For slaves to have children was often risky and sometimes even painful—for the children as well as their parents. If times got tough or if the slave owner saw opportunity for profit, the healthiest boys and girls were sold.

Even though he was faced with worry, Basusu learned to cope. When a second son was born to Chati and Basusu, Mr. Jordan sent word through Sally that he was very pleased. She repeated her words to Basusu. "Massa Jordan say yo' an' Chati are very good slaves. He says wid people like yo', his plantation will always have slaves." Immediately, a change came over Basusu's countenance like a fast-moving rain cloud. Sally and Chati could not get a word out of him. Sally was stunned; she thought that he would be happy for such news. But Basusu knew exactly what it meant, and it sent him instantly into a deep depression. However, these moments of depression strengthened his resolve to be free one day.

Later in the week, Basusu was asked to drive Mr. Jordan to town. During the trip, Mr. Jordan inquired as to the name of the baby.

"Gregory, Massa Jordan. Gregory," Basusu replied. Mr. Jordan nodded his head in agreement to the baby's name.

"Mrs. Jordan told me your new son is a healthy one," Mr. Jordan stated matter-of-factly.

"Yessuh, Massa Jordan. He sho is." Basusu warmed to the thought of such a healthy infant. Many children born to slaves suffered health problems because slave families were not nearly as healthy as their white masters' families.

"You are making a fine new family for the plantation." Basusu wasn't sure what that meant. Was Mr. Jordan simply making conversation or alluding to his plans to retain the Mensua family as his slaves permanently?

"Yessuh." Inside, Basusu was as frightened as he was furious.

When Basusu came home that evening, he could not eat. Chati insisted he tell her what was bothering him. She sat across from him at the table, waiting for him to talk to her. She knew him well by now; he'd eventually talk. He played with his food, pushing the chicken and gravy from one side of the plate to the other. Without looking up, he said, "Massa say we makin' a fine new family fo' dis plantation."

"Well, dat's true, Basusu. Yo' know we belong to Massa Jordan." Chati clasped her hands, hoping to state the facts as congenially as possible.

Basusu showed anger that Chati had never seen before. He pounded the table and shouted at the top of his voice. "*Yo'* belong to him. Me an' dese chilun belong to nobody but me! I am African! We is free!"

Chati simply stared at her husband. His outburst, though warranted, caused her great alarm. She silently prayed that somehow, someday, Basusu would come to terms with his life.

Sadly, Basusu went to the back porch where he sat on a step—the image of a dejected man. Chati followed him and sat close to him, putting her arm around him and resting her head on his shoulder. Knowing she came to comfort him, Basusu looked into her eyes and kissed her gently on her forehead. Chati's quiet presence gave him hope and assurance. Soon, he began to feel better.

That night in bed together, Chati cuddled him and spoke very softly, so softly that he strained to hear. Then he realized she wasn't talking to him. "Lawd," she murmured, "save us. Help us, Yo' servants. Keep us togetha. Keep our chilun safe." Basusu fell asleep peacefully while she was yet praying.

Not more than a year later, Chati was pregnant again. And again, Basusu felt both fear and joy. He tried to explain to Chati that it was not the children that bothered him. Rather, he was afraid they would be taken away, sold, or traded to another plantation owner. He had seen wives taken from husbands. He had seen children of other slaves taken away.

After chapel on Sunday, Basusu and Chati met Rosie, a new field hand Mr. Jordan bought from another plantation. She told how one day the driver took her from the field and made her get into a wagon. As she was being taken away, she saw her husband protesting. Rosie cried as she explained further. "De overseer tol' him to stop makin' a fuss. But ma man tried to come near me. De overseer grabs him an' when I leavin' ma man was bein' tied to de whuppin' tree." She sobbed hysterically.

Basusu asked about her children. "We have no more chilun," Rosie sobbed, reaching for the cloth that Chati held to her to wipe her face. "Three girls an' a boy. All taken 'way. Dey not even on de same plantation!" Chati could sense Basusu's fear for their children, and for the first time, she embraced it as her own.

The Mensua family was blessed with another male child. He was named "Joseph." Basusu liked neither the name Joseph nor Gregory, but as long as his first son had an African name, it was acceptable for him. In Africa, the firstborn son carried on the family name's responsibilities and traditions.

THE JORDAN PLANTATION,
NEAR BRUNSWICK, GEORGIA—1851

Like Basusu, Mr. Jordan had a large family, comprised of three sons and a daughter who were just a little older than those of Basusu, even though he himself was much older than Basusu. They were Jerry; Bobby; Timothy; and Mary, "the baby," who had been given her mother's middle name.

Many times, other slaves joked that Basusu seemed to be competing with Master Jordan. Perhaps they were right. On New Year's Day, 1851, Chati had a little girl they named Jennie. Ironically, there was the same number of children in Basusu's family as there was in the master's family, an advantage they were not aware of at this time.

In the spring of that same year, the Jordans' firstborn, Jerry, had become seven years old and was considered of age to attend school. It was Basusu who was chosen by Mr. Jordan to drive the carriage to take Jerry to his first day of school. The entire Jordan family came along including Mr. and Mrs. Jordan and all their other children. Basusu felt more than pride and honor; he felt trusted, especially when Mr. Jordan appointed him to drive Jerry to school every morning and then fetch him at the end of the day.

Glynn Academy, the school selected by the Jordans for their firstborn son, was in the town of Brunswick, a seaport town built eighty years before on a mere 385 acres. It was an hour's carriage ride from the plantation. Though the Jordan Plantation was three times that size, Brunswick was now a busy town with broad streets named after places in England and Colonial benefactors. Every morning, Basusu drove Jerry past the town docks where a half-dozen schooners had been tied up to receive their cargos of rice, cotton, indigo, and fruits.

Substantial quantities of goods came from the Jordan Plantation, so much that Jerry often exclaimed, "Look, Basusu, there's wagons of my rice! And over there, my cotton! And there, baskets of peaches and plums from Mother's orchards!"

The academy was not one of those "manual labor schools" the Jordans spoke about with disdain. Glynn Academy did not require its students to perform farm work to pay for their education. On the contrary, it was a school attended only by white children whose parents could afford the tuition. As one might imagine, the Jordans were more than proud to have their children attend such an academy. It was often the point of conversation at their social gathering.

PART 3

THE JORDAN PLANTATION, BRUNSWICK, GEORGIA—1853

CHAPTER 12

Clandestine Education

By the twenty-fifth year of Basusu's life, all the Jordan children except Mary were in school. The Jordans made certain that the Glynn Academy teachers kept the future of their children in mind every day, for they had high aspirations for their sons. They planned for Jerry to be an attorney, Bobby a doctor, and Timothy a politician. They talked so much about their children's future lives that the teacher even addressed them accordingly.

During school, therefore, Jerry was called "Jerry the lawyer," Bobby was called "Bobby the doctor," and Timothy was called "Timothy the politician or statesman." A classical education was offered at the academy; so in addition to reading, mathematics, and writing, the Jordan boys were taught geography, literature, and history. The older children, Jerry and Bobby, were taught spelling and grammar, and later, German and Latin.

At the end of each school day, Bobby, Jerry, and Timothy came home to play with Basusu's children, playing games in which the Jordan children took turns in their respective roles at play. As the children grew and played together, the Mensua children gradually learned to read, learning from the Jordan children. Moreover, they also began to envision a future surpassing that of a slave. Presently, their tasks were limited to light housework such as gathering wood for the stove and occasionally helping tend the yard; but in the future, those tasks were calculated to give way to the daily life of a field hand.

On one occasion, Sam came home from a time of playing and told his father that he wanted to be a doctor.

"Where yo' get dat idea, Swamasa?" Basusu asked, stunned.

"Me an' Bobby was playin' today. Bobby was de doctor. I had to be de sick one. We friends, so I want to be de doctor too," he enthusiastically replied, searching his father's face for a sign of approval.

Basusu, forcing a smile, immediately remembered how inadequate he felt when he couldn't read the note Chati wrote for him when they first met. He certainly did not want the same thing to happen to his sons, yet he felt certain that if Mr. Jordan found out they were learning to read, they would be in serious trouble. Through his children's "passive education," as well as discussions from dinner guests at the Jordan plantation, Basusu had learned that over eight decades ago, Georgia established a law forbidding the teaching of reading and writing to slaves. He felt hopeful that his sons were progressing further educationally than he had, yet he was uncomfortable at the prospect of being found out. Though Chati knew that the boys were learning to read by being around the Jordans and knew too well that it was against the rules, she ignored it and hoped for the best.

The older Sam, Gregory, and Joseph grew, the more clever they became. Their daily close contact with the Jordan children was beneficial, as if they too were attending school. Indeed, they were being exposed to ideas that were denied to (and not even considered for) other slave children. Mr. Jordan was aware but not disturbed that his own children played with the Mensua-Jordan children. Their interaction and imitation of school only served to reinforce the education that his sons were receiving. In his mind, the Mensua-Jordan children were bound for the fields—or at best the yard—when old enough, which would promptly halt all further interaction with his sons.

Jerry, Bobby, and Tim played like brothers with Sam, Greg, and Joe. Of course, there was Jennie Mensua-Jordan, the pride of Chati's life, who played freely with little Mary, the pride of Mrs. Jordan's life.

In the evenings, Basusu and Chati would sit for hours and talk about how their children were growing taller, more handsome, more beautiful, and smarter. Chati saw the children as they frolicked around the big house and knew that her boys were learning to read. Now she openly worried that Mr. Jordan might object to the education that was taking place. She feared that Basusu would be held responsible for allowing the education of their children to occur, even though it was taking place inadvertently. Basusu, however, directed his fears to God in prayer, hoping for direction and an answer.

Sally, noticing her grandchildren writing words and reading them aloud to each other became distressed and feared the worst. On a cool autumn morning she found an opportunity to address Basusu concerning it, as he rummaged through a drawer in search of a missing tool. She sat next to him at a stool, mending clothes, and broached the subject.

"Basusu, I see de boys readin' now," Sally said while mending a shirt belonging to Jerry.

Basusu momentarily looked up from the drawer and stared outside at the colorful leaves, which signified a new season. He sensed Sally's concern for the welfare of his family.

"Sally, I know dat de boys can read some but ain't notin' to worry 'bout," he replied matter-of-factly.

Sally laid the shirt into her lap and stared at her son-in-law in disbelief. "Do yo' know whad yo' sayin', Basusu? Yo' know de trouble dat will happen over dis?" she hissed, reaching for the shirt only to let it lie once more. "Slave chilun not 'posed to know notin'. It's de law, Basusu."

As the leaves tumbled in rhythm with the wind, Basusu weighed Sally's words. *It's de law, Basusu . . . It's de law . . . Slave chilun not 'posed to know nothin'.* Something churned deep inside his spirit, and he felt peace about what he was about to say. He located the tool that he needed before replying.

"Sally," he started, facing her. "Da boys mus' learn to read."

Sally was dumbfounded. Reaching to grasp Basusu by the wrists, she looked carefully around to make sure they weren't seen by anyone before she spoke, then intently looked at him.

"Basusu Mensua!" Basusu knew Sally was serious when she referred to him by his full name. "Yo' goin' get us in trouble wid' de massa. Once he fin' ou' it's no game, it's over fo' us. Readin', writin' is not dat important." She softened her tone then continued, "Yo' gotta tink 'bout yo' life . . . 'bout yo' family's life. Slave families been beat'n, separated, an' sold 'cause of tings like dis." With that she released Basusu's wrists and turned her attention once again to mending the shirt, certain that this would be the end of the matter.

Paternal instinct coupled with tribal pride overshadowed the possible consequences of his decision. Basusu knew that this was an answer to prayer and that he would have to take the risk for his family's future.

Feeling that Sally would never understand his position, Basusu thought about how to let her down easy. He knew that Sally was only trying to protect his family and that her love for them was not an issue. In fact, it was the core of her position—she loved them all so much and didn't want anything bad to happen to them. But Basusu was a father now, in accordance with being a husband and a son-in-law. He viewed things differently and hoped against hope for a future for his family. He had to convey to Sally, a woman who had been a slave all of her life, what he was feeling. Taking a deep breath and silently uttering a prayer in his mind, he seated himself next to Sally.

"Sally, yo's a good motha to Chati and me an' yo' love dem boys . . . an' Jennie." He sensed Sally relax. He paused to let the words sink in, then continued, "I know dat yo' don' want no trouble from de massa. I don' want trouble too." Leaning in closer to her and lowering his voice to a whisper, he continued, "Sally, I got dis faith in da Lawd dat says let da boys read an' write an' tings. I know de law an' 'bout all de trouble but . . . some kinda way, it's okay to do dis."

Sally thought for a moment then responded. "If da Lawd put dat in yo', den I will believe yo', but jus' 'cause it's da Lawd—if yo' say it's da Lawd—yo' still gotta use yo' head, boy," Sally said, lightly tapping Basusu on his temple.

Basusu chuckled. "Sally, right now I gotta use . . . wha' da preacher say? Faith!"

"Whad Chati say 'bout dis'?" Sally asked, ignoring Basusu's remark about the preacher.

"Notin' yet 'cause I ain't said notin' to her," Basusu replied flatly.

"Dis faith done made yo' crazy, boy." Sally folded her arms and stared at him.

"Chati will agree wid me." Basusu met Sally's stare.

It was Sally's turn to laugh. "Chati's not dat crazy. Dat girl don' like no trouble." She rose from her stool to meet his gaze straight on. Although Sally was a big woman, Basusu now matched her height. Sally continued, "How yo' know wad she will say, Basusu? Yo' got some special way dat see her mind? Hmm?" A few moments of silence passed between them.

Basusu's eyes glistened with hope as he responded, "I got sometin' betta, Sally. I got da Lawd's faith."

Basusu began to have dreams about his children being free. In his dreams, they were free from slavery and free to read and write just like the master's children. These dreams allowed him to experience a measure of freedom that he could only fantasize about. These new dreams were so pleasant that when he lay down, he would deliberately start thinking about them, which induced him to fall asleep so pleasantly. Basusu prayed to God that one day, some way, his sons would experience freedom even if he didn't. Also, he pretended not to know anything about his children learning to read and write just in case Mr. Jordan asked him about the boys' learning.

In the evenings when Basusu was free, he watched his sons intently when they all had a chance to be together as a family without interruption. Over and over, they rehearsed the lessons that they had learned from the Jordan boys. They would rehearse words and letters and even medical terminology that, although they didn't fully understand, relished the activity of it all. Many evenings, they simply played with one another as siblings not relinquishing their imagination to the serious issues of reading, writing, or their future. Basusu was concerned when almost a week passed without the boys showing any interest in their educational skills until one evening Sam abruptly stopped playing with Jennie and said, "I wan' to be a doctor when I grow up."

Basusu was excited at Sam's declaration and privately wished that he would become a doctor. He recalled that whenever the Jordans' family doctor came to the big house, he was shown much respect and esteemed highly. In Basusu's village, a man was esteemed for *who* he was instead of *what* he was; but in America, a man was measured by his level of success.

Although he did not agree with this philosophy, Basusu realized that if his children were to have a decent, if not altogether fair, attempt at any measure of relative success, he would have to get his family away from the plantation. As free blacks, Sam could achieve his ambition. Basusu's heart surged with African pride and dignity that often lay dormant, suppressed by a system of injustice and inequality. But he felt in his heart that his faith in God would not fail him.

Basusu realized the potential that Sam possessed to be a doctor as the childish play games of "doctor" blossomed into a closer reality. The prospect of such a thing elated him, and he allowed the boys to continue learning. Nevertheless, how to facilitate it was beyond his comprehension. In order for one to be a doctor, one had to be properly educated and trained. To his knowledge, what else did slaves become besides a slave themselves, with life as it was.

Chati pushed her thoughts aside, for she could not imagine any type of successful escape from the plantation. She wished that all of Basusu's desires could be a reality; then they all would be happy. But right now, his fanciful notions of freedom interfered with their daughter's rest; and for that, Chati was annoyed.

CHAPTER 13

Base Heard of Free Slaves in the North

Around the plantation and over dinners served to the Jordans, Basusu heard quite a bit about slaves escaping to the North, where they were free. However, he never really entertained the notion too deeply because he had also heard about many slaves being chased down by slave catchers and brought back home. Some were whipped terribly by their masters; even masters' wives would take turns whipping. And some were whipped and then hung to die.

But now, in light of his sons' desires, Basusu was thinking about ways to obtain freedom. He despised the idea of his children going to the field like he had to do. In the North, slaves were free, albeit not on equal footing with white folk. The more Basusu thought on this, the more he wanted to flee. He was not like Chati, who had been a slave all her life. Basusu knew the feeling of freedom—he had tasted it. There could be no other way for him . . . or for his family.

Every once in a while he would say to Chati, "I wonda whad de North is like," to which Chati would reply, "Why yo' askin'? Why yo' talk 'bout de North so much? We ain't neva goin' know whad de North looks like."

"Don' be too sho," Basusu would often reply. Chati continued to take it all lightly.

That particular night, Basusu had a terrifying dream. He dreamed that Mr. Jordan wanted to send Sam to another plantation. He dreamed he ran away with his family, rather than losing Sam. They almost made it to freedom and safety, but the slave catchers' dogs found them. The dream so agitated Basusu that he lay on his back, then on his side, then on his belly. He began to yell when the dogs and whips closed in on him. Awakened by Basusu's turning and yelling, Chati shook him. "Whad's de matta? Basusu, whad's de matta?"

To Basusu, Chati's hand was the vicious dog in his dream. He pushed it away. It attacked him again, but this time he used both hands to seize it with a powerful stranglehold around its neck. The dog's teeth were bared. It shook its head from side to side and was snapping at his arms. Basusu once again pushed the animal away. Suddenly, Basusu opened his eyes, and he looked for Chati. She wasn't on their bed. He found her, awake and frightened, on the floor. He realized now that he had thrown his own wife off the bed.

"Oh, Chati! Juba, Juba." He lifted her carefully off the floor and placed her on their bed. "So sorry. So sorry. I hadda bad dream."

"Whad was it 'bout? Yo' was squeezin' my neck real hard. I cou' not wake yo' up."

"De dogs! Dogs!" he answered.

"Dere are no dogs here. Yo's in de house. We's in bed," Chati assured him.

She put her hands gently around his neck and tenderly pulled his head to her breast. "A dream, Basusu. It was jus' a dream."

Nevertheless, Basusu feared his dream would someday become real. Sam was now seven years old and was quite a big boy for his age. Soon he would be sent to the fields, and Basusu feared what would happen to him at the hands of some brutal driver. Besides, there was no shortage of horror stories about the mistreatment of children who were sold to other slave owners.

Chati knew how Basusu felt about the future of his children; and ever since his confrontation to her, she did everything she could do to help. Coming to understand his heart's desires for his family caused her to support his decision and bold step of faith. She herself was able to read and write a bit, so she taught as much as she could to the children every chance she got and unsuspectingly used circumstances that placed her sons in contact with the Jordan boys. Often, whenever the children came around she would say to them, "Go an' play wid de others. I got work to do," which seemed innocent but was quite intentional. It was her way of encouraging the children to interact. She knew how much her own children benefited while the Jordan children were doing their schoolwork.

Every other Saturday, Annie Mae Gilmer, a respected tutor hired by Mrs. Jordan, would visit to give the Jordan children special instruction. "Miss Annie Mae," as she was called by both the Jordan and Mensua children, was a teacher at Georgia Female College and a niece of Governor Brown.

On one occasion, while the children were playing school, Mrs. Jordan came by. She was delighted to discover what the children were doing. Later when she told Mr. Jordan about it, they both concluded that their own children were learning so much because they were playing teacher with Basusu's children as pupils. It would not be wise to interfere, they thought.

On another day, Miss Annie Mae asked Mrs. Jordan how it was that his children were learning so fast and remembering so much. Smiling first to her husband and then to Miss Annie Mae, she said, "My children are pretending they are you. They are teaching Basusu's children."

"Oh," she said with a look of disapproval. "I see."

Mr. Jordan spoke immediately, lest Miss Annie Mae embarrass herself. "Miss Annie Mae, what my children are doing is good for them. By explaining what you are teaching them, they come to understand better and remember things longer. So don't worry. I have everything under control and fully approve of this process."

"Mr. Jordan, with all due respect, your slaves are learning to read and write, and that is against the law. There may be advantages for *your* children, but I cannot imagine *any* advantages to slaves becoming educated," Miss Annie Mae retorted. Clearly disenchanted by the situation, she tersely continued, "Mr. Jordan, you are a respected plantation owner in this community and highly esteemed. What will others think about this obvious display of unlawful behavior? There will be consequences for your decision one way or the other. Hopefully, it will not be to your disadvantage." Turning sharply on her heels, Miss Annie Mae headed for the front door.

A new evening pastime developed for Basusu and Chati and their children. After the evening meal and with Sam taking the lead, the Mensua children began to teach their parents whatever they had learned from the Jordan children after school. The children had become the teachers, their parents the pupils.

With great enthusiasm, Basusu and Chati learned how to read a few basic words and write short sentences. For the first time since setting foot on foreign soil, Basusu felt free again. It was a different type of freedom—freedom of the mind—but the most liberating type of freedom, he realized. Basusu's confidence soared at the prospect of grasping a basic command of the English language. He realized that it would take time, but he welcomed the challenge.

Normally, by age seven, slave children are put to work somewhere on the plantation. Basusu's children were at or near that age, and Mr. Jordan wanted to send them into the fields; but Mrs. Jordan intervened, insisting that the benefits for their own children were more important than sending the Mensua children into the fields. Spending some leisure time in their study one evening, the Jordans talked of the benefits of more hands in the fields.

"Can't they study in the evening?" Bill asked.

"Bill, how can anyone find energy after a long day in the field," Joan countered. "Besides, can't you see that there is much work around the house to be done? And don't you agree that every opportunity must be taken to assure proper preparation of the boys' education? Their goals are that much more within reach with the extra practice they have with the Mensua boys." Joan anxiously awaited her husband's reply.

Bill Jordan was at a crossroads. *If I continue with the educational process, I'll risk my reputation. If I don't continue, my boys will not progress as swiftly as they are.*

Staring at some papers on his desks, Bill replied, "Joan, I cannot give special consideration for the Mensua boys. They're slaves, and it's time for them to go to work. And I need them in the fields. That's where they belong."

Clearly taken aback at her husband's reply, Joan Jordan would not relinquish her position. "Bill," she began, "our children *need* this extra interaction. They *have* to practice with other children besides themselves. Their game allows each boy a play-learning partner, so to speak." She regained her composure and gently crossed her arms, allowing time for the anticipated outcome. She didn't have to wait long, but the outcome was not what she expected.

Striding across the room toward his favorite chair, Bill retorted, "Hear me, Joan. It's time for the Mensua boys to do what they are supposed to do. That's why they are on this plantation—to work and labor. I have a business to run and a reputation to uphold, and neither will suffer at the hands of . . . slave children not doing their jobs." With that, Bill Jordan lit his pipe, took a few puffs, and planted himself in his armchair, his face taut with anxiety and concern.

Joan had never seen her husband this stressed over such a simple situation before. She had witnessed him deal with everything from crops gone bad to runaway slaves to men trying to cheat him. She couldn't quite put her finger on what unnerved him so, but then a thought came to her. *He's scared. He's scared of the threat from the tutor, and he doesn't want to admit it.*

As if he could read her mind, Bill spoke, "I'm not about to break the law for anyone or anything, Joan. I know that our boys learn and retain more by interacting with Base's boys, but you have to understand something. Slaves, even children, must work, not play, especially when they are learning *something* about reading and writing in the process of playing. Let's not act as though they are not benefiting. They are." Pausing to refill his pipe then deciding against it, he continued, "Bobby, Jerry, and Timothy will learn just fine on their own. They're smart. Right now, I need hands in the fields, and the Mensua boys are all I have." Knowing that this statement was not entirely true as there were enough house slaves to trade positions with, Bill shuffled uneasily in his seat and hoped his wife would put this issue behind them.

Joan waited. She waited because it was wise to wait before responding too soon. Her husband was right to some degree, and she understood his dilemma. But her chief concern was the fate of their children's education. She didn't care what any tutor threatened them with. Delicately rising from her seat, she approached her husband and sat on the armrest of his chair. She waited for him to acknowledge her presence; and when he did, she responded.

"Bill, you're right. It is against the law to allow slaves to read and write. But in the process of playing, it occurs a little bit. But who's to say which of our slaves don't already know some things educationally? You cannot stop a person from learning—it happens. But let's look at the bigger picture. Our sons are doubling their educational position by having friends who are eager to play school with them. And besides, they don't always play educational games. Sometimes they just play together as boys; and even in that setting, the Mensua children are learning. We can't stop that, Bill."

Taking advantage of her husband's thoughtfulness to her response, Joan pressed on. "Bill, you are a respected and noteworthy plantation owner in this region. Your reputation is impeccable. Men don't question you; they emulate you. Do you think they would really believe that you are teaching slave children to read for their own advantage? Of course not. They know better than that." Waving her hand in the air as to dismiss the notion altogether, she said, "Don't worry about that tutor. How will her word stand against your reputation? She's looking for an axe to grind. She's just jealous over our boys' favorable circumstances, and that she doesn't have control over it; that's all."

"You have a way of making things appear real smooth, Joan. You're gifted," he chuckled, turning to come face to face with his wife.

Joan smiled. "Thanks," she said. "It's just how I see it. Well, what do you think you should do?" Joan thought it best to allow her husband to have the final say although she clearly knew the effect her words had on him.

Outnegotiated by his wife, Bill agreed, with only a little prideful reluctance, to the Mensua boys working around the house. Mrs. Jordan made sure that the chores were light, having noticed that when the boys were tired, they were not alert enough to interact with her children and their schoolwork. Surely the Mensua children were being used, but everyone benefited.

As time went on, the Jordans received all sorts of compliments on their children's intelligence. Often, their sons' academic achievements were the topic of conversation at social gatherings in the big house and elsewhere. No one said a word about Basusu's boys' participation except merely acknowledging that they played the part of pupils and with the exception of Miss Annie Mae, who continued to tutor the boys with restrained disdain toward their "playtime" with the Mensua boys, all agreed that this method of hands-on participation was brilliant.

Many times, Sam, Gregory, and Joseph would make the Jordan boys read to them for hours, and then they would invent elaborate scenes imagined about their lives in the future. Jerry would be the famed defense lawyer in a courtroom melodrama that also starred Sam as the judge; Gregory, Joseph, Jennie, and Mary as jurors; Bobby as the accused; and Timothy as the prosecuting attorney. Their imaginations soared beyond the boundaries of master and slave, free and bound. At such junctions, they were simply friends.

With great benefit and interest, the Mensua boys were also learning the geography of the United States and of the world. And at social occasions when they served the guests in the big house, they overheard all the important developments both political and social, particularly the changes taking place in the North, including the things "Negroes" were doing.

CHAPTER 14

Base the Wise Slave

THE JORDAN PLANTATION—1862

By the thirty-fourth year of his life, Basusu had come to be regarded by the Jordans as "the wise and dignified slave" of the Jordan Plantation. He had come a long way from Ghana, now able to speak a considerable amount of English and run the affairs of the Jordan household better than any house hand.

Though always aware of their status as sons of the plantation master, the Jordan boys felt honest, deep friendship and respect for the Mensua boys, becoming so dependent on them that they could hardly be separated from them. The older the Jordan boys became, the more they traveled—always with the Mensua sons along as "personal servants," visiting plantations and busy cities farther and farther from home.

The year was 1862, and there was disorder in the South. Georgia had seceded from the Union after two years of open opposition to Lincoln's ideas. Since he had taken office, nearly all of Georgia's nine hundred plantation owners had gathered a hundred at a time at the Jordan dining table to express their fears that Georgia's prosperity might be undermined or even banned by constitutional amendment. Because of the civil unrest, Mr. Jordan insisted that travel cease for his sons.

Already, the War Between the States was in its second year. Whenever cannon fire was heard nearby, Sally, Chati, and Basusu often trembled in fear, as did the Jordans. Basusu overheard many dining room conversations among visiting guests about plantations becoming targets of the Union Army. Mr. Jordan had kept his children home from the academy for three months ever since the town of Brunswick had to be evacuated, with residents, shop owners, workers, and the Confederate Army fleeing for their lives. Miss Annie Mae, having taken refuge on the plantation, tutored the Jordan children every day; and nearly every evening, the Mensua children were present during homework, playing the parts of pupils, the Jordan boys their teachers.

On one such evening, the Jordan boys announced to the Mensua boys that they wanted to leave the plantation—and Brunswick—for a safer place. It was also time for them to begin preparing for higher education, and they decided that this would be a practical time to go North to seek acceptance to college. It was only natural for Jerry to say, "We need you to go along with us, Sam. Greg and Joe too."

Sam looked at Bobby and said teasingly, "We can't do nothin' like that. We can't leave Massa Jordan and our parents."

Bobby said, "Why not? We'll see to it. We are not goin' for good, you know."

When Sam went home, he told his parents what the Jordan boys had expressed about leaving the plantation. It seemed so extraordinary they could hardly believe it. But it was just what Basusu wanted to hear.

"Thank de Lawd!" Basusu said, realizing the trip would be an opportunity to escape. Indeed, he thought, it would be less risky than using the Underground Railroad, the existence of which was known by most white people and certainly enslaved Africans. Basusu also had been worrying that the Jordan plantation fields might become a battleground between the Union and Confederate forces. Perhaps the Jordan mansion might be destroyed if caught in the crossfire of opposing armies.

A few days later upon returning from a town meeting, Mr. Jordan told Basusu, "My boys are going North, Base, to see about college."

"Yes, suh," Basusu replied.

As he started to walk away, Mr. Jordan added, "I would like you and your boys to go along to take care of them."

"Yes, suh," Basusu answered, trying to keep his mind focused on the conversation. "We be happy to go, suh. We take care o' dem, suh."

Basusu hoped this was not another wild dream. When he went home that evening, he told Chati what Mr. Jordan had said. Chati became so alarmed, she thought her heart stopped. She turned pale and said, "If yo' an' de boys go North, I ain't neva goin' see y'all no mo'! Evah!"

"I don't tink dat's true, Chati." Basusu looked out the window, trying to determine where the sound of musket fire was coming from. "Ev'ry day de fightin' gets worse. Can't stay here forevah, Chati." That night the Mensuas had a long conference about going North. The main concern was what would happen to Sally and Chati if they ran off.

"No, we can't do it," Sam said, shaking his head after giving it consideration. We would put Gran'ma Sally and Mama in danger. They would probably be punished, maybe even killed. We can't do it."

Thoughtfully, Joe said, "Well, if they are goin' for an interview, they will have to come back. And then go again, won't they? Let us go and come back to show we're faithful slaves. Then we get everybody away on one o' the next trips."

"Sound good," Basusu replied. "But whad if we neva go again? Dis may be de only chance."

Basusu loved Chati, Ma Sally, and his daughter Jennie so deeply he could do nothing to hurt them, nor could he live without them. That was precisely why Mr. Jordan was not afraid to send Basusu and his boys with his sons. Right then and there, Basusu decided that he was willing to sacrifice his own freedom and let the boys escape.

Clearing his throat, he began, "Sam, Joe, Greg. I know dat dis will be too hard if I go 'long, so I tink to stay wid yo' motha an' Jennie. Yo' freedom is more 'portant den mine. I'll tell massa Jordan dat Chati is not feelin' good an' dat I mus' stay wid her."

"Papa," said Sam, "Massa Jordan will know you planned it all, and you all will be in trouble. We will not do anythin' to hurt you or anyone in dis family. Papa, we gonna stick together no matta what."

Basusu had nothing but admiration for his eldest son. He was willing to endure and to hold together for the sake of family. *He thinks like a tribal chief,* Basusu thought to himself. "Swamasa," Basusu began, immediately capturing everyone's attention by formally addressing Sam. "In my village, men always make de way for de village. Right now, dis family is de village. De time has come fo' yo' an' yo' brothas to be free. God is answerin' my prayers. Dis is His way."

Sam swallowed and remained silent for the duration of he evening. He realized that his father was in a tough position and that there were no easy answers. Before resigning himself to bed, he offered a petition to God. "Lawd, if dere's a way for us all to go, show us."

Early the next morning as the twilight gave way to the sunrise, Basusu was tending to the needs of the trip. He scurried about, checking the carriage wheels and frame. His heart was heavy as he knew that his boys were about to embark on a journey for their freedom. He hoped that Mr. Jordan would cooperate with his excuse and allow him to remain at the plantation.

Surveying the landscape, he was reminded of familiar markings. There was the tree. As a toddler, Sam used to play and rest under the shade of the massive oak tree. When his brothers became toddlers, the trio would cling to Chati's skirts throughout the day as she made her rounds, doing chores. Basusu scanned the fields. The workers were already out, beginning another laborious day, harvesting crops. Noted among the workers were a few small figures. Squinting, Basusu could make out the frames of several young children. *A slave is always a slave. Notin' changin'. Notin' getting' betta fo' nobody but de massa.*

Basusu's thoughts were interrupted by the sound of voices approaching. He turned to see Mrs. Jordan approaching. Alarmed, he thought that perhaps something had foiled their plans, but to his surprise, Mrs. Jordan also wanted to go along with the boys and named Chati to go along as her personal attendant.

Can dis be true, Lawd? he silently prayed. He continued thinking, *Almos' all de family goin' North. Dis must be de chance to get free."* But then he argued with himself, *Sometin' ain't right. Whad 'bout Ma Sally? An' Jennie?*

Travel was slow in those days, and adequate time had to be given for any kind of journey by carriage for it was many miles to reach the railroad line to the North. It was Wednesday, and the interview was the following Tuesday.

The Jordans and their personal servants left home on Thursday of the week before the interview. To see them leaving, one would think they were moving or going away for a year. There was only one problem: all the Jordan boys wanted to go, even though Bobby and Tim were not old enough for college. They would enter a private college preparatory school, and Mary would continue her schooling in Brunswick when the town became safe again. All Basusu's children would be required to go on the trip, for they had become the personal servants of master Jordan's children. In a way, they were one family.

The Mensuas became excited about the trip. While Sam and Jerry were veteran travelers, this would be the first time that they were taking a trip of this distance. Basusu had traveled around the state with Mr. Jordan a bit, but this was beyond his wildest dream. Chati had hardly left the front steps of the big house, and it showed, for she was asking questions about everything—and she got lots of answers. All the boys were eager to show off their travel experience. It was a beautiful sight to see these nine people leaving for the North like one family.

CHAPTER 15

Trip to Boston

BOSTON—1861

Three days later, the group arrived in Boston, tired and weary, but very grateful that they encountered no fighting between the armies. Several times during the trip, they had to leave the train and continue by stagecoach because the tracks and stations ahead had been sabotaged, sometimes by the Union, sometimes by the Confederates. All day Monday was spent traveling around Boston, Mrs. Jordan shopping as if she planned to open a store when she returned home. Often, Basusu thought of how he could escape, but he needed his family, and that restrained him from doing anything.

On Tuesday, the Jordan boys went for their interviews one by one. With the recommendations they brought and their financial backing, each interview was a mere formality. Their school of choice was an expensive private school, having facilities from preparatory school through college level. Therefore, all three Jordan boys could attend and be together at one institution. When the news that all three boys were accepted reached Mrs. Jordan, she was very happy; only moments later, however, the realization came to her that in order to begin their schooling in Boston, her sons would have to leave home. She now began anticipating their absence from home. She would miss them so much.

It also dawned on her that with her sons in Boston, the Mensua boys would have to be assigned to the fields, a change that would amplify her sorrow—because she had grown to love them as her own. The Mensua children were privileged, not as usual slaves; and this particular family had occupied a place in Joan's heart.

On Wednesday morning, the families started home again. Everyone hated to leave; everything was so different and interesting in Boston. The Mensuas lost what seemed to be a moment of freedom.

THE JORDAN PLANTATION—1862

The Jordans arrived home Saturday evening, tired but delighted to be back home again. Though weary from their long journey, the Mensuas decided to have a serious talk before retiring to bed.

The trip up North had opened their eyes in a way that Basusu could not dream. For the first time since he left Africa, he saw free black people walking the streets. Sam was able to pick up a few black publications, showing how freed Blacks were forging ahead in their quest for freedom. But what was most exciting was that they found out that up North there were black individuals who were doctors, teachers, and publishers. Admittedly it was on a small scale; but compared to the South, any such achievement seemed great.

Basusu now realized there was no doubt they would be required to accompany the Jordan boys to Boston in the fall, which was just a few months away.

The Mensua boys had not been idle while in Boston. They learned the name and address of a freedom fighter named Joel Brown. But how would they communicate with Joel without being discovered? Slaves were not allowed to read and write; writing letters would be dangerous. They had to find a way to reach Joel. Next morning, everyone returned to work as normal.

During their evening meal together, Basusu and his family gave thought to selecting a way to communicate with Joel Brown, Greg insisting that writing a letter was the only effective way.

"Yo' cannot write lettas to dat man, Joel, widout bein' found out," said Chati.

"I figured out a way, Mama," Greg said.

"Whad yo' mean?"

"Well, Mr. Jordan is making Tim keep in touch with the school in Boston, and sometimes he has me mail those letters. Maybe I can send one to Joel Brown without anyone knowin'."

"I don' know," Basusu said. "Dat's not safe. Yo' betta be careful, Greg."

"Don't worry, Papa," Greg said. "There is a way, and we'll find it."

Gregory had tricks up his sleeves that neither Chati nor Basusu could ever imagine. For instance, he knew that only privately they were known as the Mensuas. Publicly, they were Jordans and any correspondence that went out by the name "Jordan" was not suspect. Nonetheless, one problem remained to be solved: would anyone notice to whom it was sent? Joel Brown was well known in the North for his efforts to free slaves. If a letter sent to him were discovered, it would spell absolute disaster triggered by the embarrassment the Jordans would suffer.

That same day during study time, Gregory decided to try something new. Tim, now fifteen years old, was spending more time studying to prepare for an entrance exam, which he had to pass in order to enter college. Because of his deep interest in politics, Tim often wrote letters and speeches advocating various causes—some invented, others real. These he would read to his brothers and the Mensua brothers when they practiced their education sessions together.

Gregory wondered whether he could utilize Tim's interest in advocacy. He broached the subject one afternoon as the two of them were organizing Tim's schoolbooks and papers.

"Say, Tim, I heard some talk in Boston 'bout something called the 'Freedom Movement.' Did you hear 'bout that too?" Gregory asked, placing Tim's textbooks together on a table.

"Yes, there's a man named Joel Brown who has become a public figure, having attracted both admiration and scorn," Tim replied, while scanning some papers.

"Maybe we ought to write him a letta of protest. Mistah Brown's work might cause trouble in a good relationship between many good slaves and their gentle masters. Don't you think so?"

"I think," Tim said, laying his papers aside, "that Joel Brown has begun a campaign that is not likely to succeed. Furthermore, many slaves who escape do not even make it to freedom as they imagined they would. I'm glad we don't have this problem on our plantation." He resumed the papers again, obviously at a loss of what to do with them.

"If I were a politician, I would certainly write a letta of protest," Greg said.

Innocently, Tim suggested, "Then why don't you write one for me?"

"You know I would not be allowed to do that," retorted Gregory, glancing at the papers Tim held to see if he could be of assistance.

"Don't worry, no one will ever know," Tim said, offering the papers to Greg.

"Okay, but who are we gonna write to? We don't have any address or anythin'," Greg asked as he filed the papers accordingly.

"Just send it to anyone up there," Tim replied. "No one is going to take notice anyway. It's just an exercise." Noting that Gregory had handled the papers accordingly, he glanced around the room. Eyeing his textbooks, he grimaced but picked them up.

"I'm taking these to my room to study. You won't see me again until dinner."

Elated, Gregory immediately set about to write the "letter of protest" to Joel Brown. He closed his letter by explaining he and his family were going to be in Boston when school would begin and would like to meet with him to talk about the many slaves who die or are murdered on their way to freedom.

When Joel Brown received the letter, he immediately saw through it. He was used to receiving letters saying one thing but meaning another. He was, however, a little puzzled about the quality of the writing, but he remembered meeting Gregory and noted he possessed intelligence that was advanced for a slave. Greg had signed the letter, "Timothy Jordan," but he reminded Joel who he really was.

Joel replied by writing how happy he would be to meet with him when he was in Boston again. Though the reply was addressed to "Mr. Timothy Jordan," Mrs. Jordan noticed the letter and opened it out of curiosity. Joel cleverly phrased his reply to praise Timothy's advice, giving Timothy's parents cause for pride.

> Thank you, Mr. Jordan, for your thoughtful advisory letter. Please accept my assurance that in my advocacy of rights for slaves I will place on the highest priority the preservation of good relationships between masters and their slaves. I will do that because of your advice that such relationships will stabilize the political climate and promote economic development among plantation owners.

Mrs. Jordan was impressed and rushed to show her husband the reason for her excitement. "Timothy truly has the makings of a politician!" she exclaimed.

That evening, Tim was hugged and congratulated by his parents, brothers, and sister Mary. Before going to bed, he told Greg about Joel Brown's reply. Convinced that the entire family would be in trouble if the Jordans found out who really wrote the letter, or the reason for Greg's letter, Basusu forbade him to do any such thing again. Gregory was completely untroubled.

There were now three months to live anxiously through before the trip to Boston, and careful preparation had to be made. The secret nature of the Freedom Movement made everyone nervous. One thing was in their favor: everyone knew that the Jordan boys were going off to school and that the Mensua-Jordans were going with them on the trip.

About a month later, Gregory convinced Tim that courtesy required a reply to Joel Brown to let him know his letter had arrived safely. In his next letter, after showing it to Tim for approval, Greg slipped a note into it asking Joel Brown not to reply. Greg also wrote, "We are going to be a part of your Freedom Movement!" At bedtime, he told the family of his latest move. They became optimistic but still nervous. Basusu reminded Greg about being careful and taking pains not to cause any trouble to the family.

As the time for the departure drew nearer, the talking, both truth and gossip, was everywhere on the plantation—in the chapel, in the fields, in the slave quarters, and in the big house. And now, among the Mensuas, the code was "freedom movement." The Jordan boys prepared for their new school in Boston by intensifying their own studies, with the Mensua brothers as their pupils. The result of all these activities was that the slave Jordans were as prepared as the white Jordans for the trip.

Finally, August arrived! All the boys were finishing up the packing. Jerry and Bobby had to take a qualifying exam before entering school. The exams were given two weeks before school opened. All along, it had been decided that they would go to Boston, take the exam, and stay until school opened. The parents, knowing that the boys were going to be away for a long time, wanted to spend as much time as possible with them before they left permanently. A controversy arose: why couldn't they go and come back?

Joe and Gregory, hearing the discussion around the house, knew that if the Jordan boys went to Boston and then returned after those exams, it would be advantageous for them. Mr. Jordan certainly would send the Mensua boys along with his sons, which would allow further contact with Joel Brown.

In a few days, the boys were on their way to Boston, following the same route they had taken before. No one suspected that the Mensua boys might escape or that the Mensuas' own freedom movement was under way. Once the boys were out of sight, all restraints were lifted. They were just a bunch of kids together.

Taking advantage of the light atmosphere, Greg prodded, "Don't you think, Tim, that we should try to find Joel Brown and have a good debate with him, jus' to show him we Southern folks are smart too?"

"Why not?" Tim said. "That could be fun."

They arrived at Boston two days later, tired, but in good spirits. The Jordan boys rested that night, and the next day was spent reviewing for the exam. After accompanying the Jordan boys to the testing room, the Mensua boys left to look for Joel. Joel Brown knew precisely how to handle things. He had been at it for a long time now. He even agreed to have the "debate" as soon as the Jordan boys could arrange it. Most importantly, Joel Brown knew that they were coming, when they were coming, and how many were in the family.

With exams over, the Jordan boys agreed to contact Joel Brown for the debate. Timothy really wanted to try his hand at it—with a well-known, experienced opponent. So they went out to visit Joel Brown, the Mensuas leading the way to his small office, which was in a church in a part of town where there were many stagecoach offices.

Gregory let the Jordans initiate introductions and arrangements.

"I'm the Timothy Jordan who wrote the letter you very kindly answered, Mr. Brown. We came hoping we could have a friendly debate with you before we have to return. We must leave for home by train tomorrow evening."

"Well then, how about doing that now? I'd like to find out what you young men can do. Come, sit down," he said, offering the chairs.

Each of the Jordans settled comfortably in the brown leather chairs Mr. Brown had arranged around his desk. The Mensuas, however, took their places discreetly and quietly on the one simple wooden bench in the vestibule. They heard Joel Brown ask about them.

"Who are those boys?" he innocently asked.

"Well, they are the slave boys who were designated by our father to be our personal servants in our travels," Jerry explained. "We have known them ever since childhood. They are very trustworthy."

"Tim, why don't you begin what you want to discuss with me," Joel said.

"Thank you, Mr. Brown. This is an honor." Tim was excited but, thankfully, not nervous. Choosing his words carefully he began. "I understand that you are against slavery, and so you help slaves from the South escape to the North. But from what I see and hear, these people are worse off when they get here. How do you justify the many slaves who die trying to get to this so-called freedom land? Look at our boys there; we never had any trouble with them. We live and work together like one family. Isn't that right, Greg?"

Greg immediately stood up, answering, "Yes, suh, Mr. Brown, dat is true. We have a good life on the Jordan Plantation. So I also am very worried about what you are doing. Don' you know that not all us slaves want to come North? And as Master Timothy says, how 'bout those who die tryin' fo' freedom?"

Joel Brown was very philosophical in his answer. "Well, you see, gentlemen, freedom is more than having a place to live and food on the table. We in the North might not have much, but we are able to determine our own destiny. And that's what freedom is all about. Besides, freedom is not only something worth living for; it is also something worth dying for. I know that many have tried to be free, but one day's freedom is worth dying for. Don't you think so?"

The debate went on into the afternoon. Whenever Tim and Sam seemed to make a good point, Joe and Gregory giggled like they were enjoying it. Joel Brown ensured the boys the victory, and in the end the boys left elated.

The next evening they were on their way home; two days later, everyone was home safely and full of glee. That night, the Mensuas had what had now become their "freedom movement" talk. Their plan had worked; they were able to meet with Joel Brown and plan the return with the Jordan boys. They were also glad that Tim was high in self-esteem. He had not only "won" a debate with *the* Mr. Joel Brown but also felt confident that the Mensua boys were on his side.

The boys shared a quiet laugh. Their hope and prayers were that all of them would be asked to accompany the Jordan boys back to Boston.

When Joe and Greg had been alone with Joel Brown, talking about the possibility of entering school themselves, their speech and knowledge convinced him of their abilities to succeed in formal education. They explained how they were used as the Jordans' study partners. Joel Brown was excited due to the fact that there were schools in Boston offering places to black students, but many of those places could not be filled. Once he found out the extent of the Mensua boys' education, he wasted no time preparing for their freedom as well as enrollment in school.

CHAPTER 16

Plans for the Big Move

Several weeks before the time of the big move, the Mensua family became increasingly fearful. What if something went wrong? What if their participation in the Freedom Movement was found out? They made certain they appeared calm, accepting of their lot, and cooperative. It was slave life as usual.

Two weeks prior to departure, Mrs. Jordan spoke to Sally and Chati, informing them that Mr. Jordan was not sure he could go with the boys. Now if Mr. Jordan did not go, someone would have to stay behind to look after him. Everyone became worried. If it worked out that way, who would be required to stay? What if it were Chati or Ma Sally? What if Basusu were required to stay? It would complicate the whole plan.

Ma Sally spoke up. "Well, I'm nothin' but an ol' woman now. If anyone stays it sho'd be me, so be it. Yo' lives are jus' startin.' I sho don't have much left in mine. 'Sides, I don' know dat I could be happy in Boston anyway. An' I can' even read or writes."

"No, Ma!" the children cried in unison. "We not leavin' yo' here.

"Mama, it will work ou' fo' all of us," assured Chati. "We're not leavin' widout yo'. How could we leave yo' here?" Chati shook her head and reaffirmed her position.

"Dem boys ain't growin' up slaves all dere livin'. No, suh! But I sho don' wants us leavin' yo' here on dis plantation," Basusu said.

Sam was just sitting through it all, but now he could not hold out any longer. Rising to his feet and taking a position next to his father, he exclaimed, "Don't you undastan'? Anyone left behind . . . she would be in trouble. She would have to tell where de others are . . . we must go together or none at all."

"I don' know," Basusu said. "I jus' can' see yo' boys bein' slaves all yo' lives. No matta if I can' go, yo' gotta be free."

Reminiscing, Basusu told them a story he had heard as a boy in Africa. "My papa tol' me dat wid men, animals, and nature, some gotta die dat some may live."

"What does dat mean, Papa?" Sam asked, clearly alarmed. "We don't want anyone to die; we all want to live." He stared at Basusu, awaiting an answer.

"Dat's de way it is, boys," Basusu affirmed. "Dat's de way it is."

It was the custom of the day for a well-to-do family to have an attendant for each family member, particularly when traveling. The problem was that there would be one more member in the Mensua family than in the Jordan family if Mr. Jordan did not take the trip. But the Mensua boys were never without ideas. They had learned to find solutions, to seize opportunities. "What can we do," they asked themselves, "to be sure that everyone goes on the trip?" Shortly, they had a suggestion for their father.

"Papa," Joseph said, "yo' got to show Massa Jordan dat yo' gonna be mighty sad after the boys go off to Boston. He knows dat yo' always admired dem. Tell 'im you'll be betta if you go to Boston too. Tell 'im you want to be with them as long as you can."

A few days before the trip, Mr. Jordan sent Sally to Basusu with a message. "Basusu, Massa Jordan wants yo' to get out de new carriage. Take 'im ta town right away."

Waiting under the portico as Basusu drove up, Mr. Jordan was dressed in a fine business suit, one that Basusu had never seen before. Jumping from his bench to the ground, Basusu opened the carriage door for Mr. Jordan to enter. The morning was chilly, so he took out a blanket and laid it on Mr. Jordan's lap and legs.

Inhaling, Basusu savored the smell of this new carriage. Expensive aromatic leathers covered the upholstered seat Bill Jordan was sitting on. Mr. Jordan told him he had the carriage "imported" from a place up North called Pennsylvania. The craftsmen who built it had varnished the oak moldings that bordered mahogany panels, which were polished to a deep, dark brown.

Basusu resolved to give Mr. Jordan a comfortable ride—not too fast, not too slow. A few miles from the big house, Mr. Jordan spoke, "You have been taking care of my new carriage very well, Basusu."

"Tank yo', suh. I been usin' dat special oil yo' give me for de leather. Rubbed it in good, suh!"

A little farther along the road, Basusu ventured to bring up a new subject. "Massa Jordan, I don' know whad it gonna be like wid yo' boys gone 'way, suh. Sho woul' like to 'tend to dem one mo' trip to Boston, suh." Ordinarily, a slave like Basusu was expected to answer questions, not initiate conversations, but today he was compelled to say things that might persuade Mr. Jordan to send him to Boston. Bill Jordan was silent. Basusu wondered if his silence denoted anger and worried that his words might be considered presumptuous. After a considerable pause, Mr. Jordan responded, "You know, Base, I can't imagine what it will be like myself." His eyes brimming with tears, Bill Jordan began to weep openly. Basusu reached over and touched him on the shoulder. "Dat's all right, suh. Us Mensua family gonna be sad too. Very sad, suh. Ma whole family, suh, wants to be wid yo' boys as much as yo'd let us. We sho gonna miss 'em."

Realizing that he was counseling and touching his master, Basusu quickly took his hand off his master's shoulder, mumbling an apology. To his surprise, Mr. Jordan reached over and touched *him* on the shoulder. "I'm all right, Base. I'm sorry. I should not be so upset anyway." Both men continued their conversation in light of the boys becoming men until they reached town.

Joan was waiting for him in the parlor when her husband returned home that evening. Rising to meet him, she found solace in his embrace. "Bill," she said, "I'm so glad to see you. I've been miserable all day, thinking about all the boys leaving us at once."

Bill stroked his wife's hair as he glanced out the window. "That's how I've been feeling too, dear. A few minutes of silence passed between them. Recalling his day with Basusu, he continued, "Today, it dawned on me just how close our boys have become to Base's boys. Chati and Base have been taking care of our children with as much care as we have."

"And with as much love," Joan added, resuming her seat to continue what appeared to be a conversation of deep concern for them both. "And Sally, that dear old lady, has become like our boys' grandma. Have you noticed how much respect they give her? She does so much for them."

"I know what you're getting at, Joan," Bill replied. "But somebody has to be in the house. We can't take everyone with us to Boston. We are not going to close down this plantation just because the boys are going to school." With that, Bill Jordan nestled himself in his favorite wing chair, closed his eyes, and rubbed his forehead, a sure indication of exhaustion.

Joan considered her words and thought it best to lay everything out on the table at once. "I know you want things to run smoothly while the Mensua boys are gone, but they don't run things; they assist with our sons, not the house. We've got plenty of slaves in the fields, the yard, and the house, Bill. With the new driver for the fields and the overseer, things will run normally while we're in Boston. And I know in my heart—you do too, Bill—that Ma Sally deserves to come along. She has feelings just like us, you know."

"We'll see, dear. We'll see." Bill resigned himself to finish this conversation at another interval as he flipped through mail and periodicals that were within reach.

"No, Bill, please let's not put this off," Joan persisted as gently as she could, seating herself on the edge of her seat. "There's something else to consider."

"What's that?" he asked absentmindedly.

"Appearances, Bill. Our friends in all our social circles, as well as your business associates here and in Boston, would probably think you are having financial difficulties. We just can't rush up to Boston and then turn around to rush back. What would they think if I, your wife, went unattended by my personal servants Chati and Sally?" Joan quipped.

Tossing his periodical on the coffee table, Bill asked, "Since when has Sally been your personal servant?" He crossed his arms and awaited a reply.

"Dear, you're not in the house long enough to see just how much I depend on them both," Joan retorted. Just then a thought occurred to her. "Have you ever known one of our dinner parties to have a single flaw? They've trained all the other house hands very well. That's precisely why your business associates look forward to coming here."

Joan knew by the look of resignation on her husband's face that she had won him over. They all could go. Inwardly, she smiled. She could take both Chati and Ma Sally and enjoy unrushed shopping and sightseeing. It made the plantation lady look good to have two women attendants, and Joan Jordan certainly would not trade shopping even for her husband's companionship. As for the Mensua boys, they were indispensable to carry the Jordan boys' trunks and to make them look the part of sons of a financially successful father and Georgia plantation owner. Mary was going, and Jennie would be her personal servant. Nothing could look better than a young girl like Mary having her own attendant.

A trace of anxiety remained. Mr. Jordan might change his mind at the last minute. He might relent and go along just to make sure slaves behave as slaves should. He knew the Mensuas were more like family and in his heart he trusted them, but he might decide to go along to control interactions. This possibility worried Mrs. Jordan as well as the Mensuas.

August came, and school was scheduled next month. Excitement filled the air because Mr. Jordan now wanted his sons' arrival in Boston to occur at least one week before school started, allowing more time for them to adjust and settle in before the first day of school. On a few occasions, he complained to his wife about so many people leaving the house at once, but each time she calmly answered, "Bill, dear, we have our position to maintain. Besides, nothing's going on in the house while we're away. We've not one party to host."

It was now the last week of August, and packing took most of everyone's time—the Jordans giving orders and directions, the Mensuas doing the work. There were no complaints; they did not want to cause the slightest disturbance. They were afraid Mr. Jordan's mind would change. Mr. Jordan's mind, however, was on the war, filled every day with worries about where battles would be fought. He deeply wanted to be at home if the fighting spilled into his fields.

The Jordans decided to leave on Thursday to arrive in Boston early Saturday morning, intending to spend the weekend settling the boys and shopping before returning home by Friday of the next week.

Thursday afternoon, as they left the plantation, the overseer allowed the slaves to watch the departure, cheering and waving. Two carriages were needed for the travelers, with Basusu driving Mr. Jordan's favorite one, and Kwasi driving the other.

At the train station, there was more jubilation; the stationmaster reported the tracks were clear and intact all the way to Massachusetts. The Jordan boys embraced their father on the platform and then waved to him from open windows until he was out of sight. Each of them now breathed slowly; finally they felt safe and relaxed for the first time after weeks of preparation. The Mensuas each felt the thrill deep inside that came from realizing they were actually a part of the Freedom Movement.

During the train ride, Basusu looked out of the window, watching parts of his new landscape flashing by. He thought about his life since he had been brought to the plantation. He tried to remember details about his boyhood in Africa—his father, mother, grandmother, and Akosua. It was hard for him to remember how they looked. Mostly, he just looked at Chati. He knew her frequent smiles were meant to comfort him.

Thankfully, it was the boys who led various conversations. They talked about the train, the noise, and the dust and smoke getting into their car. For the benefit of Mrs. Jordan, Basusu, Chati, and Ma Sally, and their young sisters, Mary and Jennie, the boys showed off their experience as visitors to Boston and what to expect in the big city, recalling places they passed through on their previous trips.

Two days later, the train trip ended without incident. *Boston, here we are,* thought Greg. The luggage and trunks were transferred onto the stagecoach, which Mr. Jordan had arranged by telegraph to be waiting for them.

The Mensuas eyes searched the platforms. Where was Joel Brown?

CHAPTER 17

Back to Boston

BOSTON—1862

The stagecoach brought the Jordans and Mensua-Jordans to a part of the city called Duck Square, where the dean of the school had made reservations for them at a hotel called the Cocked Hat. Mrs. Jordan walked briskly and confidently to the registration desk, closely followed by her sons and then the Mensuas, who trailed behind carrying part of the luggage. The trunks had been left on the coach for a later trip to the boys' school.

Mrs. Jordan was not prepared for her encounter with the desk clerk.

"Mrs. Jordan," he said, "we were not informed that members of your party were Negroes. We have no accommodations for colored people. Perhaps you can make arrangements for their accommodations elsewhere." The clerk rang the bell to call the hotel staff, and Negro boys in uniforms promptly appeared.

"Mrs. Jordan, your colored people can put down all your luggage. Our boys will bring everything up to your room."

Clearly upset by the turn of events, Joan had no recourse but to band everyone together to head for the school. Everyone climbed back into the coach for a ride to the campus, which was

138

not far away. Upon arriving, Mrs. Jordan explained her dilemma to a school administrator, hoping that he could suggest where the Mensuas could take refuge. He was understanding; he had authority to allow the Negro members of Mrs. Jordan's party to stay in a basement room. It was nothing fancy. There was no running water, no toilet. *Is there an outhouse?* they wondered.

The Mensuas were now alone, Mrs. Jordan and her children having returned to the hotel. Sam spoke first, almost mockingly. "So, Mr. Politician, where is Mistah Brown? Where is dis Mistah Joel Brown?"

Gregory tried to keep everyone calm but to no avail; all their fears spilled out at once. Everyone was talking; no one listening. Finally, the noise and disorder died down.

"Whad can we do?" Chati whispered.

"Well, somethin' will happen; somethin' has to happen," said Greg. Joe agreed: "Something will happen."

Basusu said, "Chati, if dis Mistah Brown don' come, we not takin' de children back. It gonna be too late fo' us, but dese boys ain't gonna be no slave like me no mo'."

Chati was beside herself. She lowered her voice to a barely audible one. "Whad wou' yo' tell Massa Jordan if we go back wid no boys? We betta tink to be dead!" Basusu met Chati's eyes and placed a finger over his mouth, indicating for her to silence herself until they could talk privately.

Late night approached, and the noise of the city was unfamiliar to the slave family huddling in a cold building, discussing several scenarios and possibilities and having no supper. Coupled with the fact that they had traveled several days and were now faced with limited resources for comfort, the Mensuas were tempted to become discouraged. Sensing the atmosphere, Sally spoke up.

"It's time to put all dis tinkin' down fo' now and rest de best we can." Surveying the surroundings, she distributed sleeping arrangements. Making beds out of piles of clothes from their bags, the Mensuas focused on trying to sleep, the cold basement storeroom offering not even a small measure of comfort.

In the still of the night, certain that everyone had fallen asleep, Basusu arose to his knees. Bowing, he prayed, "Lawd, it's been a hard time today gettin' here an' now all dis . . ." He scanned the room where streetlights emerged through cracks in the walls. He continued, "Lawd, I trustin' Yo' to do whad my fait' is believin' Yo' fo'. Dese boys got to be sometin' mo' den a slave. Dey got to be mo' den I am." Basusu became as still as the night, receiving hope and encouragement from the Lord. Shortly thereafter, he resumed his resting position.

Sam was awake, having listened to his father's prayer. In his mind, he added, *Lawd, make me to be as much as my fatha already is.*

At daybreak, Chati and Jennie left to attend to the needs of Mrs. Jordan. Their walk took longer than the coach ride yesterday; and upon finally arriving at the hotel, they presented themselves to the desk clerk. "We here to 'tend Missus Jordan," Chati said.

Moving fast because he didn't want it to appear he was admitting Negroes, the clerk called a bellboy over. "Take these two up to suite 316. Take them up the back steps right away." The clerk then remembered he had a message waiting to be delivered to one of the Jordan boys. "Boy, wait. Bring the big colored girl back here." Hearing him, Chati returned on her own to the desk. "Do you know Mr. Timothy Jordan?" he asked.

"Yes, suh."

"Mr. Joel Brown left this note. Give it to Mr. Tim Jordan. Now go with the bellboy upstairs." He abruptly turned on his heels and briskly walked away.

As they passed an open back door, a Negro suddenly darted into the hall and stopped Chati. "Are you with the Jordans?"

"Yes, suh," Chati nervously replied.

"I'm Joel Brown. Tell Mr. Tim Jordan I can see him this evening."

"Yes, suh," Chati answered. She was smiling but trembling from excitement. Lowering her voice to a whisper she said, "We been lookin' fo' yo', suh. De boys are under de school. De tird big house."

Joel Brown walked as fast as he could, straight to where the Mensuas were.

Upon hearing a soft knock on the door, Sam cautiously approached and opened the door. When Greg saw Joel, he froze as though he had seen a ghost. "At last!" Greg exclaimed. "You found us! But how?"

"Whad's de matta?" Basusu said, as he made his way to the door, having not clearly heard the conversation.

"Dis is Mistah Brown," Greg proudly announced.

Joel walked in as if he had an appointment. He got straight to the point.

"When are you leaving?" he asked.

Greg spoke up. "Monday."

"Okay. Conduct yourselves as usual each day. Late Sunday night, I'll be back. I want you on a train to a place called Philadelphia. I'll be there at the station to show you how to find that train and to get your tickets too. Now don't worry."

Basusu came forward. Things seemed to be moving too fast. "Ain't gonna be de slave catchers 'round de train place, Mistah Brown?"

"What slave catchers? You are too far north to worry about slave catchers. They can't get you here. Don't worry. Leave it to me." Sensing Basusu's uneasiness, he smiled as he spoke softly to him, eye to eye. "You've come this far; don't lose faith now." Basusu let out a sigh of relief and silently thanked God for Joel Brown.

Joel Brown left as abruptly as he came. For a while, the Mensuas just looked at each other, admittedly happy but scared at the same time.

Greg broke the silence and said, "I can't believe it. Can you, Sam? Let's go and tell Mama."

"Don't be silly; it was Mama who sent him here," Sam reminded him.

"I forgot . . . I must be losin' my mind. We got to go now. Maybe the Jordans want us." Greg was clearly excited at Joel Brown's proposition of freedom, and he had a hard time containing it. He was reminded to calm down and behave normally; and when Basusu and Sally felt he was composed, they all set out for the hotel.

At the hotel suite, the Jordan boys were in the lobby discussing Joel Brown's message. Joined by the Mensua boys, Tim told Greg that he had received Joel's message, explaining that his mother and brothers did not think it was a good idea to debate with him.

Greg feigned disappointment. "I was really lookin' forward to it," he said.

Chati, who was listening, said, "Yo' boys ain't come here to do no debating. We got work to do fo' Missus Jordan."

Basusu expressed worry. "I hopes we ain't late. Missus Jordan look like she waitin' on us!"

"Boys, you are all just in time," Mrs. Jordan said happily. "There are some stores and markets open today. I need you all to carry boxes of goods I will buy." Basusu was relieved and very glad that they were not in any trouble for arriving late. The day's chores were carried out with the usual care and acceptance.

Mrs. Jordan continued, "We'll also take a nice stroll so you all can see the sights. We can even visit the churches. So come on. You all can follow me. Later, we are going to have a picnic lunch in a park I found yesterday." The Mensua boys carried covered baskets of luncheon food Mrs. Jordan had directed the hotel kitchen to prepare.

The day was like a family outing, Mrs. Jordan visiting many stores and thoroughly enjoying the process of selecting goods to buy. She even asked Ma Sally and Chati their advice on utensils and cookware for the kitchen, tablecloths, and cloth napkins for the dining room, and curtains for bedrooms. Some goods would have to be shipped back home. It seemed to Basusu and his sons that they were carrying most everything Mrs. Jordan bought.

A pleasant picnic was a welcome pause for everyone, yet it was a mere intermission in the women's shopping spree. By early evening, they had returned to the Cocked Hat. Mrs. Jordan dismissed the Mensuas, bidding them to return to their room at the school. She wanted to spend more time with her boys alone.

All seven of the Mensua family left for their little basement room with no expectation of returning to Mrs. Jordan's hotel the next morning. Tears welled up in their eyes even before they turned to walk away. Mrs. Jordan thought they were crying over having to leave her sons.

Back in their room, the Mensuas sat with everything packed, waiting. The more they waited, the greater their anxieties. *Did Mr. Brown already come fo' us?* Basusu thought. *Maybe we 'posed to wait fo' him at de train place. We don' know how to get to de train place!* Just then they heard a knock on the door. Everyone's heart seemed to skip a beat. Opening it cautiously, Sam saw Jerry.

"My mother sent me to tell you she wants to see you very early in the morning. Come about an hour after dawn," said Jerry. He noticed that their bags were packed and neatly piled on the floor against the wall. "How come you are packed already?" he asked without suspicion.

"Well, suh, we jus' wan' to have everytin' packed 'way so we don' leave notin' behind," Chati said, forcing herself to speak steadily.

"Good thinking," Jerry said. "You have to come early anyway."

Suddenly, Chati ran over to Jerry. "Oh, Massa Jerry! We gonna miss yo' so much!" She began to weep. Basusu stiffened at the outburst and prayed fervently in his mind that Chati would not accidentally give away their plans.

Jerry put his hand on her shoulders and said, "Miss Chati, we are going to be all right. We will come home on school vacations; you will probably have to attend to Mother again, and soon, because she isn't finished with her shopping in Boston," he teased.

He turned and said goodnight. As he went out the door, he said, "Don't forget that you have to get my mother's packages to the train station and will have to make several trips."

He left, and everyone felt weak. "Whad if Jerry had come when Joel was here?" Bobby blurted out.

"Papa, whad's goin' on?" asked Jennie, who had been spared the details of the plan to escape.

"Notin's goin' on, my chile. Notin'." Basusu stroked his daughter's head.

Being only eleven, Jennie was very close in age and emotions to little Mary Jordan. No one could be sure that she would not foil the plans, being too young to appreciate the consequences.

Their waiting resumed.

Chati sat down on her bag, Basusu standing by her side. Slipping her hand in his, she closed her eyes and held tightly. Her expression was peace and tranquility. She began to pray softly, her words so melodious and comforting that everyone became calm.

"Dear Lawd Jesus, help us to be strong an' keep us trustin' dat dis is Yo' way fo' us. We don' know no otha way, Lawd. Tank Yo' fo' Yo' peace wid us now. Tank Yo'." Lowering her voice so that Jennie couldn't hear, she whispered, "An', Lawd," Chati choked back tears. "Keep Yo' han' wid Missus Jordan an' dem boys. Be wid Missus Jordan takin' de way back home."

Sally found a cloth and discreetly passed it around for the adults to dry their tears.

Shortly, there were two sharp knocks on the door. Joel had told them that he would knock twice. Basusu slowly approached the door.

"Who's dere?" he inquired.

"Joel Brown. Open up!"

Basusu quickly opened the door and surveyed the outside surroundings. The streets were quiet.

Joel noticed Sally and Chati reaching for their lanterns. He sternly warned them.

"Don't light your lantern. Just pick up your stuff and follow me."

Jennie began to whimper. "Mama, where we goin'?"

"Neva min', my chile. Jus' come along quietly. Everytin's fine. We talk layla, okay?" Jennie merely smiled, but her large eyes indicated that something was amiss.

The escapees left the premises the back way off the school grounds to the train station, Joel leading the way. Once there, he firmly said, "Just do what I tell you. Exactly what I tell you. Exactly. Nothing more, nothing less!"

Looking around a few times, Joel beckoned to a white man standing on the platform. "Basusu, this man is John Barclay. While you are on the train, you all belong to him. Pretend you are his slaves. Do whatever he says, like he is your master."

Basusu's eyes betrayed his amazement and worry. Joel continued, "Unless you want them slave catchers to get you, you better do what I say."

"Yo' say dere no slave catchers here," Basusu snapped.

"Don't worry," Joel laughed. "I'm jokin' a little, Basusu." Taking notice that Basusu was still unnerved, he continued on a more serious tone. "Put your trust in the Lord . . . and in me, Basusu," Joel whispered, easing Basusu's fears. "Mr. Barclay is really a preacher. He'll get you to Philly by tomorrow." Patting Basusu twice on the back, Joel Brown disappeared into the train station.

The train puffed and screeched to a stop, steam from the brakes swirling around them, making Basusu feel like he was in a dream. A black man in a uniform stepped down from the train to the platform and shouted, "Train to Philly! Train to Philadelphia! All aboard that's goin' aboard!"

The Mensua family followed John Barclay into a passenger car, pretending their luggage was his. He spoke only to order them about. Joel Brown sat near them but kept silent. As they traveled through the night, they slept fitfully. In the morning, they were startled by the shout of the conductor. "Phil-a-del-phi-a!" He sang the word. "Phil-a-del-phi-a! Be sure to take all your belongings! Phil-a-del-phi-a!"

The engineer did not apply the brakes gradually. Twice they lurched forward as the train slowed. They got up, gathering their bags, and looked through the dingy windows at the houses and factories of Philadelphia.

Dutifully, they followed John Barclay, who stepped to the platform like a proud Southern owner of the slaves behind him. Leaving the station, they walked for a few blocks, fascinated by the red brick sidewalks. They followed John Barclay and Joel to a small white-shingled house that had marble front steps, like many of the houses they passed. In unison, John and Joel knocked on the door.

A black lady opened the door. "Come in! Come in!" she said. They all filed in. The lady said, "Sit down, everyone. Make yo'selves comfortable. Nice to see yo' again, Joel. Thanks to God you're here safe, John."

"This is Miss Nash, Ellie Nash," said Mr. Barclay, "and this is her husband, Matthew Nash." Then he turned to Joel Brown and said, "You know where you can find me if or when you need me." Then he left. The Mensuas nervously took a seat, and Joel began telling Mr. and Mrs. Nash all about the Mensuas.

CHAPTER 18

Base and his Family on the Run

PHILADELPHIA—1862

Back in Philadelphia, Sally, Chati, and Jennie were feeling just as sad as Mrs. Jordan and Mary were feeling. They missed the orderly routines of their lives in Brunswick. Jennie, especially, moped about hardly talking to anyone. Born and raised on the plantation, she could not understand why leaving was such a good idea. After all, she was quite privileged for a slave, never working the fields, spending most of her time in the big house, and eating good food every day.

On a particularly dreary morning, Jennie became quite melancholy. Taking in the view outside, she sighed deeply. Philadelphia was quite unlike the Jordan plantation. Gone was her view of flowers and peach trees; instead, Jennie stared at gray buildings and gray skies. Everything, even the people, seemed gray to her. She squeezed her eyes shut and tried to imagine herself back at the plantation.

Tears came to her eyes as she thought of Mary. *If I was home an' not here, me an' Mary would be playin' 'bout now,* she thought.

Not willing to deal with her thoughts alone, Jennie ventured to ask a question.

"Whad was so bad 'bout de plantation?" she asked.

It was time, Ma Sally realized, to give Jennie a lesson in slavery practice. She looked at Chati to let her know that she would answer her granddaughter.

"Chile, yo' betta tank God yo' ain't dere no mo'," Sally said.

"Why, Grandma?" Jennie asked.

"If yo' growed up an' dere was no work fo' yo' in de house, an' yo' was no good in de fields, dey sell yo' an' we would neva see yo' 'gain. Everyone ain't lucky like yo' mama to fin' a husband right dere. Sometimes, dey send dem 'way to breed an' sell 'em little ones. Chile, yo' will understand one day, ain't dat right, Chati?" Sally seemed satisfied with her answer and hoped that Jennie would accept it.

"Yeah, Mama, dat's right. I'm glad yo' tol' her," Chati said, carefully weighing Jennie's expression for any sign of anger, confusion, or fear.

Feeling a need to drive her point further, Sally continued. "See, chile, when yo' grow'd up yo' wou' not be 'lowed to play wid Miss Mary no mo'. Does yo' understan'?"

Little Jennie heard, but her only wish was to be home with Mary. She acknowledged her grandmother and dutifully nodded her head, blinking back tears. By now, the older members of the family were slowly adjusting to life on the run, but no one's head was yet clear. There were still moments of confusion; however, their biggest hurdle was yet to come: schooling for the boys.

Over the next few days, Joel Brown made several visits to the Mensuas to get all three boys enrolled in one of the schools that had been established with political and financial help from abolitionists. The talk excited the boys, but their parents were somewhat apprehensive about it. Basusu agonized over the separation that would come soon. He poured out his pain and fear to God and to Chati, both of whom comforted him in his hour of need.

Basusu tried, but he could not make time stand still. Two weeks later, Joel Brown was back to take his sons off to school. But before the departure, they had to decide on the new names they would be known by. Miss Nash had told them that the safest, most prudent thing for escaped slaves to do was to change their names, even if it was just temporary.

With Joel Brown's help, Sally became Bessie; Chati became Clara. Sam became Rob; Gregory picked Sol, which was short for Solomon; and Joseph chose James as his new name. Jennie was delighted about the idea of changing her name. She chose Sarah Jean. Basusu, with as much reluctance as resentment, picked Jake.

Joel Brown returned the following day to discuss the matter of schooling. Samuel and Greg would attend the same school, but Joseph had to be enrolled in a different school because of his interest in law. The idea of splitting up the boys was disturbing to both Basusu and Chati because the family had never been apart before. But Joel Brown convinced them that it might not be bad after all, because if anything happened, everybody would not be caught.

"Do de slave catchers go to dese schools?" Basusu asked.

"No," said Joel Brown. "Slave catchin' is not allowed in these schools. The schools I picked for your sons are connected with churches that help slaves escape from the South. They are like sanctuaries; they cannot be captured there." Reassured by Joel Brown's explanation, Basusu relaxed some.

"And another good thing, Basusu," Brown added, "your boys can come home on weekends."

PHILADELPHIA—SEPTEMBER 1862

The prospect of their sons returning from school on weekends pleased Basusu and Chati very much. The boys, however, were very frightened. It was the first time that they were ever apart

149

from the family. It was almost unbearable, but they adjusted by the day.

During that first week of school, a teacher, astonished at his ability to read, write, and to understand difficult material, asked, "Rob, what school did you attend before?" Sam related the story of being a slave but did not give him any specific details.

On the weekend when they returned home, there was jubilation, with everyone wanting to know how everything went throughout the week. Each boy reported his experiences, all claiming that the hardest thing to do was to use their aliases and to be separated from each other.

"How 'bout yo' schoolwork . . . can yo' do it?" asked Basusu.

"Well," said Sam, "my teacher is spendin' a lot of time with me in the evenings, showin' me how to take notes durin' lectures. He's also showin' me how to catch up where I had no learnin'."

Sam turned to Chati and asked, "How did you do all week, Mama?"

Chati smiled. Sam also had her interest at heart. Even from a youth, he cared deeply for his mother. "Fine, boys, fine. A little bored . . . not gettin' out every day and doin' tings like back on de plantation. But we fine. Mr. Brown is fixin' to get us work sometime soon."

Sam was puzzled. He turned to his father and asked, "What are yo' goin' to do? Ain't no plantation 'round here."

"Don' yo' worry," Basusu reassured. "I gonna get somethin' to do. Yo' papa's still a warrior, right?" At that he grabbed Sam, embracing him and patting him on the back. Looking around on the others, he said, "Yo' all okay; yo' all warriors like me! Yo' still fightin' fo' freedom. Yo' jus' make sho yo' gets dat schoolin' in yo' head. Den nobody make no slave of my sons. Maybe one day, we all go back to Africa an' live free." His eyes gleamed at the mention of his home. All three Mensua boys and Jennie stilled themselves, lest they interfere with their father's impromptu moment of hope.

When the moment passed, Gregory spoke up. "Papa, we will do our best fo' you an' Mama."

Even before dawn on Monday, Basusu awakened. As was his habit, he checked the weather. But due to the restrictions of his whereabouts, he simply peered outside. The view in Philadelphia was a far cry from the Jordan Plantation. The city, with its noise and fanfare, was strikingly different from the country life he had known for the last twenty-three years. And although Basusu had ventured into the city with Mr. Jordan on numerous occasions, he was simply not prepared for daily living in the city.

Stepping away from the window, Basusu's mind flooded him with anxious thoughts. *Wha' now? Is dis really freedom? Yo' can't even go nowhere alone . . . Chati's sad . . . Jennie's sad . . .* Basusu pushed past those thoughts and thought of his village and his sons instead. He understood what it meant to be free; and now, no matter how difficult, he must afford his sons the same privilege.

Thinking that he was the only person awake at this early hour, he was startled to hear a noise. He stopped to listen carefully and heard the sound of dishes rattling. Miss Nash was already in her kitchen mixing up her biscuit batter that he loved. Not wishing to reveal his presence, he remained in the front room, quietly pacing back and forth. Something dawned on him—he realized he wasn't happy because he wasn't earning his keep in Miss Nash's house. On the plantation, he worked, and for that he had clothes, food, and a place to sleep. Here, he felt no sense of accomplishment.

Basusu masked his disappointment throughout breakfast, not wanting Chati, Sally, or especially Jennie to feel his pain along with theirs. He tried to comfort himself in the fact that the family had only arrived a little over a week ago and were just beginning to settle into a routine. But that's precisely what he lacked—a routine. He was used to working and organizing his life for Mr.

and Mrs. Jordan; and although free, he knew not what to do with his freedom.

There was a knock on the door. Instinctively, the Mensuas stiffened and held their breath.

"Who's there?" Miss Nash called out, stealing a glimpse at her nervous guests as she approached the door.

"John Barclay. Can I come in?"

Miss Nash's face brightened, and she opened the door. "Mr. Barclay, come right on in, of course." Miss Nash took both his hands in hers and led him into the kitchen, where the rest of the family were still seated around the table.

"Look here, everyone! It's the Revered Barclay. Just look at them, Reverend. They stuffed with my biscuits and gravy. But I saved some in the oven for you." She laughed, urging the reverend to sit down.

"I don't have much time to stay, but I heard about some work for Basusu and Chati, and Sally, if they are interested," Reverend Barclay said, directing his words to Basusu more than to Miss Nash.

Basusu leaped out of his chair. "Oh, yes, Reveren', we wants to work!" Sally and Chati nodded in agreement.

"Good, good. Then come with me now to meet some very nice people. They have a house too big for themselves to take care of." The reverend headed for the door, followed by the Mensua trio, with Jennie scurrying to catch up.

Reverend Barclay led them to a house situated on the top of a hill. It reminded Basusu and Chati of houses they had seen on the smaller plantations. When the reverend knocked on the door, he said, "It will take a while for the lady to answer as this house is so large. We'll have to be patient." Eventually, a lady answered.

"Oh, it's you, Reverend! Do come in. Are these the nice people you've been telling me about?"

"Mrs. Barrington, this is Jake and Clara." Basusu and Chati peered from behind Reverend Barclay into the kind green eyes of a petite red-haired lady. Victoria Barrington was a stunning lady, stunning in a classy sort of way. A bit older than Chati, she personified a youthful manner cloaked in wisdom beyond her age. Her eyes twinkled as she spoke kindly to the Mensuas.

"Well, I'm glad to meet both of you, finally. I've heard wonderful stories about you and your family from the Reverend." Turning to Mr. Barclay she said, "I know you are very busy with appointments today, so please feel free to attend to your business. But on your way out, could you look in the garden for Mr. Barrington? Please tell him to come and meet Jake and Clara."

Chati liked the Barrington house from the moment she walked in. And Victoria Barrington was eager to show the Mensuas her collection of crystal prisms until her husband came. Chati immediately noticed how dusty they were. *Dis lady need us,* she thought.

"Here I am, dear!" A robust man of dignity and English courtesies, Walter Barrington's presence filled the room. Quickly and delightfully shaking their hand, he said to his wife, "Suppose I show Jake around the estate while you show Clara and Bessie around the house?"

Basusu followed Mr. Barrington through the house until they were outside. "May I depend on you, Jake, to take care of the grass, the firewood supply, the flower beds, the horses, the barn, and all the other outdoor buildings?"

"Yes, suh, Mistah Barrington!" Basusu was excited about the responsibilities.

"And anything in the house that needs to be done?" asked Mr. Barrington.

"Yes, suh."

"You know, Mrs. Barrington and I are from Europe. Have you heard of England, Jake?"

"No, suh," Basusu lied.

Basusu's answer was a quick reflex act because he was fearful to display the knowledge that resulted from listening to his sons' accounts of their lessons as "pupils" of the Jordan sons. He could have given a discourse showing he even knew that Georgia was named to honor King George II, that the king signed a charter specifying how Georgia was to be ruled, and that the whole idea of the charter was James Oglethorpe's. Indeed, Basusu could have identified King George III as the king for whom Brunswick was named, because that king was from the House of Brunswick.

Mr. Barrington persisted. "Haven't you heard of England, Jake? England . . . where the king is."

"Uh, yes, suh."

Basusu's answer went unheard, for Mrs. Barrington and Chati had found them. Victoria Barrington called to her husband. "I told Clara, dear, that she and Jake are welcome to have their meals here."

Already, Basusu and Chati's worries had evaporated; the Barringtons were unlike the white people they knew in the South. So that night when they returned "home" to Miss Nash's house, they were eager to tell her all about their day.

"I ain't neva met nobody from Europe befo'," Basusu said, recapping his conversation with Mr. Barrington.

"Yeah, I see he ain't no Suthnuh'," continued Chati.

"He sho is a nice man."

"He's got a piano!" Jennie exclaimed, her fingers rolling along the edge of the table in pretense of keys. "And dey got a daughta jus' a few years younga den me," she continued with excitement.

"Dat man a gentleman . . . a fine gentleman," commented Miss Nash. "But you be careful," she warned. "All white folks up here ain't like dem Barringtons."

CHAPTER 19

Union Skirmishes Increased

THE JORDAN PLANTATION

Things had not gotten back to normal. Skirmishes between Union and Confederate forces had become more widespread. The Jordans' apprehension increased each day and night, for their home increasingly had become a haven for friends whose distant plantations had been destroyed—by vengeful Union soldiers.

Worries about what might happen to his plantation did not displace Bill Jordan's resentment toward his wife. He continued to blame her for the loss of the Mensuas, reproaching her every morning. Joan did not let his ranting bother her, for her greatest problem was not having Sally and Chati around. She did not know that she had developed such a bond between herself and the two slave women, and often she was in tears. Whenever Bill asked what was wrong, she could not tell him, but it was because she missed Sally and Chati so badly. Now she realized that they were more than mere slave hands; they were family.

Mattie and Cassidy were doing their best to fill the places of Sally, Chati, and Basusu; but they were not successful. Sally and the others had been there so long they knew the routines and expectations. When the Jordans entertained guests, Mrs. Jordan could leave everything in the capable hands of Sally. But now she had to constantly tell Mattie what to do and often had to show her how to do it. Little Mary was feeling better now, but she was still very lonely. Jennie was her only real friend. She needed someone to play with, and no one could take the place of Jennie.

PHILADELPHIA—MAY 1863

Sam, Greg, and Joe were doing very well in school. By now they had learned the fundamentals of academic life and were making the very best of their opportunity. Many were the moments, however, when they felt saddened by their separation from their boyhood friends, always wishing they could see Jerry, Bobby, and Tim again.

BOSTON—JUNE 1863

The first year of schooling for both the Mensua and Jordan sons had come to a successful end. Now the time had come for the Jordans' sons to return to their plantation. Their trip took more than a week, for many train stations, trestles, and miles of track had suffered the destructive effects of the war. They spent as much time on stagecoaches as they did on trains. When their train finally arrived in Brunswick, they were met by their anxious parents, who were so relieved and happy that they wept openly and freely.

During the ride to the big house, however, they were quiet, each aware that once again they were returning home without their most valuable family of slaves.

"Mother, who is the new driver?" Tim asked, breaking the silence. Joan swallowed hard, pretending to be thinking about something else and not wishing to get involved with such a volatile topic. She turned to Tim and tried to speak to him with her eyes. *That question,* she thought, *is just the one to get your father going again.* But then Bill spoke.

"He's our new yard hand," Bill said, answering for Joan. "Cassidy. Do you remember him? That's his name."

"Is he the one who's taking Base's place, Father?" asked Tim. Sensing that Tim wasn't going to let the matter drop worried Joan. Bill spoke again, turning his explanation into a complaint.

"Cassidy is no Base. He's slow. Slow to learn. Slow doing anything. He even thinks slow," Bill said, clenching his jaw and glancing angrily at Joan.

"But he works well with Mattie, whom we assigned to the kitchen," Joan said. "And boys," she added, "don't mention or talk about anything going on outside of the plantation in front of Mattie and Cassidy. Ever since Lincoln signed that despicable proclamation a few months ago, slaves have been a real problem to our friends all over Georgia."

"So don't talk about anything that might be considered inflammatory to the slaves around the house. Is that understood, sons?" Bill asked.

"Yes, Father," the Jordan boys chimed in unison.

"Well, tell us how you are doing in school," Bill said, much to Joan's relief. "All that book reading filling your head?" he joked.

Jerry took up the conversation. "I have to tell you, Father, that the news of, and the reaction to, President Lincoln's Emancipation Proclamation was received mostly favorably in Boston. There were very angry debates in our classes, Father, and I always felt my views supporting slavery were in the minority and most unwelcome."

"Well, that's too bad," snapped Bill. "Let's see if them Northerners can work a plantation without slaves. They'd be bankrupt in a week! Are you boys ready for some real work?"

"We're looking forward to getting back to plantation business, Father," Jerry said.

They arrived home, and Cassidy drove the carriage under the portico. Before the carriage was halted, the boys leaped off it like wild goats, jumping and prancing about. Little Mary heard the commotion that could only be her brothers and rushed out to meet them. One by one they picked her up, swinging her around and around.

"Come on in, boys," Joan said. "It's time for you to eat some good home cooking. Mattie's a good cook."

"You haven't had anything good to eat all year long," joked Mary. "Look how thin you are!" She kept patting them on the head and thumping them on their shoulders. "I taught Mattie how to make Sally's peach pies. And that's what she made for dessert." Hearing that, the boys dashed inside and ran to the kitchen to make sure Mary wasn't teasing some more.

Once dinner was over, the boys strolled around the plantation, looking around to refresh their memories and to see things that made them happy. When they reached the slaves' cabins, Bobby saw Kwasi, Basusu's old friend. Kwasi was sitting on the cabin step, alone and solemn. *Would Massa Bobby 'memba me?* he wondered.

"Kwasi!" Bobby called. Kwasi smiled and stood up at once, nodding his head happily.

When Bobby had come near enough to him, Kwasi ventured to say he missed Basusu. "I do too, Kwasi," admitted Bobby. "My brothers also miss him. We especially miss Base's sons."

Their quiet moment together was interrupted by Tim. "Bobby! Here! Look at Mother's orchards."

The brothers stood together, silently and sadly, looking with disbelief. "Mother's orchards used to stretch from here to the ridge. Now look at them," Tim said.

"Looks like our boys engaged the Union here," Jerry said. "Look! Acres of blackened trees. Not a single leaf. Makes me wonder where Mattie got the peaches for the pies we just ate. Mother must really be upset by this."

Later on in the evening, when everyone had settled down, the boys could not hold out any longer. Tim was the first to apologize.

"Father, we are sorry about Base and the rest escaping. We just could not imagine anything like that happening. Really, Dad, we did not even suspect it until it was too late. We always just thought they were one of us."

You've learned a tragic lesson, boys," Bill said. His calmness both surprised and relieved Joan. "A very costly lesson, boys. Things will never be the same around here again."

The boys all looked glum and repentant. But then Jerry blurted out, "I guess slaves are always slaves . . . and they will always try to escape. Can you blame them, Father?"

When Jerry realized what he had said might offend his father, he covered his mouth with his hand.

"Sorry. I didn't mean that way."

It was too late. Even with the quick apology, Bill exploded into a rage, which was all too familiar to Joan and Mary.

"I cannot believe what I just heard!" yelled Bill. "From my own son! Is that how all of you think?"

No one spoke. Mother, daughter, and sons—all knew that any dialogue with him, whether he was angry or calm, would be pointless. They knew nothing could change his view.

"You all don't understand, do you?" he continued, turning his head to look at each family member one by one. "I am in the plantation business. You are too! All of you! Do you know what that means? You must have hands to work with! Hands! Not my hands! Slave's hands! I'm not sure all your studying is doing y'all any good. Maybe Boston is not the right place for plantation sons. All that talk about emancipation up there that y'all been listening to won't pay any school fees. You got to make money to live like this."

"Oh, Dad . . . please . . . we're really sorry," Jerry said, a pained look on his face. "We don't mean that it was all right for Base and Chati and Ma Sally to run."

"All of them!" Bill shouted. He slammed his fist on the table. "All! All! All!" he shouted, his fist slamming the table each time he said the word.

Bill Jordan left the table in disgust, his family left to deal with the aftermath of his outburst.

PHILADELPHIA—AUGUST 1863

Basusu and Chati had worked their way into the routines of life at the Barrington house quite well. It did not take Basusu long to master his job. After all, he had much more responsibility back on the plantation. While Chati too had proven herself to be a valuable house hand for Mrs. Barrington, her only difficulty was that she could not always understand the Barrington's English accent.

Two important problems had been solved for Basusu and Chati, most certainly because of the good nature of the Barringtons. First, Basusu, Chati, Sally, and Jennie were living in the house's servants' quarters, sharing a room at least four times as large as Basusu's original cabin on the Jordan Plantation. The idea for them to live in the Barrington house was proposed by Mr. Barrington himself, which astounded the Mensuas even though they had known that the people in the North were different. Also, the Barringtons were Europeans and didn't have the "slave owner" mind-set.

The second problem to be solved was anticipated by Mrs. Barrington. At school's end, she said, "Clara, what are your boys going to do when school lets out in a few days?"

"Oh, Missus Barrington, we been worryin' 'bout dat too," Chati admitted.

"Clara, it would be acceptable to Mr. Barrington and me if the boys shared that room above our carriage house," she said, nodding toward the outside.

Chati and Basusu were joyous and thanked the Barringtons profusely. Even the carriage house attic room was a thousand times better than Basusu's former slave cabin. Later that afternoon in the kitchen, Chati threw her arms around Basusu and her mother. "Oh, Mama! Oh, Basusu! We all togetha 'gain! Tank de good Lawd!"

By the end of summer, the Mensuas were convinced they had improved their lives significantly. The boys had a room they were proud of, quite unlike conditions on the plantation. Mr. Barrington had even offered to pay the boys for the work they did, but they declined his offer. Instead, they kept the carriages and the carriage house clean and well organized. The boys were noticeably proud that their parents and Ma Sally were actually being paid for the work they did on the Barrington estate.

The gentle nature of the Mensua sons as well as their mental ability impressed the Barringtons. They wondered how the boys learned so much even before attending formal school. Mr. Barrington, the proprietor of a small manufacturing company, vowed that if there was anything he could do to help them, he would gladly do it.

A few days before school resumed, Mr. Barrington had a private talk with Joe. "James, you and your brothers have made my carriage house look much, much better than it was before you came here. I want you to know Mrs. Barrington and I truly appreciate all you boys have done. You three are fine sons to your parents."

Joe was warmed by his kind words. "Mistah Barrington, you made it possible for our family to be togetha. There's no way I could ever explain how important your kindness and generosity are to us all."

"Your family has earned our respect. In fact, James, all of you deserve our respect."

Joe said nothing for a few moments. It had felt good to hear Mr. Barrington say the word "respect." He returned Mr. Barrington's smile.

CHAPTER 20

The End of the War

JUNE 1864

The Mensuas were as apprehensive as the Jordans every day of the boys' second year of schooling. There were many events to worry about—or cheer about, depending on who they were or where they were during the previous year. On the other hand, the Jordans were delighted about the Confederate victory at Chancellorsville in Virginia but glum about defeat first at Gettysburg and then at Vicksburg, Mississippi. Bill Jordan was embarrassed by the surrender at Fort Hudson and the sweeping defeat at Chattanooga. Not even victory at Chickamauga cheered him; he was merely glad the fighting was three hundred miles away from his plantation. Lincoln's words at Gettysburg were salt to the wounds to his self-esteem and Southern pride.

The situation grew worse later in the year. Jordan and his fellow plantation owners felt threatened when General Grant took over the Union armies. Lincoln's reelection cut open Bill Jordan's mental wounds, but nothing so devastated him as General Sherman's destructive march through Georgia.

The Jordans and selected house and yard hands crowded in the mansion's cellar while Union soldiers burned their fields and orchards. Soldiers set their slaves free, many of whom, however, did not want to "be set free," choosing instead to hide until the soldiers left.

Union soldiers also torched or demolished nearly all the slaves' cabins. Even Basusu's old cabin was aflame. Had not the soldiers been distracted or perhaps ordered to move on to the next plantation, the Jordan's treasured mansion would have been the next target.

When the Jordans emerged from their hiding place, they gathered on the grand porch, silently looking at the smoldering fields all around. Realizing her husband was near tears, Joan put her arm around his waist. "Look, dear, our slaves are returning," she said, hoping to offer some measure of comfort. "Poor things; they were probably so scared they didn't know where to hide."

"We'll have to make them put up tents until I can get some materials for rebuilding the cabins," Bill replied. "Thank God our house is still standing."

Joan held him more tightly now and began to sob. Cannon fire could still be heard, rumbling toward them from over the hills. Bill saw that the noise alarmed the slaves who had gathered near the porch. "Don't worry anymore," he shouted to them. "The soldiers are going away . . . that way," he said, pointing northeast. His words brought them little comfort. Many slaves simply stared at the charred fields while others cried, partly for fear and partly for relief that something was being done about slavery.

Bill turned and looked intently toward St. Simons Island. "Hear the bells, Joan? I wonder how the old Oglethorpe and Hamilton places look now." Together, arm in arm, they walked to the steps on the southern portion of the porch, which completely encircled their mansion. From there, they could see Joan's herb garden, untouched by the enemy. They walked through it between the raised beds, enjoying the fragrances and colors of thyme, mint, dill, and rosemary, which was Mary's favorite. At the southern edge of the garden, they gasped; the gate to the family cemetery had been knocked down.

A quick look at the vandalism made both of them cry. Four generations of gravestones were either smashed to bits or knocked down. "This is miserable," Bill said through his sobs. "Just look at my father's grave." The headstone was broken in two. Joan helped slide the pieces together and read the words carved into the granite: "William James Jordan II, born 1790, died 1825, pneumonia, faithful husband and loving father." The stone of his wife, Martha Emily Jordan, was intact and still standing vertical.

Just beyond was Bill's grandfather's grave. It too was desecrated. "Spite!" Bill shouted angrily. "Just look at this! Smashed so much to bits you can't read it anymore." He knelt on the ground, attempting to fit the pieces together again. When he realized pieces were missing because they had been kicked away, he cried harder. "Joan, it used to say 'George William Jordan, Colonel, Revolutionary War.' It had the dates of his birth and death. All smashed to bits now, and I don't remember what those dates were, Joan."

Joan squeezed her husband's hand and nudged him on from the destroyed gravesites. "We'll make do, Bill. We can reconstruct everything, for we still have your great-great-grandfather's Bible. Every important event since your family came to America has been written in it, here and there." Bill did not reply and Joan continued, "I hope that's some consolation to you." Bill Jordan continued to stare blankly at the desecrated graves.

The worst grave they discovered was that of Bill's great-great-grandfather James. He had landed with James Oglethorpe at St. Simons Island in 1736, Oglethorpe's second voyage to America. The condition of the grave was more desecrated than the others.

Bill tried hard to remember what his grandfather had told him about his ancestors, where they came from and what they did. "I was only two when my father died, Joan. So much of what I know about my family I learned from my grandfather. Have I ever told you that?"

"Let's go back to the house, Bill," she broke in.

Consumed with his thoughts that were wrapped in his grief, he asked, "Did I ever tell you my grandfather George not only fought in the war against England but also helped cut the timber used to build the ship *Constitution*? The timber was cut right on St. Simons." Bill blinked back the tears.

Joan rested her head on his shoulder as they walked. She had heard that story many times.

PHILADELPHIA—SUMMER 1864

The Mensua boys were given work in Mr. Barrington's factory. They were very proud and were not expecting the bad treatment they would receive from other workers. On their first day, while Mr. Barrington's shop foreman reluctantly showed them around, they heard slurs, some whispered, some intentionally loud. "Niggers! Niggers! Now we got stinkin' niggers here," nameless faces said.

Almost all of the workers' faces showed disgust or contempt. Mr. Barrington's was the only friendly face. Immediately, detecting general rejections of the Mensuas, the very next day Mr. Barrington ordered all his employees to shut down the machinery and assemble. Using a bench as a step to reach a worktable in the center of the factory, he turned slowly to face everyone. "Gentlemen, let's not pretend you haven't noticed the new hires," he began, staring directly at his audience.

He paused in speaking but kept turning and made eye contact with each employee. Then he spoke more loudly. "The new hires . . ." again he paused and then resumed, punctuating each word with his index finger on his own chest, "are my hires."

Hearing that, not one worker mumbled or even dared shift his weight from one foot to another. Mr. Barrington continued, "These chaps—Rob, Sol, and James—will be working with me in my offices upstairs. Already they have given me new ideas that will make us produce more, more easily, so my factory can make more profits, so all of you fellows can keep your jobs. Were it not for these three chaps that some of you have insulted from the start, many of you would have had to be fired. Now get back to your machines. Don't let me catch you making fun of them; don't let me hear you calling them names." Mr. Barrington scanned the faces of his employees carefully and thoroughly. About to step down from the table, he changed his mind to nearly shout, "And by the way, all you fellows, there will be no second chance for anyone! Remember that!"

His words put an end to the problem. In fact, talk among the white workers changed. Now they were wondering how Negroes, who were ex-slaves, became intelligent enough to work for Mr. Barrington. *How did they learn how to add, to subtract, even read and write?* they wondered.

At the Barrington house, Basusu and Chati worried when they heard about how the workers treated their sons. But Mr. Barrington assured them that the only way to incur change was to stand up for what one believed. These words encouraged Basusu who, being the son of a warrior, embraced strong character.

SEPTEMBER 1864

For the Mensua brothers, their experience at the factory intensified their desire to change the world, not just for themselves, but for all other freed slaves. Being free themselves was not enough.

The more they studied and the more they talked with their teachers and other Africans who had escaped to the North, the more they realized how necessary Lincoln's idea of emancipation was. Greg was the most sensitive to that idea. So interested was he that he wrote to Joel Brown.

SEPTEMBER 28, 1864

Dear Mr. Brown,

Sometimes I get sick to my stomach when I hear stories about how slavery was for other Africans. My father and mother, Grandma Sally, my brothers and I were the exception. The suffering of my people began long ago in Africa when slave catchers stole us away. We died on the way to the ships. We died inside the ships. We had little value as individuals. That is why so many of us were taken away to America. The story of my people — my father Basusu's people — is an ugly one. Today, there are over five million slaves in America. Imagine how many have died — perhaps over ten million were stolen from my father's homeland!

Please tell my father how I feel, that now I understand why he never gave up his desire to escape. Tell him also that I want to become like Moses — I want to help my people become free. I want to become a freedom fighter like you, Mr. Brown.

BOSTON—JANUARY 1865

Cathleen Valdery was tall, beautiful, and slender with cascading auburn hair that flowed freely over her shoulders. She was an only daughter whose father was an educator and whose mother was a homemaker. Cathleen had enrolled at the same school as Jerry Jordan's to prepare herself for a career in teaching. Jerry fell in love with her the very first time he saw her at the beginning of his third year of school. They were reading in the library, opposite each other at the same table. It was only a matter of minutes before Jerry conversed with this lovely creature and finally asked her out on a date. Over the course of weeks, his admiration of her beauty fell second to his admiration of her heart; and before long, Jerry realized he was in love.

During the months of their courtship, Jerry excitedly wrote to his parents several times. His first two letters told about his love for Cathy; in the third he mentioned she was the daughter of Northerners. His mother's reply gently described his father's outrage. A sentence saddened him. "I hope, that is, your father hopes, you aren't thinking of marriage to this girl." Marriage was exactly what was on his mind.

Later during the year, Jerry opened a letter from his father that disturbed him very much. As he read, he could hear the anger in his father's voice.

MAY 26, 1865

My Son,

What are you going to do with a Northern woman on our plantation? At least what's left of it! What's wrong with the fine crop of Southern girls in Georgia?

How can you even think of marrying a Northerner? Are you not aware of what they've been doing to us down here? Last month Richmond surrendered to that weasel Grant. And our Confederate states surrendered at Appomattox. It's over, son! It is finished. They even jailed Mr. Jefferson Davis. And today, our very last Confederate army may surrender at Shreveport. Our beloved Georgia is a wasteland, Jerry. All over, we are in ruins! Union soldiers even smashed the sacred ground in our family cemetery. The best thing that could have happened to that man Lincoln happened in Ford's Theater last month.

Jerry, in my opinion, I hope and pray you put your studies of law to the use and protection of your Southern families. Your friends and family here are looking to you to protect the best interests of Georgia, son. Don't embarrass us by marriage to a Northerner. Even Lincoln's successor, Andrew Johnson, is a troublemaker. Today, he proclaimed amnesty to "us Confederates" if we would ratify that 14th amendment. Outrageous! In my prayers every day, my son, I pray you come to your senses.

With love, your father,
William James Jordan III

Several weeks later, Jerry accompanied Cathy to visit her parents. Both Jerry and Cathy were equally shocked to find out that the Valderys also were not keen on the idea of a Southern and Northern match.

CHAPTER 21

Jerry Disinherited

In Boston, Bobby and Tim were concentrating on their studies as intently as they could. Jerry, in the meantime, had set his mind on continuing his relationship with Cathy in spite of opposition from both their families. Still desiring to become an attorney, however, he resumed his college studies and hoped that his father would not cut off his financial support as had been threatened.

It was not until later in the year that the school notified Jerry that his tuition payments were in arrears. He realized that his father was serious after all. He immediately wrote to his mother, seeking help. While her reply supported his father, the envelope contained money. Cathy also supplied him with money whenever his mother was unable. But as the weeks passed, each letter arrived with less and less money. Bill, having found out about the secret funds, forbade Joan to take money out of the business budget for Jerry. Joan obliged but managed to amass small amounts out of her own household budget to send whenever she could.

In one letter he received in January 1866, Joan wrote,

December 19, 1865
My Dear Son Jerry,
   I do hope this letter reaches you before Christmas. Although the money enclosed is the smallest yet that I have sent you, it is the most

I can afford from my account, which like your father's dwindles more and more each month. Life has changed so much here in Georgia and, as my friend writes me, all over the South. Plantations have collapsed, a consequence of Sherman and other Union vandals. The end of legal slavery also contributed. The planting fields all over the South are virtually barren, from the battles fought on them and from overplanting, the government agents say.

The President has warned us folks that if we do not ratify that 14th Amendment, Congress shall place Georgia under strict military rule. Your father is so agitated! As if that were not enough to worry about, he cannot operate with the few slaves that have remained voluntarily. For days he has been wondering whether he should let acreage to tenants, or to share tenants, or to the sharecroppers. Your Aunt Mella reports that her plantation escaped the ravages of Union soldiers, but she is unable to manage as a war widow and has actually deeded all except a small cottage for herself to her slaves. The nearby town of Savannah officially intends to rename her plantation "Freedmen's Grove." Negroes from other areas, having heard about Aunt Mella's action, have already taken up residence there. I do hope your Christmas is blessed. You will make it anyhow. I pray for you and Cathy every night.

With Love,
Mother

JUNE 1866

Four years of schooling had ended. While the Jordans wondered whether their sons would continue their studies or return to Brunswick to rebuild the plantation, the Mensuas had no doubts what their sons would do to pursue their interests. Sam, like Bobby Jordan, wanted to become a medical doctor. Greg, like Timothy, wanted to become a politician but wanted to try his hand at teaching first. And Joe, like Jerry, wanted to become an attorney.

Bill and Joan continued to worry that Jerry might marry "that Northern girl," an issue that had become even more important than dealing with the aftermath of the war. Perhaps the greatest blow to Bill had taken place in October of the previous year when his own state accepted President Johnson's terms—and was readmitted to the Union. Readmission was short-lived, however; happily for Bill, Georgia refused to ratify the Fourteenth Amendment, which would have given full citizenship to Negroes. Union troops came to occupy Georgia almost immediately, threatening to keep Georgia under military rule until the amendment was accepted.

Jerry was as obstinate as his father and as brave as his great-grandfather George. The year was a tough one. But with the help of his mother and Cathy, he was able to survive and qualify for admission into law school. Bobby and Tim also did quite well, with Bobby getting accepted into medical school and Tim into political science studies.

When his professional studies began in September of 1866, Tim was happy to discover that his professors required him to combine classroom studies with service to municipalities. His mother was overjoyed to learn that he chose service to the state of Georgia. In Boston, he helped form the Loyal League (which some Southerners called the "Union" League) and volunteered to establish offices throughout Georgia.

For Joan, news about Tim working in Georgia offset the news that Jerry and Cathy had continued courting.

As for Basusu's sons, Sam was admitted to medical school and Joe to law. Greg was searching for a job as a teacher and would study political science at the same time. Jennie had taught herself piano and singing on Mrs. Barrington's walnut spinet that was kept in the dining room. Often, while her mother and father served dinner to the Barringtons, Jennie would play for their entertainment. At the Freemen's Baptist Church, where the

Mensuas worshipped, Jennie was always called on to sing hymns of praise and worship.

Even Basusu became involved in church affairs. Pastor Paxton, pastor of the Freemen's Baptist Church, had asked him to join the board of deacons. Though hesitating at first, Basusu accepted it as another challenge. After some time, he grew to take great pride in serving in the house of God more than all of his other duties. The solace of being in the sanctuary prior to the attendees often comforted his heart, and he rendered many thanks to God.

CHAPTER 22

Hard Times Fell on the Plantations

AUGUST 1868

Bill and Joan struggled to save what they could of the planting fields. The Jordan Plantation was no more. The sons had returned home to help and learn how their father had successfully adapted to farming without slaves. For the second summer in a row, Jerry had declined to visit.

Tim noticed how depressed his father looked. One evening, while they were walking through the cemetery, Tim asked, "Dad, you looked sad to me all day. What's the matter?"

Bill stopped at the gate and leaned with his back against the wrought-iron post. His face showed emotional pains he spoke. "Tim, it seems to me that the older my children become, save for Mary, the less and less attached to me they become. In fact, lately I am noticing you and Jerry are working against my principles."

"You mean because Jerry is courting Cathy?"

"That's not it at all, Tim. What I'm talking about is your involvement with the Union League."

"Loyal League," Tim cut in. "We named it *Loyal* because we are working to show loyalty to our country."

"How can you call it loyalty, Tim? You're helping them Negroes have a say in government. They are severely deficient in intelligence. You know that!" Bill's anger started to rise again at the thought of Negroes having any role in life other than serving him.

"Not true at all, Father," Tim retorted. "Many Negroes have learned how to read, how to write, and—"

"And how to run away!" Bill said angrily. Taking a deep breath, he pushed off the gatepost and walked behind Tim.

Tim was forced to turn around. "Dad, I helped the league develop a charter. It calls for officers like me and members—who are white people from the community—to teach Negroes the meaning of equality. We teach and encourage them to enforce their rights as citizens."

"Citizens! What makes you think slaves have the right to be—"

Tim cut him off in midstream. "Dad, things can't be the same anymore. You just have to stop fighting change. Last month, our state of Georgia finally ratified the Fourteenth Amendment."

"That's what I heard, son. You were involved with the Georgia Legislature, weren't you, persuading people in the House to vote in favor?" Bill inquired, his eyebrow arched and his arms folded, waiting for his son's reply.

"That's correct, Father," Tim coolly replied. "And that's neither an apology nor an admission. I am saying that I lobbied with pride and honor." Father and son stared at each other. Bill spoke first.

"And so did Jerry I hear!" he blurted out.

"Dad, what do you mean by saying—"

"You better not try to defend your brother. You think I don't know Jerry was in Atlanta with you?" Bill paused for an answer, but Tim did not speak.

"Your brother is courting that Northern gal. Doesn't come to see me with her to pay his respects. He doesn't have the guts to do that—but he can face the Senate and boldly speak in favor of giving citizenship rights to Negroes!" Bill Jordan, seething with rage, screamed at his son, indignant at the conversation they were having.

"Dad, maybe Jerry would have come with Cathy if he were confident you would not be cruel or rude to her." Tim, speaking in a monotone voice, tried to calm his father down. It appeared to have the desired effect.

Bill thought for a moment. "Maybe that's so, son."

The two of them spoke no more and headed back toward the house. In the herb garden, Bill put his arm on Tim's shoulder as they walked together. Tim's arm found its way around his father's waist, the two of them supporting each other—the father needing comfort, the son needing acknowledgement.

Upon reaching the grand porch, they sat together on the top step to further enjoy their new appreciation of each other. It was evening now, and Cassidy was carrying the lighted lantern that he would place atop the lamppost at the entrance to the drive that arched in front of the house.

Hearing the clip-clop of an approaching carriage, Cassidy stepped aside to let it pass. "Who is that coming, Dad?" Tim asked, squinting to get a better look.

"Can't tell yet. Cassidy doesn't seem to recognize the driver or the passenger."

Suddenly, from the upstairs window of Mary's room, they heard a screeching sound. "It's Jerry!" she screamed. "Papa, it's Jerry!"

Mary pulled her head inside and whirled around, yelling, "Mama! Mama, it's Jerry! He's here!"

Bill stood up and squinted at the carriage, hoping to improve his ability to identify who was inside. He could still hear Mary screaming with excitement as she came running down from upstairs. She flung open both of the front double doors and dashed past Tim, nearly knocking him down as he was trying to get up. She took the porch steps two at a time, her skirts flying and billowing, and ran to the carriage even before the horse was halted.

"It *is* Jerry!" she screamed again. "Papa! Mama!"

Bill Jordan stood, tidied his clothes, and cleared his throat, bracing himself for the worst.

"Would somebody please tell me what's going on?" Bill shouted. Jerry walked toward the porch, Cathy following behind. All was quiet except for a breeze that had just stirred up last year's autumn leaves on the drive, scattering them noisily between Jerry's boots. The same breeze was slowly pushing the front doors closed, but Joan opened them again. She had come to see what the commotion was about. The sight of Jerry at the foot of the porch stairs stopped her. She stood framed by the open doorway.

Jerry spoke first. "Hello, Mother, it's me. Dad, how are you?"

So much was the surprise that Bill and Joan were unable to mumble a word. Trying to control his emotions, Jerry looked back at Cathy. He turned to face Joan. "Mother, this is Cathy."

Cathy continued walking, past Jerry and up the porch steps, past Bill and Tim, gliding straight to Joan. She offered her hand, and Joan took it gracefully. "Mrs. Jordan, I am honored and happy to meet you. You are as lovely as your son said you were. He wasn't boasting after all!"

Mary, who had closely followed Cathy, stared openly at her, which Joan noticed. "Mary, close your mouth and move back a little. Give her some air; you're practically breathing down this poor girl's neck!"

"Oh, Mother, doesn't she speak beautifully?" Mary squealed.

Joan, her hand still clasped around Cathy's, took Mary's with the other. "Come, let us ladies have some tea together on the

garden porch. We have many important things to talk about."
They disappeared into the house, leaving the men alone.

Tim was first to speak, still standing next to his father on the
top step, Jerry standing in the drive.

"Why didn't you write? You could have told us you were
coming." No one answered Tim's question, so Jerry continued
after a few awkward moments. "Dad, I thought about writing to
you . . . but nothing I wrote made sense. I just—"

"That's all right, Jerry," Bill interrupted, draping one arm
over his son's shoulders. "We all feel upset about not seeing each
other for a long time. Let's go inside and talk. This calls for some
of that old bourbon I hid in the library closet. I have a feeling it
will help us bring an end to the suffering." With that, Bill Jordan
led his sons into his study.

The next morning was Sunday, and by nine o'clock all the
Jordans had set out for the Baptist church in town. Bill and Joan
led the way in their largest carriage so that Tim and Bobby could
ride with them. Jerry and Cathy followed in theirs.

It had been a long night that began with the women having
tea on the garden porch. That's when Cathy broke the news to
Joan that she and Jerry were married. Joan was stiff-faced; Mary
squealed with delight. And halfway into the bottle of bourbon,
Jerry announced to his father that he and Cathy were married.
There were near-arguments at the men's gathering; Bill raised his
voice only twice, which, thankfully, wasn't heard by the women
at the other end of the house.

During their ride to church, Jerry and Cathy felt peaceful.
Jerry closed his eyes, confident that his horses would follow
the carriage in front. "Is anything wrong, Jerry? Do you have a
headache?" Cathy asked.

"No, sweetheart. I'm just tired and was enjoying the heat of
the morning sun on my head," he replied, reaching for her hand.
He found it and squeezed it gently.

"I'm glad you had a chance last night after dinner to talk about some sensitive issues with your father and brothers. You know, I think your mom is much more flexible than your dad." Cathy softly stroked his head.

"Yes, that's the way it's always been. Mom can always make allowances. She is always the first to show love and forgiveness." Jerry took a deep breath.

"But your dad loves you a lot too," Cathy added matter-of-factly.

"Oh, definitely. He even embraced me last night before we all went to bed. He's having a hard time adjusting to me wanting to be independent," Jerry replied, straightening the reins a bit.

Cathy offered her insight. "I think he's having a hard time getting used to the new way of life on his plantation, compared to the way it was before the war."

"You're right, Cathy. Except it's not even a plantation now that Atlanta has become the state capital. He's especially upset that the legislature includes thirty-two Negroes." Jerry continued, "Cathy, my father made it all too clear to me last night that the war, the burning of his plantation, was a terrible injury to him and to the South. And every new amendment is an insult to that injury."

"He must have exploded through the ceiling when he heard about you and Tim working in Atlanta to push ratification of the Fourteenth Amendment?" Cathy countered.

"Yep . . . he mentioned that. Made me feel like a traitor . . ." Jerry's voice trailed off. He looked sadly at Cathy and then continued, "Traitor to my father, my family, my hometown . . . even to myself." He searched her eyes to bear witness to what he felt; but, thankfully, they indicated otherwise.

Shaking her head, Cathy resolved, "You're too dedicated to the cause, Jerry, to stop. Even with freed slaves in the legislature, the other Negroes are afraid to vote."

They rode in silence the rest of the way to town, both thinking about the same thing. When they arrived at the church, Jerry said aloud what Cathy had been thinking. "It's the Klan that General Gordon's been leading. That's why they're afraid to vote. They're afraid of the Klan."

On Monday, Jerry and Cathy said their good-byes and left on the train to Boston. The worst was over. Jerry was returning to Boston for more study to become an attorney, confident that he would succeed.

With Cathy's financial help, Jerry was able to pay for another year of law school. He had his sights set on a partnership with a law firm in the city, an opportunity Cathy's parents developed for him. The Valderys figured the best thing to do in the interest of their daughter was to support her decision to marry. And the best way to show that was to support her husband.

Bobby, on the other hand, had the full support of both his parents and was planning to return to his native state where he hoped to practice. Indeed, Bill and Joan were already making plans for his welcome-home party. Secretly, everyone was hoping Jerry and Cathy would come too.

Final examinations were fast approaching, but the boys' thoughts were not completely on study. Bobby had received several letters from his mother urging him to find some way to make Jerry return to Brunswick—for good.

On an occasion when they were together for lunch, Bobby decided to test the waters. "Jerry, I've been thinking about you and me and our future."

"What do you mean?" Jerry asked between bites of peach cobbler and sips of cold lemonade.

"Well, we've studied through school together . . . why not set up our professions together? In the same building even?" Bobby asked.

Jerry finished off the cobbler and wiped his mouth with his napkin. He looked thoughtfully at his brother. "That's a good idea," he replied, as he began reading a paper he wrote for one of his classes, his head bent down in concentration. Still focused on his paper, he said, "It would be nice to stay together. Our own building. Medicine and law together. As a matter of fact, I've seen some nice buildings in town . . ."

Bobby interrupted. "I don't mean here, Jerry. Georgia." At the mention of the word "Georgia," Jerry stopped reading and lifted his eyes upward to look at Bobby.

Bobby continued, leaning toward his brother, holding his gaze. "Brunswick, Jerry. Brunswick." Bobby's excitement burst forth. "Jerry, the town has been doing an admirable job of repairing the streets and buildings. I'm sure Dad would help us get—"

"Absolutely not! Boston, yes! Brunswick . . . never!" Jerry sternly replied, gathering his papers.

Bobby softened his approach. "Well, Mom wrote to say they'll all be up here in a few weeks to be at our graduation. Here, have a look at it." He passed the letter to his brother who merely glanced at the contents. "I really wish you would keep thinking about us going into practice together."

"Bobby, it's not the going into practice together that bothers me. It's where one goes. For me, it is certainly not Georgia."

Mom, you're going to have to find another way, Bobby thought as the brothers headed back to classes. *Jerry can be as stubborn as Dad.*

CHAPTER 23

Boys Graduations

Basusu and Chati were making preparations to attend their sons' graduations. Of course, they didn't have to travel as far as the Jordans; and, naturally, their preparations were modest in comparison. However, Mr. and Mrs. Barrington had offered the use of their entire home for the celebration, which added to the gala event. Sally and Jennie took the lead in planning and accounting for every moment. For Basusu and Chati, just knowing that their sons had begun and completed school was the most important and cherished thought. They were thankful to God and immensely proud of the young men's achievements.

BOSTON—JUNE 1868

Only Bobby was standing on the platform. And when the train from New York via Baltimore pulled in, Mary was the first to see him there.

"Daddy! Mommy! There's Bobby! He's waiting for us," she exclaimed.

"Is anyone else with him, dear?" Joan asked, anxiously scanning the platform for Jerry.

"No, Mommy. Except for one of those people who puts your luggage on a wagon for you . . . you know . . . a colored man."

The Jordans' Pullman did not come to a stop anywhere close to where Bobby was waiting. Bobby and the attendant followed his parents' and Mary's car all the way to the other end of the platform. The baggage porter on the platform transferred their luggage from the train to one of the many coaches traveling about in and around Boston. Joan's face expressed disappointment that Jerry was absent for their arrival. She was sad and quiet all the way to the hotel.

Bobby had made many arrangements. At the hotel, the Jordans were in their suite in a matter of moments, Bobby having made arrangements for their registration. They were in one of the newer hotels, their suite many stories up from street level. From their window they could see the evening sun sinking into the Atlantic.

A knock at their door startled them. "He's here!" Joan exclaimed. "I knew he'd come."

Mary rushed to the door and opened it. "Cathy! It's you!" Mary looked behind Cathy into the hallway for Jerry. "Where's my brother?" she asked. Everyone gathered around Cathy as she entered the room, waiting for her response.

"I know you are all disappointed that Jerry's not here," she began. "I came in his place. Please forgive him . . . he was apprehensive about how his presence would be received." Looking at the disappointed faces in the room, she added, "I can see now that he wasted his time worrying."

Joan embraced her strongly. "Daughter-in-law of mine, I am proud that you insisted on coming to greet us. Wait until I see that son of mine." They all chatted for a while, Mary happy to share a sofa with Cathy. The conversations revolved around work and marriage. When the relaxed evening came to a close, Cathy suggested she return home to Jerry; but it was Bill who protested.

"You mustn't go now. Come with us down to the hotel dining room and be our guest for dinner. Later, Bobby and Timothy will accompany you home safely by carriage."

"Please stay! Please stay, won't you?" Mary urged.

"You must be tired, so let me leave you. You need rest for tomorrow. It's going to be a big and long day," Cathy countered.

"Cathy, you will disappoint us all if you go now," Joan said, rising to her feet and heading for the door. "Mary especially. Besides, we all have to eat before bedtime, so just come along with us."

PHILADELPHIA—JUNE 1868

"Pardon me, Charlotte, for staring at you," said Reverend Paxton. "My, oh my," he continued, his smile nearly as wide as his face, "you look so lovely. That dress must be brand-new. Can't get nothin' like that around here . . . did you buy it out of town? And you too," he said, turning to Basusu. "Never saw you in a suit as fine as this, Basusu!"

Chati, pretending shyness, bowed her head slightly but kept her eyes fixed on the Reverend, who now was stepping aside to let other parishioners in. He took Chati and Basusu by the arms and pulled them closer to him so others could get by. Jennie sauntered in between them to let the preacher see her too.

"My dress is new too, Reverend. An' look at Ma Sally comin' in. She's got a new dress too. An' we didn't buy 'em. We made 'em, 'cept for Papa's suit."

"I'm glad you all came early," the reverend said. "Church is fillin' up fast for this mighty fine graduation service. Your sons are already seated upfront." A white couple and their young daughter had come into the church and approached Chati and Basusu. The Reverend was about to greet and welcome them to the service, but Chati made the introductions.

"Reverend, dis is Mistah and Missus Barrington. Dey be de nice folks we all work fo', and dis be dey daughta, Shelly."

"Well, you are most welcome in our church," said Reverend Paxton. "Please do not hesitate to take a pew with the Mensuas."

"We best be sittin' before dere's no seats," Chati said, urging her family toward the front. "But 'fore we do, I want yo' to know dat it was Missus Barrington here dat made my dress, an' my mama's. Jennie's too." Chati looked at Basusu, hoping he would have something to say in thanks as well, but he was hesitant. So Chati continued. "Mistah Barrington took Basusu into town las' week and done bought him a new suit. Just for dis celebration!" Basusu grinned broadly and nodded in thanks to the Barringtons.

As the Mensuas and Barringtons filed past him, Reverend Paxton stopped Jennie. "Jennie, dear, I'm glad you agreed to sing in today's service. You're gonna make your brothers cry again for joy." Jennie blushed at the thought.

The Jordans had a joyous time at their sons' graduation exercises. During dinner, Timothy decided to tell about the letter he and his brothers received. But after announcing his intention, he hesitated at the beginning.

Bill looked at Tim. "Well . . . are you going to go on? Don't put us in suspense. Was it a job offer?"

"Okay, Dad, I'll tell you, everyone here, about the letter. I'm just worried that you may be upset about the contents."

"And the writers!" Bobby added.

"Well, who sent the letter?" Joan nervously asked.

"There was no return address, Mother. It is from Base's boys."

Immediately, there was silence around the table. Bill had lifted his wine goblet but returned it to the table. He was showing no anger, just curiosity. His calm reaction gave courage to Tim to continue, though Joan had placed her hands over her mouth in disbelief.

Tim read the letter slowly. Joan was the first to cry. Mary followed at the mention of Jennie's name.

To all the Jordan family, we send our love. We all are well—Ma Sally, our mama and papa, Jennie, Joe, Greg, and Sam. We will be graduating in a few weeks. We thank you for the education you gave us, hoping you will be happy that we are following in your footsteps. Joe is in law, Greg has been studying government, and Sam is studying medicine. Jennie will probably study music and the arts. She is a talented singer. This could not have happened in Georgia. It is happening up here because of schools built by people who believe slavery is wrong. We are sorry we had to leave you. Even though you were kind to us, we could not stay slaves forever. We will never forget you.

The letter was passed around, Bill noting and mentioning that it was signed, "Sam, Gregory, and Joseph. Sons of Basusu Mensua."

"I'm glad they are alive . . . and I hope they are safe and well," Joan said. There was a long silence, as if everyone was waiting for Bill to make a comment.

Mary was impatient. "Oh, how I wish I could see Jennie. Chati too." Mary looked at her father and swallowed hard, an apology in her eyes for speaking before he did.

Bill picked up his goblet. "Here's a toast to Base. Let's wish them well!" Everyone drank slowly, surprised at his words.

"Mind you!" Bill continued, staring into his glass. "Not that I'm forgiving them. But they're gone. They've been gone a long time." He paused, and it was minutes before he spoke again. "And in a big sense, we helped them escape and made it possible for them to survive. We prepared them for this. Deep down, I don't know whether I am furious or just glad they're okay." Bill looked at his family, then leaned back in his chair, signaling it was their turn to speak.

Mary spoke first. "Father, what do you mean? How did we make it possible for them?" she asked.

"When your brothers played school with them, they were teaching them many things," Bill explained.

"Whatever we learned, they learned," Jerry said, turning to his sister.

"Just look at the quality of the writing," Joan commented, giving detailed attention to the letter. "It's not just the fine handwriting. Look at the words. The grammar."

"They don't talk or write like slaves anymore, do they?" Bill observed, crossing his arms and tilting his head to one side.

No one ventured to remark at that comment.

In bed later that night, Joan asked her husband. "If you should see them someday, what would you do, Bill?"

Bill looked up at the ceiling before answering. "I can't really say, Joan. I paid good money for those slaves, you know. Good money!"

Joan did not say much more. But before she fell asleep, Bill whispered, "During the reading of the letter tonight, you looked glad . . . like you were happy to know they were alive."

Turning her face toward his, she kissed him and whispered back, "Because I've always felt like they were kin, Bill."

CHAPTER 24

Sam's First Interview

PHILADELPHIA—AUGUST 1868

The waiting room was hot and stuffy, and Sam wished he had the courage to walk over to the slightly open window and open it all the way. But the other applicants sat motionless, as if they were in a contest to determine which one of them would falter first. Sam, the only colored man in the room, noticed that each of the other applicants would stare at him—until he looked back.

The black woolen suit he wore was more appropriate for fall and winter, and his leather shoes were too heavy for this kind of weather. The new white shirt he wore was heavily starched, perhaps by an overzealous shirtmaker. During the walk to this interview, the shirt crackled as his arms swung back and forth. But now perspiration had softened the starch, making the sleeves and back stick to his skin. Even though uncomfortable, Sam told himself to be grateful, because the suit, tie, shoes, and even the shirt were all a gift from Mr. Barrington so that Sam would look professional during job interviews.

The door to Dr. James McNally's office was opened again by the same woman who had been admitting applicants since nine o'clock this morning. Though Sam had arrived at eight-thirty, the secretary called only for the others who had arrived after he did.

"Dr. James Finnegan? Dr. Finnegan? Are you here?" she called. The white man next to Sam got up, and the secretary escorted him into the next room.

It was nearly noon, and Sam was beginning to get hungry. When the secretary came in again, Sam got up immediately and quickly walked over to her.

"Excuse me, madam. Is my name on your list of applicants?" Sam asked. At the mention of the word "applicants," the others in the room shifted in their chairs. Some began talking in low voices, and Sam thought he heard one of them say, "Has that man lost his mind?"

The secretary's question jerked Sam's attention back to her. "What is your name?" she curtly asked.

"Mensua . . . Dr. Samuel Mensua."

"Dr. Mensua? Did you say *doctor*?" She began checking the list in her notepad, clearly upset by the thought of a Negro bearing the title of "doctor." "I don't see it . . . how do you spell it?"

Sam patiently spelled his name. Everyone was looking at him. He was now more uncomfortable than before, sweat running down his back. He was glad for the suit jacket; it might have been heavy, but it was hiding his wet shirt.

The secretary smiled suddenly. "Oh! Here it is. Uh . . . Dr. Men . . . Meen-sue-aye . . . I see your name now. Please take your seat again. I need to speak with Dr. McNally." She whirled around and returned to McNally's office, closing the door behind her.

"What do you mean, Janice?" Dr. McNally said. He removed his eyeglasses and pushed back in his high-backed leather chair, waiting for her to explain. "You say there's a *slave* out there? A colored man? A Negro?"

"Yes, Doctor. I'm sorry . . . I didn't know. Had I known what he was, I would not have put him on the list."

Dr. McNally was clearly upset at the thought of a Negro doctor coming to him for an interview. He looked his secretary straight in the eyes. "Look, Janice. I'm too busy to deal with nonsense like this. Understand? Take him into Dr. Nevins's office; he's not in today. Tell this Meen-sue-ee 'doctor,' or whatever he is, that the position in the clinic has been filled."

Janice pursed her lips, left the office, and did as she was told. Sam understood the implication perfectly—Negroes cannot be doctors in the minds of white people. *Slaves may be free in the North,* Sam thought, *but they are still enslaved in the minds of men.*

The walk back home felt very long to Sam. But in a way he was glad; it gave him time to mull over what had taken place. It was just like interviews Greg and Joe had—always the long waiting—while white people were called promptly. Always no reason given for rejection. Always no commitments from the interviewers. Greg couldn't even get a job as a teacher's assistant. Joe wasn't even offered a law clerk's position.

"I've had enough, Joe," Sam admitted several weeks later.

"Me too. We will never get anywhere like this. I think it's time we write to Joel for some advice."

Their answer came in the form of a long letter, which had been delivered and addressed to the Barringtons. Joel Brown had become very fond of, and very trusting of the Barringtons, for they had given Basusu, Chati, and Sally jobs and housing. Moreover, they made space for Jennie and let the boys convert the upper floor of the carriage house into a large bedroom and study.

When Mr. Barrington realized Joel Brown's letter was not for him, he asked Jennie to deliver it to the boys right away. Delighted that something important had come for her brothers, she ran to the carriage house but stopped before going in.

Mr. Barrington noticed and playfully called out to her. "Jennie! That's not for you to read. Go up and bring it to them right now." Laughing, Jennie obeyed.

Upon delivering the letter to her brothers, Jennie could not be persuaded to leave the room. "I want to hear it too! What's it about?" Resolute, she sat on the floor in front of the long table that was used as a study desk. She wrapped her arms around a table leg, her eyes challenging them to pull her away. "It's time yo' included me in things that are goin' on! I'm seventeen now," she affirmed.

All three brothers realized they weren't dealing with a little sister anymore. Right before their eyes, little Jennie had blossomed into a young lady and possessed Ghanaian courage and beauty. Jennie admired her brothers and believed that her persistence and faith would pay off.

Joe opened the envelope and began unfolding the letter. He sat on the floor next to Jennie so she could see it too. Sam and Greg sat together on Joe's bed, which was the closest to her. Though she felt her brothers had accepted her presence, she did not relax her grip on the table leg.

Joe read it through from beginning to end and then returned to read certain parts.

September 28, 1868
My Dear Friends,

Get it straight, boys! This is going to be a hard struggle. But fight on, and brace yourselves, for there are worse days that lie ahead. This is the way of the Negro of this land. You have been a fighter from the start like your father. Don't give up now. You have come a long way. The Barringtons are on your side. You can trust them to help you, so do not give up!

Toward the middle of the letter, Joel Brown's advice on what to say during interviews interested all of them. Joe read it aloud twice.

You must tell your interviewers the names of your teachers. Don't wait to be asked. You must take the lead. Though you have not, and still are not, attending impressive medical or law colleges, you have been learning from established and respected men. Joe, name the prestigious lawyers who have visited your classroom. Greg, tell your interviewers the names of your instructors and the colleges they teach at. Sam, tell them the names of your teachers, the surgeons who visit from Howard University in Washington.

Don't feel you're not good enough just because your school is on a back street. I am aware, just as you are, of the new schools—Purdue, Cornell, University of Maine, University of Kentucky. I know that graduates from University of Massachusetts will get jobs faster—and more offers too.

Once again, Joe read the closing paragraph, the part Jennie liked the best.

So, for all of you, you must name your teachers. And you must tell them what you've learned. I might add that you all ought to "rehearse" your words; you should practice your delivery like you used to do on the plantation with the Jordan boys. Give my love to all, especially Jennie. Her fame in music and singing is spreading. Make sure she gets a chance at education too!

CHAPTER 25

Another Interview???

Sam was off to the first of his interviews for the week. When he arrived, there were others in the waiting room. *Whether I come in quietly or not, they're all goin' to stare,* he thought, taking a chair near a window. All the other applicants were white, some speculating that he was a well-dressed messenger here to deliver important medical reports to Dr. Garland.

Sam noticed the lamp table to his left. On it were some forms, and a closer look revealed that they were applications for the position of staff physician. Realizing his next action would attract negative attention and possibly even resentment, he pulled out his fountain pen, a special gift from Mr. Barrington, from his inside vest pocket. He felt the stares of others in the room but ignored whatever they were thinking. Before beginning to write, he recalled Joel Brown's words and Jennie's kiss and hug of encouragement given before he set out that morning.

Having finished the form, he looked about the room to see what else could occupy his time. But just as he was about to pick up a journal on the lamp table, the secretary entered the waiting room. "Dr. Morgan?" she called. "Dr. Garland can see you now."

A white man got up and said, "Here I am." The secretary nodded a polite welcome and stepped aside to admit him to Dr.

Garland's private office. Turning to the others, she announced, "Please make certain you fill out the application and give it to me. The doctor will review your application before he will see you."

Hearing that, Sam leaped to his feet and presented his neatly filled-out application.

"Is this from your employer?" she asked, scantily reviewing the application. "Were you sent here in advance of his arrival . . . to hold his place perhaps?" Condescension was on her face.

"No, madam. This is mine," Sam replied, not flinching at her rude comment.

The secretary shifted her eyes from Sam's and surveyed the other applicants. Without looking back at Sam, she shrugged her shoulders and took the form to Dr. Garland.

Sam returned to his chair and picked up the medical journal he had noticed a few moments ago. He flipped pages until he found an article that promised to be interesting. When he finished the first page and turned to the next, the other applicants exchanged looks of contempt or disbelief. Their reactions swelled when Sam pulled out a notepad from his briefcase and began writing notes about data he felt would be valuable to remember. The man sitting next to him looked to determine whether he was really writing words. The man then nodded to the others, as if to say, "He's not pretending."

Suddenly, Dr. Garland's door opened. Without entering the waiting room completely, and holding the doorknob, the secretary looked directly at Sam. "Dr. Garland wants to see you now."

She didn't even call me "doctor," Sam thought. *Didn't even try to pronounce my name.* The secretary went into the private office ahead of Sam, making it obvious that she would not escort him.

"Here he is, Dr. Garland." And then to Sam she said, "Close the door behind you."

Sam did as he was told and stood before the doctor's desk. There were two comfortable chairs he could have sat in, but neither the doctor nor the secretary invited him to sit. She disappeared behind the partition, which was her work area.

Dr. George Garland cleared his throat and read Sam's application. "You are standing here, a colored." Dr. Garland spoke brusquely, his voice deep and wavering. "How am I to know you are indeed a doctor?"

Sam was about to say what he had practiced with his brothers, but Dr. Garland continued. "How do I know you are indeed capable of doing a doctor's work in my hospital clinic?"

Dr. Garland paused, clasped his hand together, and waited for Sam to speak.

"Before studying medicine, Dr. Garland, I graduated with honors from the Baptist Society Preparatory School for Boys. That was four years ago. It's here in Philadelphia."

"Yes, yes . . . but what about your medical studies? Where did you—"

Sam interrupted Dr. Garland's line of thought. "I was taught by well-known physicians and surgeons, Doctor. The school did not look like the stately buildings of Yale. My school was the room above the dress shop, the basement of a church, the morgue at the hospital, late at night. But it was a real school—as real as the Underground Railroad. Our first professor, an abolitionist like the others, was Dr. Joseph Barnes. He used to teach biology at Oberlin College in Ohio and is now on the planning committee to establish Temple University here in Philadelphia."

Dr. Garland picked up his pen. "Did you say 'Joe Barnes'?" Doctor Garland wrote the professor's name. "He's a good friend of mine. I had no idea he was involved with such a movement, providing professional education to slaves . . . I mean, former slaves," he said more to himself than to Sam.

Sam seized this opportunity to validate his status as a free citizen. "Slaves are no more, Doctor. Not since the Thirteenth Amendment. And now that the Fourteenth Amend—"

"Yes, yes. I know. Times are changing fast—and dramatically. But you were a slave, weren't you? Where did you escape from?"

"From Georgia, Doctor. Six years ago."

"Georgia? Well they've been having their share of problems down there, haven't they? Just a few months ago, federal troops returned control of law and order to the state authorities. Georgia's been under military rule since 1867. You probably know that, don't you?" Dr. Garland tilted his head to one side and sized up the young man standing in front of him.

"Yes, I do know," Sam replied. "Georgia, the last state to ratify the Fourteenth Amendment. My brother, Greg, who is studying economics and politics, wanted to go to the Georgia legislature to debate the opposition. But that would have been suicidal." Sam shifted his weight.

"Sure would have been. Have a seat there." He pointed to one of the comfortable chairs. "So you know old Joe Barnes." Dr. Garland thoughtfully poised his pen over Sam's application. "Who else were your teachers?" he asked.

Joel Brown's strategy is working, Sam thought. Now was his chance to prove his qualifications. "Visiting from Columbia School of Nursing was Dr. Stewart Wheeler. He taught us patient care. And from Columbia School of Medicine was Dr. Lowell Schutta, who taught anatomy and physiology. Frederick Z. Henry, M.D., taught pathology."

"*The* Fred Henry? From Harvard Med School?" Garland couldn't believe what he heard.

"Yes, Doctor. He traveled from Massachusetts every five or six weeks, staying for a week at a time to teach us—even bringing his own specimens for us to study."

The doctor was clearly dumbfounded. He asked, "Who taught pharmacology?"

"We had regular visits every two weeks from George Christman, M.D., from Johns Hopkins in Baltimore. His classes would begin Friday evening and run all day Saturday and Sunday."

Sam paused to see what the doctor would say next. Dr. Garland took a deep breath and put his hands on his hips. He moved his left hand to his chin, slowly rubbing his cheek with his fingers.

Speaking bluntly, Garland asked, "What am I going to do with a Negro doctor in the hospital? Are the patients going to think 'slave'? How are we going to do this, Men-sue-aye?"

"Men-sah," Sam corrected softly and gently, realizing that Dr. Garland was not rejecting him but instead, anticipating a way to make the situation work.

"If I were you, I would get me a regular name that is more like you," Dr. Garland suggested.

"What do you mean by that?" Sam asked, puzzled at the comment.

"Well, Dr. Mensua, people need to be able to know who you are."

At the mention of "Dr. Mensua," Sam knew that he had won Dr. Garland's respect.

"Well, I'm a doctor. What's wrong with 'Mensua'? There are names harder to pronounce, yet people pronounce them. Another one of my teachers was Stanley Kirschenmann, M.D., from Germany. We all had trouble saying that at first, but we all learned how to say his name correctly."

"I don't quite know how to explain it; all I know is 'Mensua' sounds like some foreign name." Dr. Garland shuffled through the applicant forms on his desk, indicating that the interview had come to an end.

Sam thought about debating the point by saying, *Aren't we all foreign?* But the interview had gone well, and Dr. Garland promised to have him back to talk more. Thanking Dr. Garland, Sam proudly left the office and headed home.

"Mama!" Jennie shrieked. "Sam's home! He's home . . . an' he's smilin'. Smilin', Mama."

Sam had hardly entered the house when Jennie put her hands on his back and pushed him into the kitchen. Chati put the lid on the stew pot. Then wiping her hands on her apron, she rushed over to Sam with open arms.

"Yo' sho is smilin' . . . just like yo' sister's sayin'. Finally looks like yo' got yourself a fair intaview. Jennie, go get Papa. He's fixin' a wheel in de carriage house out dere."

Mother and son beamed smiles at each other. Sam gave details of the entire interview and explained that Joel Brown's strategy worked. Basusu entered, hugging his son and repeatedly patting him on the back. Sam recounted the details to his father, but when he mentioned that Dr. Garland suggested he change his name, Basusu's smile soured, a change noticed by everyone. By now, Sally and Mr. Barrington had joined the gathering.

"Y'all can call yo'self what evers yo' want. But my name is Mensua till I die." Basusu walked out, disappointed and sulking.

CHAPTER 26

Joe Faces Interview

Joseph's interview a few days later with a small law firm in the city was upsetting. He was severely ridiculed by the men who interviewed him. Once they found out that he had been a slave, the interview turned into a kind of comedy session. When Joe returned home, Jennie immediately knew he had been rejected and hurt.

"Mama, they called me 'boy,'" Joe said, disgusted.

"Who did? Who called yo' dat?" Chati asked, her brow furrowing.

"He's a lawyer downtown. Norman Westbond's his name. There were two other lawyers there . . . his partners. Once they realized I was colored, they had fun with me." Joseph fought back the tears.

Jennie embraced her brother as he continued the account. "I didn't go to a fancy law school like they did. And Mr. Joel Brown's brilliant advice didn't work for me. In fact, they hated my teachers. Westbond called Professor Spector a"—Joseph stopped, hugged Jennie tighter, and took a deep breath—"a nigga-lovin' sympathizer," he sobbed.

"It's terrible how all kinds of professional, well-educated people reject other human beings because of their color," commented Mr. Barrington. He had overheard Joseph's lament from his study and decided to offer comfort and perhaps some advice. "Norm Westbond, you say?" Mr. Barrington questioned. Joseph nodded yes. "That's shameful, Joe. But you have to expect to run into characters like that. I'm just glad I didn't hire Westbond for business. If I had, I would fire him right now."

Joe was grateful for the support although it didn't lessen the pain. "That's not the worst of it—the interview I mean," he said. "One of the laughing partners said I looked truly distinguished in my suit. At first I took him seriously, until he said he had a great job for me."

His family had gathered around him, closely by now, waiting for Joe to continue. Mr. Barrington put his hand on his shoulder.

"His yard hand. That's the job he thought I was perfect for." Joe looked down at the floor.

Sally moved closer, first taking Joe by both his hands and then cradling his face in her hands. "Dis world ain't fair," she said. Though her hands were much callused, all Joe felt was softness on his face. Her touch always comforted, always strengthened.

"Y'all know whad I'm talkin' 'bout. De Lawd ain't dead. De Lawd gonna fix it all one a' dese days. Just like Reveren' Paxton say last Sunday." Sally patted Joseph's cheeks gently. He closed his eyes and moved closer to her.

"Don't worry, son. Yo' be like yo' Papa. He ain't never let notin' get 'im down. He just keep goin' right on." Sally continued to stroke her weary grandchild's face.

By now, Basusu was back in the house. And when he heard his mother-in-law's tribute, he smiled contentedly. "Dat's right, Joe! Like yo' gran'ma say, don' yo' quit!"

Four days later, the Barringtons' mail included a letter addressed in a way that confused the postman but excited everyone in the household as it was passed along, unopened of course, to Sam. It was addressed, *Dr. Samuel Mensua.*

No one would give Sam peace or privacy. Everyone gathered around, wanting to know what the letter said. Sam cut it open carefully and neatly with the pocket knife Mr. Barrington had given him.

"This letter is from Dr. Garland," Sam said. "And it's dated just a few days ago . . . October 21, 1868." Sam hesitated, afraid to read, and therefore find out Dr. Garland's decision. Jennie came close, touched his arm, and whispered, "Tell us, Sam. What's it say?"

Sam began to read.

Dear Doctor Mensua,

I enjoyed meeting you. It is evident that you are a fine young man, your studies obviously sound. I have no doubt that you will make a fine doctor.

I am afraid that your presence in any hospital here in Philadelphia would stir up controversy among patients and staff. Please be assured that I have not closed my mind to the idea that you have a place, and future, in medicine.

Your future, I am sorry to say, seems bleak here in Philadelphia. There is much opposition here; I doubt I can change it no matter how often or how long I talk to staff.

Please stop by my office next Thursday at 6:30 in the morning. I have a proposition for you to consider and am hoping we can have a discussion before I do my rounds at the clinic.

Please continue to consider my comments about changing your name because I believe it would increase your acceptance not only among staff but also with patients.

George Garland, M.D.

Everyone was silent at the end of the reading. The thought of changing his name was as troubling to Sam as it was to Basusu. "How much do we have to give up, Papa?" Sam moaned. Basusu shook his head sadly.

Mr. Barrington offered some advice. "I think Dr. Garland is misinformed. I think his judgment is wrong. Changing your name is not going to change the color of your skin. It is the color that causes discrimination—*not* the sound of your name."

"Yes, Mistah Barrington, sir," Sam said, "but Dr. Garland thinks the sound of 'Mensua' makes white people think of me as a slave—not a doctor."

"You mean to tell me you actually believe a different name would fool people?" Mr. Barrington challenged. "You think people will accept you because you do not have an African-sounding name? Your skin is black, Sam. Your father was a slave; he was stolen from Africa. I don't know any black-skinned people who came here of their own accord and free will from Africa. Anyone here with black skin is most likely and probably a slave who was stolen or captured, call it whatever you wish, from Africa." Barrington's words came fast, making him so breathless he had to pause. He was visibly upset and frustrated with Dr. Garland's viewpoint.

Tim decided to enter the debate. "Sam, Papa, maybe people who judge by color are easily fooled by words . . . and not by what their eyes see. Perhaps if you changed to a French-sounding name, they might think you are the educated son of a French-African nobleman." He searched for approval from anyone but found none who would agree. Basusu stared at him in disbelief. Sheepishly, he recoiled.

It was Sally who broke the silence first with a screeching laugh that echoed through the house. "Yo' all talkin' in circles!" she complained. "Is yo' skin black? Den yo' been a slave. Is yo' a slave? Den yo' a slave from Africa! Go on. Change yo' name. See if'n yo' can fool dem white folks in de hospitals." Sally was as disgusted as Basusu. Together, they left the kitchen.

Mr. Barrington looked at the confused and angry Sam. "Your father holds his name sacred," he said gravely. "That's why it was difficult for him to choose an alias even if it was temporary.

And . . . it may be more important to you too, more important than you realize to keep your last name. Do you really want to go on with your life with someone else's name, Sam?"

"Dat's how it was on de plantation," Chati said. "We all was Jordan in de eyes of de Massa. But to Basusu, we was, always is, Mensua."

The following Thursday, Sam presented himself at Dr. Garland's office promptly at six-thirty. Like everyone else in the Barrington house, Sam had not attached much importance to this meeting or to the "proposition" mentioned in his letter. The whole Mensua family, as well as the Barringtons, had become involved in a yet-to-be-resolved debate about changing Sam's last name, and maybe even Greg's and Joe's. That involvement was so deep and focused that no one paid much attention to Dr. Garland's proposition.

Dr. Garland was happy to see Sam as he entered the office. "Come in, Sam! Glad you were able to be here on time. In fact, I have less time than I originally thought. A patient's condition is deteriorating even as we talk, so I must excuse myself in a few minutes. My assistants are preparing her for emergency surgery. So sit with me. Take this chair."

Taking the seat Dr. Garland had pointed to, the one by the side of his desk, Sam noticed the tray with two teacups on the desk. "Marian, please bring that pot of tea, and the cream pitcher too."

Am I going to hear a job offer? This is royal treatment, Sam thought. The secretary arrived with a steaming white china pot of tea and carefully poured for each of them. Following Dr. Garland's lead, Sam added a miniature spoonful of sugar and a generous amount of cream. Dr. Garland lifted his cup and took a small sip. Sam did the same.

Sam watched Dr. Garland replace his teacup—so thin and delicate it was—onto the saucer. Finally, the doctor spoke, "Let me tell you about an opportunity for you, but I hasten to add—lest you misinterpret—that the opportunity is in Boston."

"Boston? Why is there more opportunity there?" Sam said.

"The University of Massachusetts wants to establish clinics in many parts of Boston, especially in wards where poor people live. Those wards are populated predominantly by Negroes, and . . ." Dr. Garland didn't finish his sentence. Sam, detecting a look of uneasiness on his face, allowed him to stall. Dr. Garland took another slow, thoughtful sip of tea and then continued, "And, frankly, we are having trouble recruiting doctors to staff those clinics, the ones in the tenement wards."

"Why is there a problem getting physicians?" Sam asked, knowing full well why there was.

Dr. Garland pursed his lips. "Ninety-nine out of a hundred patients are coloreds . . . Negroes . . . former slaves. White doctors would rather take staff appointments in the main hospital or set up their practices on 'the Hill,' preferring the wealthy to the poor, obviously."

Sam sipped his tea. "Tell me about your proposition," he said.

"A few of my colleagues and I have formed a consortium under contract with the university. We are looking for physicians. That's the opportunity for you, Sam." Dr. Garland waited for Sam's reply.

Sam felt his heart beating faster and more strongly. Should he show how excited he felt? He wondered how much enthusiasm to show. He allowed Dr. Garland to continue.

"Sam, this could be good for you. You would diagnose and treat patients as they come to the clinic. You would travel from clinic to clinic, serving here and there as needed. And, most important of all, you would have hospital privileges."

"Hospital privileges? What do you mean?"

"Many of your cases are going to require surgical intervention. You will have the right, the authority, the privilege, to schedule your patients for surgeries at the hospital itself. At first, Sam, you would assist at those surgeries. But eventually, you'd be the surgeon in charge, after you get experienced in procedures."

Sam thought about that for a moment, though he wondered if he ever would have willing "assistants." What white doctors would agree to "assist" him, a Negro, he wondered.

"You really think I'll gain acceptance by the medical and surgical staff?" he asked.

Dr. Garland reached for his teacup before answering. "Sam, take it one step at a time. For many reasons, you are a special case . . . your background, your education, and yes, Sam, your color. One step at a time, Sam."

"Has to be Boston, Dr. Garland? Why can't it be here?" Sam pressed.

"Call me George, Sam. Frankly, Philadelphia is too small a town right now. There are more people in Boston . . . many more people. Larger hospitals. You'll blend in easier there."

Dr. Garland sipped the last of his tea and stood up. "I've got to go, Sam." He extended his hand, and Sam received a hearty handshake. "Sam, don't take long on this. If you decide, I'll need you there next week. There's no doubt in my mind that it will be the most important part of your medical education."

Wow! Sam thought to himself. When he realized he had not let go of Dr. Garland's hand and was still shaking it, he let go. "Doctor . . . I mean, George . . . I like your proposition. When must I let you know?"

"Sam, I need to know before noon this coming Monday. The consortium is pressing me to make all selections before the end of the day, Monday." Dr. Garland hurried to attend to his patient.

CHAPTER 27

Letter to Their Parents

PHILADELPHIA—JANUARY 1869

January 14, 1869
Dear Mama and Papa, Jennie,
Dear Greg,
Dear Grandma Sally,
Dear Mr. & Mrs. Barrington,
  Happy birthday, Jennie! Praise the Lord, you are 18 now! Greg says you are definitely a woman now, one not to be ignored anymore. Birthdays have been on our minds much these months. Last month it was Joseph's, when he turned 20. We are all becoming older, aren't we? Greg admits to 21 now. And, of course, I acknowledge to being 23. Papa, is it true, are you 40? Or are you now closer to 41? And what worries you more in these times—all the commotion over whether your sons should change their names, our move to Boston, or the fact that you are now growing older, Papa? We love you, Papa. (How old is Mama? Do you even know?) Joe and I are glad we visited for Christmas. I can still picture Mrs. Barrington's decorations all over the house. And what a surprise—decorating our carriage house-room! I can still smell the fragrances of Christmas. The candles Grandma Sally and Jennie made, bayberry, holly, pine boughs, the baking ham, the cinnamon-apple pies

you made, Mama. We could listen to Jennie's singing forever. The hymns she sang.

Christmas Eve was so beautiful I cried from happiness. Joe did too, though he won't admit it. (I saw him crying—and Mrs. Barrington too, as she accompanied Jennie on the piano.) Wasn't it particularly kind and generous of the Barringtons to have let us all be a part of their holiday celebration? After all, we are still their house servants—though they treated us as if we were guests, like the real guests who came for Christmas Day dinner. Oh, Mama, what a dinner you and Grandma Sally prepared! The hams, the pheasants, the pies. Oh, Joe and I miss your home cooking, Mama! Joe and I now have an apartment together, and we just can't cook like you do.

Not including the time we spent during Christmas at the Barringtons, we have been in Boston six weeks now. Our apartment has a kitchen and two other rooms. One we use as our bedroom; the other is our study. Joe has only a short walk to his office, while I need a horse and carriage to get around from clinic to clinic. Doctor Garland's group purchased three horses and carriages so doctors like me can get around. Already, I have assisted in surgeries I myself scheduled at Massachusetts General Hospital, a building so large I continue to get lost in it. Now I have seen surgeries that my professors were able only to describe! Presently, I am allowed to "close" the incisions. Mama, I'm good at it. It's like sewing a fabric seam. Good thing I paid attention to the sewing you did—Grandma Sally and Jennie too.

Joe has made real progress in the law firm that hired him. Thank the Lord for the connections Joel Brown and Reverend Paxton have! Joe received job offers from two law firms. He chose Siegel, Siegel, and Feinstein (possibly because their office was the more luxurious). Though Joe's responsibilities are restricted to clerking and research, he is learning from well-respected and qualified attorneys. Joe's name won't be on their sign next month or next year. But give him a chance. (There are white lawyers who have been working there for years, and their names still are not listed on the signs in front.)

Joe goes to court two or three times a week. The partners take him along to assist them in many ways, except he's not allowed to speak during the trials. Papa, Joe and I are testing the benefits of the name we are using. We are doing this temporarily, Papa! My calling card is enclosed for you to see. I chose Samuel M. Jordan, M.D. Papa, the M is for Mensua. Joe hasn't been able to have his cards printed yet, but it will have his name, Joseph M. Jordan, under the name of the firm. Joe will be identified as "Law Clerk and Research." The M stands for Mensua.

Personally, Joe and I feel the name change is not as critical as Doctor Garland believes. Soon, after Joe and I prove our abilities come from our knowledge and skills, we will drop the Jordan and spell out MENSUA!

We miss you all terribly. Isn't there some way you can send Jennie to us for a vacation? (There's room for you here, Jennie.) The trip from Philadelphia is shorter than we expected. Trains are faster now. There are plenty of stages between Philadelphia and Boston, so much, in fact, that we must be careful crossing streets here.

With much love,
Sam and Joe

P.S. Greg, did you accept that job offer in teaching? Write us right away, please. What's the name of the school?

BOSTON—FEBRUARY 1869

Sam was tired. He had been at the clinic all morning and afternoon, then at the hospital to assist at four surgeries. Having had no lunch or supper and it now being nine o'clock at night, he thought his imagination and desires for food were playing tricks on him. *Do I smell food?* he thought. *Maybe it's not coming from our apartment.*

It was. Joe was home, working in their study. "You must be tired, Sam."

"Yes. Very." Sam was out of breath. "This fourth-floor apartment is hard on the legs, especially after all the walking I did today. Is that hospital ever huge!"

"Take off your shoes. I've been keeping a pot of Mama's chicken stew on the stove. It's still warm."

Sam was grateful, though Joe's version of his mother's stew was more like soup. He sat in the study with his brother, eating directly from the pot. When he had finished, Joe closed his book and turned his chair so he could face Sam.

"Today, Sam, I discovered what may be the real reason I was hired. And you know what? I don't care; in fact, I am glad."

Sam took the pot to the kitchen sink.

"Put water in it, Sam. It will be easier to clean later," Joe said.

Sam obeyed and returned to talk (perhaps *listen* would be a better word).

"Sam, you know how you were hired to deliver, as they say, medical services to what politicians call the indigent?" Sam nodded in agreement, and Joe continued. "And how you take care of mostly our people . . . and even white people too poor to afford white doctors."

"And white people too afraid to go to doctors, regardless of color," Sam added.

"Well, today I discovered, even after Congress passed an amendment confirming citizenship to anyone and everyone born here, that our people don't have a real voice in the courtroom. Well, Siegel, Siegel, and Feinstein want me to take the lead in representing Negroes especially in court cases. That's why I'm here with all these reference books, studying so I can become as knowledgeable as the partners."

Sam was as excited as Joe. "Probably, the firm sees a financial opportunity in that area. Even though they may be motivated by financial gain, this move would also benefit our people. Just imagine . . . any black person with your firm's representation would have power in the courtroom."

For a while, the brothers looked at each other, smiling and nodding in understanding. Joe reached for his book, opening it to the place mark. Sam slouched back in his chair to be more comfortable. "Go ahead, Joe, resume your studying. I'll keep you company."

In a moment, Sam fell asleep. Joe quietly stood up, got a blanket, and covered his brother's chest and legs. The apartment would get cold during the night.

BOSTON—FEBRUARY 21, 1869
Superior Court, State of Massachusetts

"Will the attorneys for both the plaintiff and defendant approach the bench?" the bailiff called out.

Joe, looking at the judge with confidence, led the way for the plaintiff, Mr. Siegel following. He had done his homework, and Harvey Siegel was by his side to back him up. "Joseph M. Jordan, your honor," Joe said, loud enough to be heard by everyone in the room.

It was indeed heard by everyone, including Jerry Jordan, who was present merely to watch and listen to Harvey Siegel in action. Jerry fixed his eyes on the man standing next to Siegel, the man who identified himself as "Joseph M. Jordan."

The moment Joe turned around to return to the plaintiff's table, Jerry recognized him. Joe's face was unmistakable for anyone else's. During the walk from the judge's bench to the table, Joe kept looking from the papers he was carrying to Harvey. Before sitting, Joe casually looked toward the spectator box but did not notice Jerry, who at the last moment lifted his notepad to block his view.

Convinced that the person he was watching was Joe, and eager as he was to make himself known, his better sense told him that it would be an inappropriate time to approach him. When Joe turned his back, Jerry discreetly excused himself from the spectator box and left the building.

CHAPTER 28

Jerry Meets Joe

BOSTON—FEBRUARY 27, 1869

The early morning wind made Joe's ears hurt, so he pulled his dark-blue woolen hat down over them. He was sorry now that he had forgotten to take his gloves along. He crossed North Main Street so he could have a close look at the outdoor thermometer that hung over the door of Harrison's Hardware.

"Forty-two degrees!" Joe said aloud. "If it weren't for the wind, this could be a cold morning in Georgia." He took a look at Tom Harrison's window display of kitchen sink faucets and wished he and Sam had one for their apartment. He turned away and continued walking, glad that his office was only three blocks away.

"Good morning, Mr. Jordan," Lynn said the moment he entered. As he approached, he pulled off his hat, stuffing it into his coat pocket. Lynn held up a bundle of papers and folders for him to notice. He rested his briefcase on her dark oak receptionist's desk to free both hands and cover his frozen ears with his palms. She waited, smiling.

"Mr. Jordan, you'll have to uncover your ears so you can hear what I have to say."

"Okay, Lynn. But another minute out there and my ear lobes would have shattered. I'll take my papers. Thank you."

Lynn called out after him as Joe strode away. "Mr. Siegel Senior said you should see him as soon as you came in. I think he's still in the conference room upstairs."

Joe took off his coat with his free hand as he went upstairs. He liked many things about this building that the Siegels owned—the offices, conference rooms, and even a law library inside. The firm's name was hand-lettered in gold leaf on the front window for passersby to see. The window was large, admitting the late-afternoon sun into the reception room to warm and comfort both Lynn and waiting clients. At that time of the day, the lettering would also cast a shadow on the wall behind her desk so that the names of the three partners could also be seen on the wall. The shadow had become a sundial for Lynn; she could tell the time by its position on the wall.

Save for one room, all the flooring was covered in thick, expensive carpeting. Most everyone here spoke softly, as all the carpeting and oak-paneled walls promoted reverence and dignity. At the top of the stairs was the conference room. The double doors were open, and Joe saw Harvey Siegel standing by the window at the end of the room. This was the only room that was not carpeted, and Joe liked the way voices echoed here. Four tall, narrow windows faced Bayberry Park, and Harvey was looking out at the seagulls splashing in the pond. He turned when he heard Joe's footsteps.

"Morning, Joe! I've been anxious to show you something I know will excite you." Motioning toward the long table, he put his hand on Joe's back to hurry him along. A newspaper was opened to show the front-page story.

"Just look at this! 'Congress Proposes Fifteenth Amendment.' I was so excited to see this I couldn't wait for you to come in. When this becomes ratified—even before it is made law by ratification—

you will have federal basis to support your cases. Now what do you think about that?"

Joe turned the paper so he could read it better. "It says here that 'neither race, color, nor previous condition of servitude shall be reason to deny the right of citizens of the United States to vote.' And look here, Mr. Siegel . . ."

Harvey Siegel didn't attempt to conceal his enthusiasm. "I know! I know! This amendment is written not only as a federal law but also extends to all the states. This may need time to reach the ratification stage. There are still many states reluctant and resistant—just like they were for the fourteenth and thirteenth. And take a look at this separate story. The reporter interviewed legislative people in various states of the opposition." Harvey pointed to another place on the paper for Joe to read.

Joe read fast because he too was excited, but a sentence slowed him down. He read it aloud, "According to Timothy Jordan, a legislative assistant for the state of Georgia, passage of this proposed amendment is a welcome, just, and deserved extension of the previous two amendments abolishing slavery and confirming citizenship rights to freed slaves."

"Imagine that," Joe said. "I know this assistant . . ."

Harvey didn't let him finish. "Joe, there's someone here who said he knows you. From the way he talked about you, apparently you've known each other a long time. He admires and respects you very much."

"Where is he?" Joe asked, tossing the paper aside.

"He's in the private reception room. He preferred not to wait in the front reception room; he wanted to surprise you. I'll tell him you're here and have Lynn show him to your office."

Joe liked his own office. It was on the street-level floor; the partners and senior attorneys had theirs on the floor above. But he too had a window, which faced the park. And he was adjacent to the law library. After arranging the papers and files Lynn had given him earlier, he turned to check on the seagulls in the pond.

A gentle, familiar voice made him turn his head slowly. "Joe . . . it's really you."

There, standing in the doorway was Jerry, smiling. Joe smiled too. He felt relieved; all the worries he had about seeing the Jordans again dissolved. He walked toward Jerry, who was the first to extend both his hands.

Joe spoke first. "Jerry, how did you find me? How did you know where—" He was unable to finish, for Jerry had first grasped his shoulders and then embraced him fully with both arms. When he let go, Joe stepped backward slightly. They looked at each other, studying each other's faces as brothers would who haven't seen each other for a long time.

"Joe, I saw you in court a few days ago. Why, I knew it was you just by the sound of your voice."

"It's been a long time, hasn't it, Jerry?"

"I'm twenty-five now. And married . . . to a Northern girl. A Yankee. And, oh, is my father mad!" Jerry smirked at the thought of his father.

"We have so much to talk about! But tell me how you found me?" Joe urged him on.

"You're not listening, Joe. I saw you in court. I watched you win your case. I saw old Mr. Siegel with you, so I assumed he was your mentor and that you were a member of this law firm." Joe interrupted him to take him by the arm to the chairs by the window. They both sat down.

They were silent a while, just enjoying the sight of each other. Then Jerry spoke.

"When you and your family left us, we couldn't believe it. We were in shock. Mother was scared. Father, of course, was furious. Only recently has he softened."

"He's been having a hard time, hasn't he?" Joe asked.

Jerry paused, choosing his words carefully. "We escaped the war. And then . . ."

Joe began to remember the plantation and the things he loved there. He sensed something amiss. "What happened to the house . . . the fields?"

Lynn knocked and entered, carrying a tray. "Mr. Siegel asked me to bring you two gentlemen some tea and sweetbreads. I'll just put them here on your conference table, Mr. Jordan, and let the two of you continue." She pulled the door shut as she left.

"I haven't done this in a long time, Massa Jerry," Joe joked, as he stood up and poured a cup of tea for Jerry. "Still take your tea with lots of cream and sugar?"

But Jerry did not laugh. Instead, he gazed up into Joe's eyes and began to cry. Joe put the cup back on the table; and when he had turned back, Jerry was standing with open arms. They embraced. Jerry stepped back and rested his hands on Joe's shoulders. "Joe, I am glad that you are a free man. I will pour your tea now."

CHAPTER 29

Georgia in Turmoil

Joe couldn't hardly wait for the end of the day to come. But now, he was in a last-minute meeting Mr. Siegel had called just at closing time. Throughout, Joe worried that he would be delayed in getting to his and Sam's apartment before Jerry. He wanted to tell Sam that Jerry was coming for a visit, and if Jerry came early enough, they could even have supper together. Joe worried that Jerry might arrive before Sam knew about it.

Joe's worries were so intense that he had trouble concentrating on Mr. Siegel's subject, which was truly very important. It dealt with Joe's assignment directly. He forced himself to concentrate on Siegel's words, thankfully, in time to hear the disturbing news.

"Just this morning, I showed Joe the papers . . . I was so happy. I thought at last we would soon enjoy federal backing in the work I assigned to Joe." Siegel picked up the newspaper. "Just look at this headline," he exclaimed, holding it so everyone at the conference table could see it. No one failed to detect the anger in his voice. "Congress proposed an amendment that would entitle freed slaves to vote. I was ecstatic until a few hours ago when I received this telegraphed dispatch from our associates in Georgia." Siegel's expression, and even his voice, was pained.

"What does it say?" Joe asked. "Has Congress changed its mind?"

"No . . . worse. The state of Georgia is in turmoil again! Georgia has totally rejected the amendment, even expelling twenty-eight of the thirty-two Negroes admitted only last year to Georgia's House and Senate. Congress again has kicked Georgia out of the Union." Siegel, exasperated, thrust the paper down.

Everyone began talking at once, expressing surprise and apprehension. When Siegel held up his hand to quiet them, the room was hushed. "As if that's not enough, federal troops— again—have been sent to Georgia to preserve law and order." His words echoed in the room; everyone was silent until Joe offered an observation.

"My brother, Gregory, writes regularly to Georgia. He's written many times that carpetbaggers increase their exploitation of landowners and freed slaves every day."

"And he's probably told you about Governor Bullock?" Siegel inquired.

At the mention of the governor's name, Abe Feinstein smacked the table with his hand, startling everyone. "That man is evil! He's done nothing but stir up trouble since tricking his way into office," Feinstein shouted.

The meeting extended well into late afternoon; and when Joe rushed past Lynn, the wall was shadowless. The grandfather clock told him it was nearly six o'clock. Jerry planned to be at the apartment at six-fifteen. Joe rushed all the way home, not even noticing Tom Harrison's wave to him from his store window. There were crowds of people on the sidewalks and much stagecoach traffic in the streets, yet Joe appeared to be the only one anxious to move fast.

When he finally arrived at his apartment building, he took the stairs two at a time. At the fourth-floor landing, he was breathless while searching for the key. He heard laughter from inside his apartment—a woman's. *Who could it be?* he thought. *Is that Jennie?*

Has Jennie come for a visit too? He put his briefcase down, trying to do so silently, but it fell over against the door with a thump. Now he had both hands free to search his pockets. "Where's my key? Where's my key?" he mumbled in frustration.

Suddenly, the door was opened, Sam standing there laughing. "Try your inside vest pocket, Joe. I'll bet it's there," he said. "We have visitors. Come on in."

There at the table was Jerry, and standing by his side was a young woman.

"You must be Joe," she said.

"And you are, of course, Cathy," Joe replied.

"Jerry's Yankee wife," she giggled. They all laughed together.

Joe looked at his brother, who now had busied himself with pot and ladle, pouring out a thick soup into bowls on the table. "Sam! You had time tonight to make dinner?"

Sam smiled mischievously at Cathy and Jerry. "No, Joe. This will be our first taste of authentic Yankee bean soup. Cathy made it at her house and brought it here for our reunion supper tonight. 'Impromptu,' as she said."

Joe took the pot from Sam and brought it close to his nose, delighting in the aromatic steam rising up. "Cathy, this smells so good. Even our mama will want to know how to make this."

"Never mind 'Mama'!" Sam added. "*I* want to know how to make this!"

For a while at the table, the three men and one woman ate without speaking, just enjoying the sight and company of each other. The boys talked of what had happened since they last saw each other.

"Mary's eighteen now," Jerry said. "Can you imagine how she'll react when she sees Jennie again?"

"Oh, my goodness!" Sam said. "They will be so happy to see each other again."

"*Hysterical* is probably a better word," Jerry commented. "Jennie is likely to be as enchanted with Cathy as Mary already is."

"It has something to do with my Boston accent," Cathy explained. "Mary likes to hear me talk. It was that way from the beginning."

"I'd like to talk about something serious," Jerry said, changing the subject. Father's health is not good. He's been complaining about stomach pains. Sometimes very severe pains."

"Has he been getting medical care at home?" Sam asked.

"He's been to nearly a dozen doctors in Brunswick, and no one has improved his condition," Jerry said. "I'm especially worried now. Mother wrote last week to say that Father will be coming to Boston to look at a business venture. She said he has made up his mind to travel here in spite of his pain."

"I doubt she will allow him to travel alone," Cathy said comfortingly.

"If history is an indication," Jerry agreed, "Mother will definitely accompany him."

"And so will Mary, Bobby, and Tim," Joe added.

"Will they be staying at your house?" Sam asked cautiously.

"Yes they will stay with us, although our house is rather small compared to the plantation home," Jerry said. "Thankfully, we do have enough room to accommodate all of them during their stay here in Boston." Joe and Sam looked at Jerry, and then at each other. Their faces showed worry more than confusion. "Father has softened markedly over the years, especially about Cathy. At first, he was enraged that I even courted a Yankee girl. Now, Mother tells me, he seems pretty content I found such a good and faithful wife." Jerry said, beaming at his wife.

Cathy pretended to be self-conscious. "We do have an exceptionally large dining room in spite of the smaller size of the other rooms," she said. "For some reason, our little house came with a dining table that seats sixteen."

"That's why Cathy wrote to Mother. She has invited everyone to dinner the day after their arrival," Jerry announced. Cathy looked at Jerry, speaking with her eyes. He nodded in agreement.

Turning to Joe and Sam, she said, "We want not only the both of you to join our dinner party but also your mama and papa and sister, Jennie, too."

"And Ma Sally too," Jerry added. "Especially Ma Sally."

CHAPTER 30

Jennie Receives Invitation

PHILADELPHIA—MARCH 18, 1869

Jennie had just come home from school and was about to enter through the side door in hopes of finding her mother fussing at the kitchen stove. She was always hungry after the long walk home. *Mama will have something good*, she thought. *Pies still warm. Or maybe chicken soup tonight*. But instead of seeing her mother, she saw the postman coming through the front gate.

"Mr. Chigaudia! Mr. Chigaudia!" she shrieked, running to intercept him. "I'll take the mail in to Mistah Barrington."

The postman waited at the front gate, sorting through his bag. "Why, hello, Jennie. Here's the mail for the Barringtons . . . Oh, wait a moment, here's another letter. From Boston, Jennie, and it's got your name on it!"

"It's from my brothers! My brothers wrote me a letta!" She squealed with excitement, the postman backing away to give her more room. "Oh, I can't wait to open it inside. Thank you, Mr. Chigaudia!"

Though she pounded noisily up the wooden front porch steps, she entered the house quietly and walked softly and fully ladylike in her search for Mrs. Barrington. She found her in her sewing room. "Missus Barrington, the postman just delivered dese lettas for you and Mistah Barrington."

"Thank you, Jennie. My goodness! You are out of breath. Have you been running?"

"The postman gave me a letta. Look! It's addressed to me. Only to me. From Boston! I'm sure it's from Sam and Joe." Jennie held the letter tight, anxious to open it but just as nervous not to.

"Well, I am sure you are anxious to read that, Jennie. Your mama's in the kitchen, which, of course, is why the whole house smells so good." Mrs. Barrington carefully threaded a needle then continued, "I certainly look forward to our evening meal tonight. Jennie, will you bring me a cup of hot tea with some cream this time? But read your brothers' letter first and see if your mama will allow me to have a bit of that heavenly cinnamon apple pie she took out of the oven a while ago."

Jennie turned to rush off to the kitchen, the unopened letter clutched in both hands.

Without turning around to see who had just come into the kitchen, Chati sang a welcome. "Well, good afternoon, chile! Ah knew it was yo'. Heard yo' yellin' to de mailman. Heard yo' comin' up de front porch. All dat noise might have scared Missus B. into stickin' herself wid a sewing needle."

"Oh, Mama! I got a letta from Boston. Gimmee a piece of pie and I'll read it to yo'. Where's Grandma Sally? Where's Papa?"

"I heard Missus B. say she wanted tea. And a bit o' my pie," Chati said, reaching for the kettle. "Yo' papa's workin' de garden wid Grandma. Let's just yo' and me hear what's in dat letta. Right now, chile."

Jennie carefully slit open the letter with her mother's favorite kitchen knife, then handed it to her to use to cut the pie.

"Mama, it's dated February 28." She turned pages until she got to the end. "It's from Sam and Joe. Ooooh, I wonder if they're inviting me to come and stay fo' a while wit' them. I ain't even seen their apartment yet." She took the letter and her plate of pie to the kitchen table and began laying down each page side by side.

"Is dat wad yo' gonna do, chile? Lookin' only for de parts yo' wants to hear? And dat pie's not fo' yo'. That tea's not fo' yo' eitha! Take dem to Missus B. right now. I'll go get yo' papa and grandma."

Jennie hesitated, still scanning for the hoped-for invitation to visit Boston. "Okay, Mama. Okay. I'll take her de tea an' cake . . . I mean, pie." Reluctantly, Jennie laid the letter down.

They both left the kitchen at once, Chati calling after her. "An' when we all get back here, I want to hear dat letta from de beginning!"

Basusu and Ma Sally needed no encouragement to come into the house. In moments, they were seated around the table, except for Jennie. She was too excited to sit, taking all the pages in her hands and reading aloud as she paced around the gathering.

"Mama, they've addressed this letta to me; to you, Papa and Mama; to you too, Grandma Sally." They all listened intently and happily to Sam and Joe's accounting of many day-to-day events in their lives as physician and lawyer. There was not even a hint of an invitation to Jennie to visit them in Boston until page four had been reached. But the invitation was not exclusively for Jennie.

When Jennie realized the invitation to visit was not just for her, she stopped reading aloud. The others grew more and more impatient the longer she read to herself. Finally, at Sally's urging, she looked up, her eyes and face expressing amazement.

"Mama, Papa, Grandma! Yo' won't believe dis! They are inviting me to Boston to stay wid dem from March 26 to April 4. And that's okay because I will be on spring break then. On March 28, they are having a dinna party—"

"Chile! Will yo' stop skipping 'round," Chati broke in. "Go back where yo' left off and read it word fo' word."

"Okay, Mama, I will. But listen to dis. They want yo' an' Papa an' Grandma, an' Gregory, if we can get him, to go to that dinna."

Now Basusu showed his own exasperation. "Dawta! Go back an' read from where yo' stopped 'cause—"

"Oh, Papa, yo' won' believe this," Jennie interrupted. "Massa Jordan's going to be there. He wants to see yo' . . . everybody . . . he wants to see everyone. And Missus Jordan too. She'll be there."

Basusu suddenly pushed his chair back and stood up, the others wondering whether he was feeling surprise or fear.

"Papa, don't be alarmed," Jennie coaxed. "Listen to this . . ."

Jennie, tell Mama and Papa and Grandma not to be worried or fearful. Things have changed, especially attitudes. The Jordans do not want to take us back to the plantation. There is no more slavery in this country ever again. All the Jordans want to do is be reunited with us.

Reunited, Jennie.

Mary, especially, wants to be reunited with you. She's eighteen, Jennie; and Jerry says she has missed you so much.

Tell Mama that it's been Mrs. Jordan all along who has softened Mr. Jordan's heart. More than ever, Mrs. Jordan thinks of us as family. That's why she was hurt when we escaped. Jerry and I had a long talk about that.

We are going to have the reunion dinner over at Jerry and Cathy's house. Cathy is hoping you will all arrive together. Try to get the Barringtons' permission to leave together so that you all arrive on the 26th. You can all stay in our apartment. Cathy so much wants Mama to help her prepare the dinner. After the reunion, Mama, Papa, and Grandma can return to Philly on the 29th, so they won't have to be away from the Barringtons so long. You, dear sister, can stay with us (and Mary) until you must return to school.

With Love,
Joseph and Samuel Mensua

CHAPTER 31

The Mensua Family In Fear

BOSTON—MARCH 27, 1869

Shouldn't dat gran'son o' mine been here b'now?" Ma Sally asked Joe. "We's got t'git up early in de mornin' t'go help Cathy cook dat big dinner. Where's dat boy?" She went over to the cookstove and repeatedly stirred the chicken stew she had been fussing over since early afternoon. She was disheartened with the condition of her stew. "Are yo' sho yo' don't have a lid for dis pot, chile? My stew's gittin dry 'n' dry. Jennie, bring me mo' water." Ma Sally then looked at Joe, waiting for his answer to her first question.

"Well, Gran'ma, Sam almost always comes home before it's real dark," Joe said. He saw worry on everyone else's face, for they had been delaying dinner since six o'clock, waiting for Sam to come home. Joe went to the dining table and began fidgeting with the position of knives and forks, trying to come up with an explanation that could ease their tension. "Maybe this time . . . most probably . . . Sam didn't have time to come home for dinner with me and had to stay at the hospital because he couldn't leave his patient," he said, trying to offer a solution.

"But look how late it is, Joe," Jennie observed, almost whining. "It's after eight-thirty, and it's dark out now."

"Can't get no darker than 'tis now," Chati observed. "Just look outside." More worried than ever, Sally looked out the window by the side of the coal stove. All she could see was the sidewalk on the other side of the street. There wasn't enough light to identify any of the walkers—only street corners had lampposts. Basusu came up behind them to have a look too.

"Don' put up too many gaslights in dis part o' town, huh?" he noted.

"No, Papa," Joe answered. "This is the best we could afford . . . and this is the toughest and most dangerous part of town."

"But I wish there were more streetlights out there," Jennie said uneasily.

"Now you all shouldn't be worryin'," Joe said. "Let's put lots of water in the kettle and make tea for everyone." He was as tired as everyone else. Together with Sam, his mother, father, sister, and Sally comprised six people sleeping, eating, and living in an already small apartment.

"No, let's all eat now," Chati said. "Afta da meal, we can have our tea. Den we ought to get ready fo' bed. Mama, yo' can set 'side a nice plate of da stew for Sam. He can have it when he gets home."

One by one, they fell asleep. Basusu was the last to close his eyes, but he was unable to sleep for long. He was worrying too much about the whereabouts of Sam. There was a little light by the window overlooking the street below, and that's where he kept watch by the window until midnight. After adding more coals to the stove, he went downstairs and out into the cold of the night, walking back and forth in front of the apartment house. He wanted to walk the route Sam would be taking to come home from the hospital clinic, but he didn't know the way. Joe would know, but he was sleeping.

Across the street, groups of men and women were drinking liquor from bottles they passed around. *Dey are a rowdy bunch,*

Basusu thought, as they roughly pushed and shoved each other around. Sometimes a serious fight broke out. And always, they would block the path of a passerby on his way home, probably someone who had to work late. The rowdies menaced and intimidated each other as well as anyone who passed by.

Eventually, those across the street from Basusu noticed him. "Hey, nigger! Come 'ere, nigger!" they called to him. "Play a bit o' poker 'ere. Come on, have a drive 'ere!"

Basusu was glad he was big. He walked toward them to show he wasn't afraid of them and stopped at the curb. "No, tank yo'," he called over to them. "Got my own bus'ness to 'tend to." He waved them away with his big hands, then turned to walk to the corner. Back and forth he walked, from the corner to the street entrance of Sam and Joe's apartment house. At times he would go into the hall to warm up.

Soon the gray light of dawn chased away the rowdies. The street became silent, but still no sign of Sam.

Basusu looked up at the windows of the apartment and saw Jennie looking out. When she noticed him, her look of worry changed to a smile—but briefly. Although nervous that her brother wasn't home, she was glad her father was outside keeping a watch for him.

The night passed, giving way to the dawn's first pink light, without any sign of Sam. By seven o'clock, the sun rose high enough to flood the street with light and warmth. Both pedestrian and stage traffic increased by the minute, making it harder for Basusu to keep a lookout for Sam. Once more, he went to the corner to look up and down Tower Street.

There he was! Sam was walking his way, carrying his satchel. When he spied his father, he called out to him and quickened his stride. "Papa! Have you been waiting for me out here? How long?"

They met and embraced nearly halfway into the street, with carriages and stages swirling around them. Realizing their precarious position, they made their way to the safety of the sidewalk.

Jennie too had noticed from her fourth-floor vantage point. Raising the window sash, she leaned out and shouted, "Sam! Sam! Hurry on up! Papa, bring him on up!"

Sam didn't expect to face the commotion at his belated arrival in his apartment. The women had finished dressing and gathering up what they needed for their day's work at Cathy's house.

"My chile!" Chati cried. "Yo' have no idea how much we worried 'bout yo' last night."

"Mo' den last night," Sally added. "I ain't hardly slept all tro de night 'cause o' yo'."

Sam rushed to give Sally a hug. He squeezed her hard, then released his hold to look her in the eyes. "Oh, Gran'ma, I'm sorry. I just couldn't leave the clinic. Not even for a little while for supper. It's a long story." Sam kissed his grandmother on the cheek, took a seat, then continued, "You'll never believe—"

"Neva yo' min', chile," Sally said, pretending exasperation. "We wimin don' have no time to hear no long story of yours. Tell us later when yo' comes ovah to Massa Jerry's house."

Sam didn't push the issue. "Well, what's for breakfast? I'm hungry. No supper. No breakfast. What's to eat?" he asked.

"Sam, you can have that plate of Gran'ma's chicken stew," Jennie said laughing. She had wrapped her arms around him the moment he had come into the apartment, and now she half dragged, half pushed him to the cookstove. She took the covered plate down from the warming shelf over the stove and gave it to him. "This gonna to be the best breakfast you've had in a long time." She put the plate in his hands and kissed him.

Sally heard Jennie's comment and said, "Sam, don' yo' go tinkin' yo' sista made dat. Chick'n Sally Stew, dat's what it used t'be called." Every one stopped talking in order not to miss what Sally would say next. "Now, I'm goin' t'call it 'Worryin' Stew,' 'cause dat's all ah did makin' it!" Everyone laughed at her remark, Basusu laughing the hardest.

Chati appeared, making haste for the door. "C'mon, Jennie; we got to go! C'mon, Mama!" she insisted. Breaking up the giddiness of the crowd, Jennie and Sally grabbed their shawls, and all three women rushed out the door.

With the latching of the door, Sam was at the table, enjoying every spoonful. Halfway through, he looked up at his brother. "Oh, Joe, I do hope you stood by Gran'ma's side, watching her every move as she made this!" He heartily ate the succulent stew, relishing each spoonful.

"No, I couldn't. She had it simmering even before I got home from my office yesterday," Joe apologized. "So tell us . . . what kept you at the clinic?" Basusu and Joe took chairs over to the table and sat down, waiting for Sam to finish his plate.

Sam took his time, even getting up to search the pantry for a piece of bread, which he used to sponge up all the gravy on the bottom of the plate. "So creamy!" he swooned. And then, to the annoyance of his father and brother, he asked, "Where's the pot Gran'ma cooked this in? Has it been washed yet?"

"Sam! Dere's no pot to lick. Enough with the eating! Out wit' it! What kept yo'?" Joe and Basusu demanded.

Sam laid his bowl in the sink, then rejoined his father and brother at the table. "You'll never believe this. But you have to because it's true," Sam said. "But this is going to be such a shocking story I'll be needing a cup of tea," he announced, noting the steaming kettle on the stove. "Will you two have tea with me?" he asked in a tone designed to frustrate them even more.

"Okay, we'll have tea with you, Sam," Joe countered, not caring that his annoyance was evident. "And it's just as well. Papa needs something to warm him up; he froze half to death all night, waiting outside in the cold for you." Pushing his chair back, he rose up to pour the tea.

CHAPTER 32

An Astonishing Story

Finally and thankfully, the tea having been poured, Sam began his story.

"I was getting ready to leave at about five-thirty, when the nurses told me Dr. Garland wanted me immediately and ready to assist him in emergency surgery."

"Is dat de same docta who took a likin' to yo' in Philly?" Basusu asked.

"Yes, Papa, the same Dr. Garland—George Garland—who recommended me to these clinics here." Sam paused a moment, then continued.

"Papa, working these clinics has been so very helpful. I've assisted at many surgeries and am learning the principles of diagnosis and treatment. Dr. Garland visits the clinics often, always asking for me to go along with him on rounds."

"What's dat mean? Goin' on rounds?" Basusu asked.

"That means I go with a senior doctor from patient to patient. Sometimes, the other doctors tell me the disease the patient has. But most of the time, they test me—"

"That's when they don't tell him the diagnosis, Papa," Joe broke in. "They make Sam ask questions of the patient so he can learn the symptoms."

"That's right," Sam continued. "I also examine the patient. And then I tell my teachers, the doctors I'm on rounds with, what I believe the diagnosis to be. I'm also asked what medicines I would prescribe, or what surgery I would do, Papa."

Basusu smiled, nodding his head proudly. "Swamasa, yo' do de surgery in de clinic?"

Sam had not heard his African birth name since he was a boy on the Jordans' plantation. To hear his father using it now meant only that Basusu was feeling much pride. Sam smiled, reaching across the table to place his hand on his father's.

"Papa, all the surgeries are done in the general hospital. Our people have to go to the clinics first for a diagnosis. Most of the patients I do surgery on or assist with are Negroes like us."

"Most of the time, Papa, our people are called 'colored' here in Boston," Joe explained.

"Last night, out in de street, I was call 'niggah'!" Basusu exclaimed.

Sam rubbed his father's hand comfortingly. "I know, Papa, I know. And I'm sorry. There are some doctors who won't give any medical care to our people. That's why there are these clinics. It's doctors like me, and white doctors who believe in the abolition of slavery, who work in the clinics. And there are patients who are white who absolutely refuse to have me even present when they're being examined."

Basusu thought about that for a moment and then looked at Joe, who had begun to laugh.

"Papa, Sam has assisted in many, many surgeries on white patients."

"How's dat if dey don' want no African slave takin' care of dem?" Basusu angrily asked.

Now Sam began to laugh in earnest. "Because, Papa, when they are out, sleepin' because of the anesthesia, they don't know who's working on them!" Basusu joined in the laughter.

"Well, here's the part of the story you won't believe," Sam said. "When I caught up with Dr. Garland, he was already in the operating room. The best, most well-equipped OR in the whole hospital. And that meant the patient was a white person, someone important and wealthy."

Basusu leaned forward. "Who was de patient?"

"Papa, when I got close enough, I realized it was Mistah Jordan. Our old 'Massa Jordan.'"

"You don't mean it . . . Bill Jordan!" Joe cried. Basusu sat back in his chair, speechless, gazing at Sam and waiting for more.

"When I saw Mr. Jordan on the table, at once I recalled that Jerry had told Joe and me that Mr. Jordan was having problems. He had been complaining of stomach pain. Dr. Garland told me that Mr. Jordan was brought in unconscious. He awoke only long enough to touch his abdomen to show Dr. Garland where the pain was. Garland told me the patient might have appendicitis. He wanted to remove the appendix and have me assist."

"And that's what kept you so long?" Joe asked.

"No. The excitement began soon after Garland made the incision. Then, Nurse Susannah Plemons, the surgery nursing supervisor for neurology, came in and told Dr. Garland he has to do emergency surgery upstairs on a patient who suffered terrible brain injury in a horse accident."

"An' den wha' happen?" Basusu impatiently asked.

"Well, Dr. Garland told me to remove the appendix and close up. He said I'd seen plenty of these with him and other doctors before. He said it was time I handled it alone. So he left."

"So what kept you so long?" Joe pressed.

"It was not a simple appendicitis. The appendix wasn't infected at all. Something else. I never saw this condition before, and only now do I know what it's called. 'Intussusception of the small intestine.'"

"What's that mean?" Joe said, a baffled look on his face.

"It means a part of the small intestine had become telescoped or sucked into a part of the bowel. The remedy was very simple. I just pulled the small intestine out and moved it to a better position."

Basusu looked disgusted. "Yo' had yo' hands 'side his stomach?"

"Papa, we wash our hands first before doing surgery. And I wasn't inside his stomach. I was inside the body cavity." Seeing that this didn't relieve his father's pained expression, Sam continued. "Anyway, I looked around and discovered a tumor attached to the small intestine. It did not look good; probably as it grew, it had pulled the intestine. I think the tumor caused the intussusception."

"So Dr. Garland removed the tumor?" Joe asked.

"Dr. Garland didn't return until after Mistah Jordan was taken to the recovery room. I did the whole thing. Removed the tumor—and closed the incision. Even the nurses assisting me never saw such a condition before. I finished the operation and decided to stay by Mistah Jordan's bedside until he woke up. When he did, I had to give him a sedative for the pain. He didn't recognize me. And then he slept peacefully. I then learned that Missus Jordan had been in the waiting room all through the night while I was at Mistah Jordan's bedside. When I released Mistah Jordan to a regular hospital room, she came in and briefly saw me for the first time since . . ." Sam paused to swallow hard.

"Our escape seven years ago," Joe continued thoughtfully.

"Missus Jordan probably is still at the hospital," Sam said. "Let's go over to Jerry's and tell them what happened."

Out on the street, the Mensuas were once again reminded of the difficulties they and other Negroes faced. Many empty coaches passed them by, only to stop a half-block away to allow white people to board.

A coach was necessary because Jerry and Cathy's house was located up on "the hill," an exclusive white Boston enclave. After attempting with no success for over a half hour, and being most anxious to be on their way, they resorted to walking.

"Most probably Mama, Jennie, and Gran'ma had a hard time like this earlier this morning, trying to get a coach to stop for them. One of us should have come down to the street to help them," Joe commented.

Sam suddenly spoke up. "Hey! I've a great idea. Why didn't I think of this sooner?" Joe and Basusu waited for his answer. Sam began walking at a faster pace, but in the opposite direction. "C'mon. Follow me. I can use the carriage the clinic assigned me. Just four blocks to the little stable where I keep Max. Come along with me. Max can pull us all to Jerry's. He's a good horse."

The Mensua men enjoyed a beautiful ride to Jerry and Cathy's house. Some other carriage drivers were perturbed seeing Sam at the reins and not one white passenger in the carriage. But when met with icy stares, Joe smiled while Basusu took advantage of the moment to greet the drivers in his most dignified manner. "Good morning, gentlemen," he would say in perfect English, not expecting a reply, which suited him just fine.

Upon arrival at the Jordans', Sam harnessed the horse and all three men hastily headed for the door. Sam knocked and Jerry opened the door. "Ah, finally, you Mensuas arrive! Come in. You have time for just a bit of bourbon to warm you up. And then we're going over to see Mother and Father at the hospital. We have something to celebrate!" Jerry exclaimed as he looked out the door to see how they traveled to his house.

Cathy, Mary, and Jennie immediately came to the door, Mary and Jennie arm in arm. "These two have been locked together practically all morning," Cathy said, shaking her head in a playful manner. "They even tried to set the table that way."

Cathy helped Basusu take off his coat. "Basusu, you and your sons don't know, but Jerry's father had to be taken to the hospital yesterday afternoon. He was in such terrible pain . . ." Cathy paused to blink back tears.

"Dat he fell down on de floor in a faint," Chati finished the statement. "Cathy was here alone wid Mistah and Missus Jordan when it happened."

"I thought he was dead," said Cathy, barely audible among her sobs.

Jerry spoke up. "Everyone, put on your coats. Let's leave right away. We can have drinks and dinner later. Let's start our reunion in Father's room at the hospital. He'd like that, you know."

Everyone agreed and began retrieving coats, capes, and hats. Though each person was cooperating, Jerry felt he had to further explain his need to rush. "All I know is that Father has had some kind of surgery that baffled even experienced doctors. When I brought Mother over, the chief of surgery told me a young surgeon saved his life," Jerry said. "He said something about some kind of mass that, if gone undetected, would have killed him. Let's go. I want to meet that young surgeon."

"Dear, here's your coat," Cathy said. "And do you think you can calm down long enough to help me put on mine?" she teased. While helping her, Jerry realized Sam's carriage was too small to carry all of them to the hospital. Turning to Sam, he asked, "Can Mary and Jennie ride with you? I'll take everyone else in my coach. I'll go out back right now to hitch up the horses." Sam agreed, and Basusu followed Jerry to the stable and carriage house attached to it.

When the doors were opened, Basusu was stunned. There before his eyes was the most beautiful carriage he had ever seen. The seats were upholstered in fine leathers so aromatic that they incensed the space inside the carriage house. He walked slowly around the carriage; it was in perfect condition. "I always loved de smell of—"

"Leather," Jerry completed. "I remember, Base, that you loved breathing in the smell of leather."

Basusu continued studying the carriage as he pushed it out with Jerry. "Dis looks very familyah," he said, nearly singing the words. He rubbed the oak moldings and let his fingertips lightly caress the red-painted panels.

Jerry could hold back no longer. "Base, this is the carriage both you and father loved so much. I've had it restored to its original condition. It got a little damaged during the war."

"Oh, Massa Jerry, I am so happy!" Basusu was gleeful and lighthearted. He remembered how everything worked and hitched it up speedily.

Jerry motioned to him to take the reins. "Base, my dear friend, the honor is yours." Proudly and with elegance, Basusu drove to the front gate. When Chati looked with curiosity and suspicion at the carriage, Basusu said, "Believe yo' eyes, woman! Dis is ol' Massa Jordan's carriage. De same one I used to take care of."

For a few blocks there were no conversations. They all rode in silence, listening to the clip-clop of the horses. Basusu's memory flashed back to the days when he gave the Jordan children rides to and from school—in the very same carriage. Joe remembered the carriage ride that began their journey to freedom. Now they were together again. "I can't wait to see Father," Jerry said. "I want the doctors to tell the whole story. Most of all, I must meet the surgeon."

"Jerry, you already have," Joe whispered under his breath. Basusu smiled knowingly. But Chati, Sally, and Cathy didn't detect a thing.

Joe continued, smiling gently at Jerry. "Something amazing happened to us last night. So amazing that it had to be God's will," he whispered. "The surgeon you want to meet, you have already met . . . and know very well."

Jerry was perplexed. "What do you mean? Who? Where is he?"

Joe shushed him to avoid making a scene among the women. "Just look out the window, Jerry. He is driving the carriage following us. You know him well."

Turning his head at once to look out, Jerry stared through the glass, watching Mary and Jennie riding with Sam. All three were laughing so loudly their shrieks and giggles were likely to be heard a block away.

Jerry looked at Joe in astonishment.

CHAPTER 33

Bill Jordan in the Hospital

The ride to the hospital was a pleasant distance away; but to Jerry, it seemed to last a lifetime. He was in deep thought as to what his father would think when the news was revealed that Sam, his former runaway slave, had saved his life on the operating table.

Finally, the carriage came to a halt. Jerry aroused himself from his thoughts and turned to see if the other carriage had also stopped. He caught a glimpse of Sam climbing out of the carriage, somewhat hesitantly. *He must be so nervous,* Jerry thought.

The silence caught Jerry's attention. He turned to see that although everyone had come out of the carriages, no one among the Mensuas dared move.

"Well," Cathy began, "let's hope Bill is awake and feeling better. I know Joan must be anxious to see us too. Let's go, everyone." She turned to walk but stopped when Sally spoke up.

"Uh, Missus Cathy," she ventured. "Maybe yo' betta go an' see Mistah Jordan first, wid Jerry an' Mary. Afta, we will come."

Cathy seemed to understand their hesitation. After all, Bill Jordan was still, in their eyes, their former slave master. Yes, the Mensuas were free; but they paid a dear price for their freedom and weren't so sure about Bill's proclaimed change of heart.

"Can't Jennie come with me?" Mary stepped closer to her friend. "Father won't mind, will he Jerry?"

Jerry looked from Basusu to Cathy and then on to Mary. His mouth opened to speak, but the words failed him.

Sam moved to join the discussion. "I think that you all should go and see your father, give him a chance to recuperate and enjoy talking with his family before we come in." Jerry nodded his agreement.

Reluctantly, the Jordans parted and began to walk away. Mary looked back at the Mensuas, who remained where they were, before turning to Cathy.

"I don't understand, Cathy . . . both Father and Mother know they're here," she searched her sister-in-law's face for an explanation. "I thought they would be glad to come."

Jerry stopped walking and turned to face his wife and sister. "Mary . . . Cathy, it's more than that. Father knows that the Mensuas are here in Boston, but he doesn't know how personal this situation is. Nor do either of you." His gaze flickered to Sam, who stood with his family in the distance. "You see, Sam is the surgeon that saved Father's life."

Both women stopped in their tracks, their mouths agape. They stared as Jerry briskly walked toward the hospital.

Bill Jordan was awake but groggy. Although tender from the surgery, he was grateful for the opportunity to be alive. He looked fondly at Joan, who was taking a strong interest in a medical journal book.

"Whatcha readin', Joan?" Bill asked, his voice still slurred from the medication.

"It's one of those medical journal books—you know, the ones that reveal the latest medical procedures. It's just fascinating at how far medicine has progressed." Her face lit up as she turned the pages. "It seems as though each year another method for performing a procedure evolves, surpassing the former."

When she didn't receive a reply, she put the book down and looked at her husband. Just that quickly, he had drifted off to sleep. His face was drawn, and Joan noticed new gray hairs at his temples. She knew they were the result of the loss of slaves, the loss of war, and the loss of his son to a Northern girl. But she admired him. He had decided to let the past be the past and vowed to live the rest of his years without bitterness or regret. Gazing at him, Joan realized just how much he had been through and what it had cost him. In Georgia, it almost cost him his plantation. On the operating table, it almost cost him his life.

Her thoughts drifted to what she had seen last night. Not what, but *whom*. Samuel Mensua was a doctor at the hospital! And not simply a doctor but the surgeon who had operated, unattended, on her husband, a rich white slave master—*his* former master! It was almost too much for Joan to bear. Her mind became full of thoughts about Basusu, Chati, and, especially, Sally. Such dedicated workers they had been to her but, Joan realized, more than just workers. They were a special part of her family. She was anxious to see them.

Fondly, Joan remembered the many afternoons that both the Jordan and Mensua boys played school and how she encouraged their playtime each day. She recalled the conversation that she had many years ago with Bill about allowing the children to interact scholastically. *I had no idea where this all would lead*, Joan thought, tears welling up in her eyes. Little Samuel Mensua, destined for the cotton fields to labor and toil for her husband, was, in a miraculous turn of events, destined to the operating room to save her husband's life. "It's nothing short of a miracle," Joan mumbled under her breath.

Joan's thoughts were interrupted at the stirring of her husband. Bill awoke to find his wife staring at him, her eyes moist.

"What's wrong, hon," Bill asked, struggling against the effect of the anesthesia. He tried to prop himself up but soon realized that it would be to his advantage to remain reclining. He turned his eyes as far as they would go and was relieved when Joan approached his bedside.

Embracing his hand with both of hers, Joan looked at her husband. She chose her words carefully.

"Bill, darling, I'm just so glad that you are alive and recovering. You were very close to death and . . ." Her voice cracked, and the tears flowed. She continued, "It was nothing short of a miracle." She laughed lightly, trying to compose herself, and thought how to break the news about Sam.

Bill noticed her uneasiness and attributed it to the previous night's events. "Joan, go get some air . . . some water, maybe," he said, with noticeably less effort. A minute passed, then he continued, "You've been here . . . all night watchin' out for me. Go freshen up." He smiled weakly and added, "I'll be right here."

The Mensua family walked slowly toward the hospital. Sam was especially apprehensive about what to do. He stopped in his tracks and turned to face his family.

"Mother, Ma Sally, Jennie," he began, "I operated on Mistah Jordan last night and saved his life." He waited for the enormity of his statement to have effect before he continued. "And . . . Missus Jordan was there too, an' she saw me."

The women stared in disbelief. Their eyes darted from Sam to Joe to Basusu and back to Sam. The men nodded to affirm that what they heard was true. Jennie gasped.

"Sam, why yo' not tell us dis dis mornin'?" Sally chided. "Do Jerry an' Cathy know 'bout dis?" Refusing space for him to answer, she narrowed her eyes as she turned to her son-in-law. "Basusu, yo' know too?"

Basusu looked intently at Sally. He was about to speak when Joe spoke up.

"We were 'bout to tell everyone, but the day got going; and before long, we were on de way here." He hoped his answer appeased his grandmother.

Chati spoke up, her voice laced with fear. "We goin' to see Massa Jordan an' now we goin' tell him whad? Dat Sam saved his life? I don' know 'bout dis. He can say it's okay dat we left, but yo' know how da Massa is 'bout black folk doin' anything betta den dem white folk. He don' like dat, yo' know." Chati was visibly shaken. "Yo' know, he might make trouble fo' Sam. Den whad?" Her eyes rested on her son, and her palms became clammy.

Basusu spoke softly to his wife, who continued to stare at their child, her heart heavy. He realized the effect that a life of slavery had on her. While he was always unsettled with the thought of life as a slave, Chati knew no other life. She was born a slave in the Jordan household. He understood her fear of her "slave master."

"Chati, dere's notin' Massa Jordan can do 'bout dis but be thankful to be alive. He will be proud of Swamasa. His boys was de ones dat did de teachin' fo' him." Basusu stroked Chati's arm, and she looked up at her husband. "Trust God, Chati. God will make Massa Jordan okay 'bout all dis. He will."

"I trust God, but I don' trust Massa Jordan!" she exclaimed. She looked around to see if anyone understood her grief. A few passersby heard her outburst and took notice of the Mensuas, slowly looking them up and down, their brows furrowing. Realizing that Chati was making a scene in public, Basusu ushered the family on toward the hospital. It was the most appropriate place for them to go to without bringing any more attention to themselves. But Chati didn't budge.

In her plain brown dress adorned with soft cream-colored lace, Chati looked pleasant and comely. She no longer resembled the young "house hand" servant girl who tirelessly performed chore after chore from sunup to sundown, clad in aprons and slave clothes. Although she worked for the Barringtons, it was a pleasurable type of work. Basusu had noticed that over the years, his wife's face became serene and her persona radiated a calm that only freedom could bring about. But now, all this grace was jeopardized in a powerful episode of fear due to a sickly man who no longer held her future in his hand.

Basusu took a deep breath and grasped Chati's trembling hand. Without speaking, he led her through the hospital doors, past the general reception area, and down a small corridor that housed the janitorial supply room. He knew that they would not appear suspicious there as black janitorial workers frequented the hallway to obtain supplies. He motioned to the others to give him a few minutes alone with her and reminded them to appear calm and relaxed in the presence of the hospital staff.

"Chati, yo' got to be brave now. Yo' got to . . ." Basusu spoke firmly.

"Yo' be brave, Basusu Mensua! I don' wan' no trouble wid my boy!" Chati interrupted. She surprised even herself at this outburst to her husband. Immediately, she uttered a profuse apology.

Basusu allowed her a few minutes to regain her composure. He prayed silently before continuing.

"Chati, yo' rememba long time ago when yo' tol' me dat it was okay fo' dem Jordan boys to play school wid our boys? Yo' rememba, Chati? Yo' tol' me not to worry 'bout notin', dat it would be okay. I put trus' an' faith to whad yo' said to me, Chati. Many times, I was afraid but I knew yo' was talkin' to me to have faith."

Basusu paused for effect. He saw the realization of his words sink down into his wife's heart. Chati blinked back tears and nodded in agreement.

"It's yo' turn to have faith again, Chati. Dis man is not *Massa* Jordan no mo'. He is *Mistah* Jordan to us, de same way like to everyone out dere." Basusu waved his hand toward the reception area where other people were gathered. "Yo' not his property no mo', Chati," he said. Pulling her head close to his chest, he whispered, "Yo's mine."

CHAPTER 34

Sam Prays for Help

Dr. Samuel Mensua felt every ounce of physical drain the previous night had caused him. His bones and muscles ached as he mounted a stool, a relatively easy accomplishment but one that exhausted his body even more. His psyche was the most fatigued part of his being. Coupling the mental effort it took to perform surgery with the pressure of such critical situations resulted in both physical and mental exhaustion.

Exhaustion he could deal with, but no amount of education or training would ever suffice to prepare him for such a crucial moment as the one he experienced the night before. He never dreamed of having to perform such a risky surgery on his former slave master—alone.

His thoughts strayed lazily to the marvelous dinner that had been so meticulously prepared at Cathy's house. It had gone untouched by everyone. He secretly wished that he could enjoy the feast that very moment.

Thoughts of food and physical needs dimmed against one reality: *God helped him to save Mr. Jordan's life.* Sam allowed his head to drop as that truth settled into his heart. After a moment, he buried his face in his hands and closed his eyes.

"God," he began a simple, inaudible prayer, "I thank You. Thank You for not lettin' Mistah Jordan die on that table last night. Thank You, God, for guidin' my hands to perform that surgery." He paused and considered the room before him.

"God, I don't know how this will all turn out, but I trust You. Help Mistah Jordan to recover . . . . Amen."

Sam opened his eyes and looked straight into the eyes of a small toddler girl, no more than two years of age. *She must have been staring at me the whole time,* Sam thought. Her clear blue eyes looked innocently at Sam, and the sides of her mouth turned upward. Sam widened his eyes, which promptly drew a giggle from the child. Her mother, engaged in conversation with the girl's sibling, turned to see what the source of her child's amusement was. She scanned the room and saw only the tense faces of others awaiting news of family members or loved ones. In particular, she noticed a thin young black man seated on a stool, his eyes downcast as if in great turmoil. Not seeing anything amiss, she resumed her conversation. Slowly sliding off the stool, Sam headed for the door. As he passed the child, he smiled, and she returned the gesture.

Such innocence, he thought to himself. *Prejudice is not inherent; it's learned.*

Leaving his family in the reception area, Sam strolled toward the medical records office. He ignored the curious glances and whispers from the white people that were present and answered their accusing stares by donning his stethoscope and affixing his medical badge to his shirt. He was used to this type of silent rage treatment. No one expected to see a black doctor, let alone a surgeon, in the "white area" of the hospital. Although people of all races congregated in the general reception area, prejudices still simmered when it came to other areas of the facility.

Sam entered the room and began to search for Bill Jordan's chart among the ones that were stacked neatly on the desk. The charts were listed alphabetically. Sam cocked his head sideways and began to read the names aloud.

"James . . . Johnson . . . Jones . . . Jordan. Here it is, Bill Jordan."

Putting on his spectacles, Sam scanned the pages, stopping at the postoperative report. He read that Dr. Garland had made an initial visit to Mr. Jordan's room and indicated in the chart that he had been resting well and that there were no initial signs of bleeding or complications. He noted that he planned to check on Mr. Jordan in two hours when the patient would be awake and able to undergo further examination.

Sam looked at his watch; twenty-six minutes remained. He sighed deeply, leaned against the counter, and began to read the report in its entirety.

Joan Jordan was frazzled; the events of the prior night permeated her entire being. She felt sticky, and her makeup felt weighty on her face and neck. She smoothed her dress as best she could and stood up.

"Bill," she called softly.

"Hmmm?" came the reply.

"Bill, I'm going to freshen up as you suggested, maybe get a little air. Will you be okay until I return?"

"Um-hmm. I'll be fine. Feel like I'll be up for a bit," he said.

"Good, good. I'll be back shortly then." She kissed him lightly on his forehead, retrieved her purse from the floor, and headed for the door.

No sooner had she opened the door than her children and her daughter-in-law bounded in.

"Jerry, Cathy . . . Mary!" she exclaimed. "Thank God you're here!" The trio motioned her to quiet down at the sight of Bill.

"Oh, he's up. He just woke up and said that he'd be up a while," Joan replied. "I'm going to get some air and freshen up." She left the door slightly cracked as she exited.

"Father!" Jerry and Mary cried in unison. "You're okay!"

"I'm okay, just sore . . . and a little nauseous," he replied.

Cathy waited at the doorway and pretended to look in her hand mirror, allowing the family to reunite, unsure how she should approach her father-in-law. He could be quite a temperamental man; and having been in his presence on less than a handful of occasions, she was clueless as to how he felt about being in this condition, especially in her presence. Her thoughts were interrupted at the sound of his voice.

"Cathy . . ." he called kindly.

She peered from the side of her mirror and caught sight of the outstretched arm of her father-in-law beckoning her to approach him. Following the length of his arm with her eyes, she finally looked at him.

What she saw was a humbled man. How humble, she wasn't sure, but she obeyed his summons and went to him.

"Cathy, how ya been?" he asked, blinking slowly.

Everyone stared at Cathy, anticipating her response.

"Been fine, Mr. Jordan. Busy, but fine," she answered evenly.

"How's Jerry been carryin' on? Okay?" he chuckled weakly.

"Jerry's been fine, Mr. Jordan." She looked at her husband, who shrugged.

"*Bill*, Cathy. It's Bill." He closed his eyes and pulled the blanket closer to his chin.

Cathy nodded. "Okay . . . Bill." When she felt the time was appropriate, she made her way to Jerry's side.

Mary sauntered to her father and gingerly sat on the end of the bed. "Father," she began excitedly, "wait till you see Jennie. She's all grown up and smart and pretty—"

"Mary, now's not the time for this," Jerry interrupted, clearly frustrated.

"Well, I was just saying—"

"Well, *I'm* just saying," Jerry countered, taken aback at the lack of consideration from his sister.

Mary frowned and turned to look at nothing in particular.

Jerry swiftly attempted to rectify the situation. "Father, forgive her outburst. It was inconsiderate." He hoped that his father wouldn't be angry with her.

"Jerry . . . it's fine, really." Bill managed to prop himself up with the aid of Mary and three pillows. He still looked uncomfortable but decided to endure it. "She's just happy to see her friend. After all, it's been a while. Right, Mary?" Speaking took a toll on him. Wincing, he tilted his head back, which promptly produced another round of nausea.

All three Jordans stood still, unsure what would happen next or what they should do next. Beads of sweat began to form on Bill's forehead. He looked pale.

Jerry became perturbed. "Where is Dr. Garland?" He sighed.

Joan tried to recall the quickest way to the main entrance. Leaving the room, she turned right, walking past other patients' rooms. Turning left then right, she proceeded down a long hallway. Nothing looked familiar to her. *I don't know if I'm going right*, she thought. Fatigued and slightly exasperated, she turned around and headed toward the sound of voices.

Dr. Garland and Dr. Mensua pored over the report together. Both doctors listened intently, offering insights and asking questions. So absorbed were they in their work that neither heard the light rap on the door, which was ajar.

Joan poked her head in the medical records room and slightly gasped. There, again, was Samuel Mensua, all grown up. Dr. Garland noticed her surprise and attributed it to the fact that a black and white doctor were corresponding together regarding her husband.

"Mrs. Jordan . . . good to see you." Dr. Garland hurriedly arranged his papers. "I was just gathering my report and preparing to review it with you and Mr. Jordan," he said nervously. He closed his file and stole a glance at Sam. To his shock, he noticed that Joan and Sam smiled a bit hesitantly, yet warmly, at each other.

Sam spoke first. "Mrs. Jordan . . . good to see you again. I'm sorry that it's under these circumstances, but I feel everything will be okay now that the danger's over for Mr. Jordan."

They know each other! Dr. Garland was confused.

"Samuel Mensua! How we have missed all of you! And look at you now, a doctor . . . no, a surgeon who saved my husband's life! Who would have ever thought?" Muttering "Excuse me," Joan breezed past Dr. Garland and embraced Sam.

Still clutching him, she prayed aloud, "Dear God, thank you for Sam and for the wonderful man that he has become. Bless him for saving Bill and for reuniting us again." She held him a few moments longer before releasing him.

Dr. George Garland was at a loss for words. "Seems like you two know each other," he ventured.

Sam laughed, then hesitantly formed a reply. "Yes, Dr. Garland. Our families know each other . . . and—"

"Sam, don't bother Dr. Garland with our little ole family history," Mrs. Jordan interjected. Confidently turning to face Dr. Garland she asked, "Didn't he perform superbly?"

Relieved that Mrs. Jordan was pleased with the outcome of the surgery, Dr. Garland replied, "Yes, Dr. Mensua couldn't have handled it better. I trusted him because I knew he could do it. His love for medicine and his past scholastic achievements effectively prepared him for what he had to do last night."

Both Sam and Joan acknowledged Dr. Garland's accolades with tears.

Dr. Garland shrugged his shoulders and said, "Let's go and check our patient, shall we?"

Bill Jordan had drifted off into a light sleep and awoke to the sound of voices, one of which he recognized as his wife's. He slowly eased his body into a position that would acknowledge her presence but grimaced when he tried to move too quickly.

Noticing his discomfort, Joan laid her hand on his arm to halt his movement. "Take it easy, Bill. Just rest and take it easy," she said.

"Mr. Jordan, I need to take your vitals and take a peek at your stitches while you're awake. Then we can chat a bit about postoperative care and let you get back to resting," Dr. Garland said.

Bill ignored his wife's arm and elevated himself as best he could to face Dr. Garland. "Doctor, whatever surgery you did, it sure saved my life . . . and . . ." He paused to let the wave of nausea pass, then continued, "I wanna thank you personally."

Sam heard the entire conversation from where he stood just outside the door.

Dr. Garland and Mrs. Jordan exchanged glances.

"What's the matter?" Bill asked.

Jerry, Cathy, and Mary waited for a response. It was Joan who spoke first.

"Bill, honey, Dr. Garland didn't perform the surgery on you. Another doctor did." She cleared her throat. "A surgeon, actually," she said.

Sam braced himself.

"Well, then I need to thank him," Bill replied, his speech slightly slurred. "Is . . . he 'round anywhere?" He reached for some ice chips to soothe his parched throat and stave off the nausea.

Dr. Garland stepped aside as Joan made her way to the door. She motioned for Sam to come in.

Dr. Mensua entered the room.

Cathy gasped.

Mary gawked.

Jerry cried.

And Bill Jordan toppled his cup of ice.

"Bill, it's Base's boy, Sam," Joan offered, stooping to retrieve the ice. She stood erect and tearfully continued, "His medical expertise saved your life. He did the emergency surgery *by himself*, without any help, Bill. Aren't you proud of him?" Joan poured on the praise as though it was one of their own sons' accomplishments.

Bill Jordan was shocked. He looked in disbelief at his family then at Dr. Garland who raised his eyebrows and tilted his head. Finally, he looked at Sam.

Silence filled the room. Then Bill cleared his throat and motioned for Sam to come to him.

Sam approached and stopped within a foot of Bill's bedside. Nervously, he fingered the end of his stethoscope. Bill beckoned him to come closer.

When Sam was within a few inches of his reach, Bill looked straight into his eyes and reached for his hand. Sam hesitantly offered it, hoping that his sweaty palm would go unnoticed. Bill clasped his hand and held it firmly, sweat and all.

"Dr. Mensua, what a privilege it is to say 'thank you' to you. You are a fine surgeon and, no doubt, you've had quite extensive schooling, haven't you?"

Sam searched Bill's face for any hint of sarcasm and found none. *He's really changed,* he thought to himself.

"Yes, sir, I have. Thank you, sir," Sam stiffly replied.

"Good, Sam. You did good by me . . . though I didn't always do good by you," Bill said much to everyone's surprise.

Sam glanced around the room and caught the eye of Dr. Garland, who was beginning to put the pieces together. Smiling, he shook his head in amazement. Sam lowered his gaze momentarily, then looked at Bill and answered.

"Mr. Jordan, you did good by me also, sir. Thank you." He meant every word.

Bill Jordan squeezed Sam's hand then released it. Sam stepped back to allow Dr. Garland room to initiate the postoperative care as he carefully paid attention and made notations in the chart.

A great feeling of relief permeated all in the room.

CHAPTER 35

Declaration of Freedom

Bill Jordan's recovery would extend over several weeks if he took heed to the doctor's orders, or several months if he did not. He did not have any intention of resisting the doctor's orders to rest, but he became uneasy at the prospect of having to spend weeks in the North away from his plantation.

"Dr. Garland," Bill drew himself as tall as the physical discomfort would allow him. He assumed a tone of firmness, speaking slowly, "I insist on knowing, respectfully, why I can't possibly travel home by train in a week." He continued as reasonably as he could. "Trains are far more comfortable now, and I can resume postsurgical care in the South quite like I can in the North," he stated.

"Mr. Jordan," Dr. Garland crossed his arms, "you must understand that you cannot possibly afford to take chances with the type of surgery you just had." He tilted his head and continued, "You almost died, you know. This was a desperately serious surgery, and traveling such a distance is simply out of the question until I am able to follow up with you." Dr. Garland waited for the rebuttal that he felt would follow. He didn't have to wait long.

"Dr. Garland, I can rest there like I can here," he snapped, leaning back to ward off the nausea. When it passed he spoke in an irritable manner, "Will this nausea *ever* go away?"

"It will, Mr. Jordan. It hasn't been even a full day since the surgery, but it will pass in time. Rest, soup, and tea are what I prescribe. Ginger tea, to be exact," Dr. Garland said. "But I'm afraid you have to stay here for a while. It will do you good to get some much-needed rest and relaxation." He caught Mrs. Jordan's eye and mouthed, "He can't go home." By the look he gave her, Joan knew it was serious.

Bill looked at Joan, who sided with the doctor.

"Bill, honey, you have to understand that Dr. Garland knows what's best for you. You can't just mosey on back to the plantation like nothing ever happened. You—"

Bill stubbornly continued. "Joan, who will run the plantation for that long without"—he paused to arrange himself more comfortably, then continued—"without somebody messin' something up? I *still* don't have capable folk like I once did."

Sensing that the topic was becoming personal, Dr. Garland excused himself to arrange for another patient's dismissal.

"Doctor's orders, Bill" was all Joan said, as she looked out the small window in the room. She did not want to stir up his emotions over the plantation workers because he might regret his decision to accept his "runaway slaves" as free men and women. She wanted and very much needed closure to this ordeal.

Minutes passed without a word being uttered. Finally, Joan turned around.

Her husband was sound asleep.

Six days later, Bill Jordan was released from the hospital with orders to rest and recuperate.

The Mensuas were grateful for more time to prepare themselves to see Mr. Jordan. The day they spent at the hospital was filled with anxiety although they didn't see Mr. Jordan. Chati could hardly keep calm, Jennie was fidgety, and Basusu and Joe were anxious. When Sam finally told them that it wouldn't be a good time to see Mr. Jordan and that it would be best, in several days, to meet at the house as planned, the family sighed with relief. Only Sally felt a pang of disappointment. Having been so nearby to Mrs. Jordan without being able to see her made Sally feel disheartened.

"Mama," Chati rubbed her mother's back. "It's okay. Missus Jordan will see yo' soon an' den yo' will feel betta. 'Sides, yo' so tired now. It will be betta to see her when yo's not tired." Chati patted Sally's back and stood, signaling the end of the conversation. She joined Basusu and Joe, who were conversing with Sam.

Sally agreed that she could wait a few days longer to see Mrs. Jordan. She wanted to be presentable and rested when she met with her and show her how much good freedom had done for her. Gone were the days of backbreaking labor, predawn risings, and the humiliation of snarls and sneers from some of the guests who frequented the Jordan household. Even still, Mrs. Jordan was kinder to Sally than most slave owners' wives, and Sally was grateful that her life at the plantation had not been unduly harsh.

Her thoughts raced back to the time when Mrs. Jordan allowed Basusu to work and live in the Jordan house so that he and Chati could marry. *Missus Jordan really had to work on Mistah Jordan fo' dat one,* she thought.

Sam's voice caught Sally's attention, and she looked across the room at her grandson who was deeply engaged in a conversation with his parents, explaining the road of recovery for Mr. Jordan. She recalled the time she asked Mrs. Jordan if Basusu and Chati could hold a small ceremony celebrating Sam as their firstborn child. Again, Mrs. Jordan had to work hard on Sally's behalf. *She was kin' to me.*

Sally's eyes misted as she thought about the pleasurable times they shared even though they were not on equal footing with each other. Upon arriving in the North, it took Sally some months to finally readjust to life outside the plantation. Although seven years had passed and she gained a new level of confidence in her freed state, she had mixed feelings about seeing Mrs. Jordan again.

"Time to go, Mama," Chati called as the rest of the family headed out the door. Sally inhaled deeply and rose from her seat. Retrieving her coat and hat, she exited the reception room.

The family reunion was scheduled a week after Mr. Jordan's release from the hospital, and the day had finally arrived. Both families were anxious but not nearly as anxious as Basusu. Pacing the living room, his thoughts ran wild. *Whad if Mistah Jordan ain't changed his min'? Whad if he still mad wid us?* Basusu swallowed hard and glanced at Jennie who was seated on a sofa, reading a book. Her lips moved as her eyes danced across the pages, and every now and then, Basusu saw her smile as she conquered a new word.

She can read, he thought. *All de chilun' can read an' write. Dere ain't notin' dey can't do 'cause dey got some learnin' now.*

Suddenly, Jennie looked up from her book. She looked straight at her father and saw fear etched in his face.

"Papa, whad's wrong?" she asked.

"Notin', chile. Jus' watchin' yo' read."

"It's a good book, Papa. Really," she answered, still uncertain of the dilemma.

"I know dat. Yo's a good girl, Jennie. Jus' like yo' mama . . . an' like mine too." Basusu blinked back tears.

Jennie rose from the sofa and approached her father. She searched his face, uttered a quick prayer, and posed the question again.

"Papa, whad's wrong?"

Basusu didn't want to alarm her, but he had to tell her the truth.

"Jennie, I don' know dat Mistah Jordan will be happy to see us 'cause yo' an' dem boys ain't no dummies. Yo' smart an' yo' know how he is 'bout dat."

Jennie looked confused.

"Oh . . . I rememba dat you don' really know 'bout how he is, 'cause you was jus' a chile when we ran. But I know how dat man is, how he make people do, an' feel, an' . . . ," Basusu ranted on.

"Papa," Jennie softly whispered. Basusu quieted at his daughter's calming appeal.

Jennie embraced her father's hands in her own and looked up. When his eyes met hers, she hugged him.

"God just tol' me to remin' you dat it's okay, dat He's watchin' out for you. You'll be brave when it's time, and Mistah Jordan will be okay too. Don' worry about it."

Jennie released her father when a knock on the door caused them both to jump. They heard a distant exchange of voices, then Chati exclaimed, "Greg! Yo' made it!"

Both Jennie and Basusu bolted from the room to greet him.

Cathy and Mary spent all morning and the better part of afternoon preparing dinner for their guests. It was just under an hour before the Mensuas were expected to arrive, and this was the first time since morning that they were able to just sit and relax.

Joan tended to her husband throughout the day and tried to lend a hand in the kitchen when she could, but both Cathy and Mary insisted that she just give her attention to Bill and keep him calm and comfortable. Now all three ladies took a break.

"How's he doing?" Cathy asked.

"He's not nauseous anymore, but he is still sore and tender. He doesn't have much of an appetite either."

"He will when Sally brings her pies over," Mary remarked. Sally had insisted that she make several pies along with a special pot of stew for Mr. Jordan.

Joan chuckled, "I hope so. To be honest with you, I think he's nervous."

Cathy and Mary laughed aloud. "Nervous? Bill nervous? What makes you think that?" Cathy asked.

"Well," Joan began, "I overheard him talking with Jerry, and he was asking all sorts of questions about Base and the family . . . kind of like he's not sure what to expect or something." Joan shrugged and took a sip of iced tea.

"Mother, were you eavesdropping again?" Mary teased.

Joan swallowed her tea and swatted her daughter. "Who, me?" she asked, feigning innocence. She continued, pressing a napkin primly against her mouth. "Well, missy, if I was eavesdroppin', it was for good reason," she drawled.

"What reason is that?" Mary asked.

"Obviously, so we would have a good conversation piece as we wait for our guests to arrive!"

Cathy and Joan burst into laughter as Mary shook her head.

The Mensuas arrived at Jerry and Cathy's front door ten minutes prior to the expected hour. As Jennie prepared to ring the doorbell, Chati caught her wrist.

"Let's pray first," she said, signaling to Basusu to do the honor.

Clearing his throat, he began to pray in hushed tones.

"Fatha God, Yo' brought us dis far an' now we are dis close to de Jordans. Be wid us an' help Mistah Jordan to have peace wid us. Tank Yo', Jesus. Amen."

Jennie rang the bell.

The pleasant chime alerted the Jordans that their guests had arrived. Mary made a dash for the door and threw it wide open.

"Jennie!" she exclaimed, grabbing her friend by the arm and ushering her inside, oblivious to the other family members who remained on the doorstep. "Mother, Jennie is here!" she called.

Jerry was hot on his sister's trail. He greeted the Mensuas and apologized for Mary's outburst.

"She's beside herself," he chuckled. "Please come in and make yourselves comfortable."

As the family crossed the threshold one by one, they felt as though they crossed a great divide. Here they were again, seven years later, in the presence of the Jordans, only this time they were free in every sense of the word. Free to live. Free to think. Free to dream. Free to face the bondages of yesteryear.

Basusu held Chati's hand firmly as his eyes searched the room for Mr. Jordan. Half expecting to see the familiar tall figure enter the room, commanding attention, he was taken aback when his eyes fell on the humble figure seated in a wing chair. Bill Jordan's features were noticeably marked by the tumultuous events of the years; but the piercing gray eyes still signaled strength and authority, although subdued.

Mary and Jennie could be heard whispering "girl talk," while Cathy arranged cups and saucers that were not in need of arranging. Sally stood next to Sam, Greg, and Joe, waiting for Mrs. Jordan to enter the room as she had done hundreds of times in years past.

Basusu silently prayed for the uneasiness in the air to be dispelled. When the silence became strained, Jerry spoke up.

"Base, Chati, come and have a seat," he motioned to the sofa located across from his father. The couple followed Jerry to the sofa and slowly sat down. As soon as they were seated, Jerry scurried back to Sally and the boys. Taking her by the arm, he motioned to Cathy to come and get the pies and pot of stew that she brought. Then he said, "Sally, you can do whatever you like . . . go into the kitchen, or have a seat, or—"

"Or join me for a cup of coffee," Joan finished. Having just entered the room, Mrs. Jordan briskly walked toward Sally, pausing only to feel her husband's forehead for any sign of a fever and to acknowledge Basusu and Chati with a firm squeeze on their shoulder and a genuine smile. She reached Sally, embraced her quickly then released her.

When the women were face to face, Sally lowered her head and began to cry, her tears freely flowing. After a few minutes, she began to speak.

"Missus Jordan . . . please fo'give me fo'"—she paused to catch her breath—"fo' lettin' yo' take dat train 'lone. I worried 'bout yo' so bad, but . . . ." She managed to continue, her shaky voice barely audible, "I . . . I . . . had to try fo' freedom, ma'am."

The large figure of Sally failed to match the frailty of her disposition. Everyone in the room was quiet, even Jennie and Mary. Jerry joined Sam, Greg, and Joe by the door while Mr. Jordan inhaled deeply and waited for his wife's response.

Joan held Sally's hand in her own and spoke to her, although Sally wouldn't meet her gaze. "Sally, that was a frightening ride home. Indeed, it was," Joan began, pausing for Sally to retrieve a napkin that Cathy offered and wipe her tears. "But I never held it against you. Life on the plantation was hard, yes it was, but I—I mean *we*—came to understand your family's choice to flee. Isn't that right, Bill?" Joan's eyes pleaded with her husband to support her.

All eyes fell on Bill. Even Basusu and Chati, who up until this time had avoided direct eye contact with Mr. Jordan, looked at him in expectation of an answer.

Bill scanned the room and looked in amazement at the people before him. Yes, they were the same people that served him and his household for many years; however, they were now free to live their lives. His eyes fell on Sam and his throat became dry. *That young man saved my life when he had a right not to,* he thought. Setting aside his pride, Bill sipped some water and motioned for Jerry to help him stand. He had something to say, and sitting down was not the way to say it.

When he finally stood, Basusu saw the Bill Jordan that he remembered and, feeling it was appropriate, stood to his feet as well.

"I want to say something to the Mensua family in the presence of everyone here," Bill announced. He looked at Basusu, then to Chati, who was still seated, then back to Basusu.

He began, "Base, you were my best driver and worker. Your whole family worked as a team; and to this day, no one has served Joan and me as well as you, Chati, and Sally. No one." He shifted his weight, then continued, "And when you escaped, I could hardly stand the thought of it. I was angry for a long, long time and not too pleasant to be around, right Joan?" Joan chuckled, nodding in agreement.

"You see, Base, I felt wronged because my wife was left all alone in this big city to manage by herself. Anything could've happened to her." Bill stared at Basusu who met his gaze. He stole a look at Chati, then continued, "You've got a wife, so I know that you understand how I felt." Basusu simply nodded.

Bill stepped closer to Basusu with the aid of Jerry. When he was close enough, he extended his hand. Basusu took it, his gaze never leaving Mr. Jordan's.

"Base, I wish you no harm, no harm at all. I've been through a lot in these last few years, and I've come to realize something." He looked up as if acknowledging God, then continued, "A man never knows what will unfold in his life." Casting a glance toward Sam, he said, "When my life was hanging in the balance, your son could've let it go . . . but he didn't. *He saved my life.* He demonstrated character and courage. He gets that from you, Base. I know you're proud of him . . . and so am I." Turning to Sam, he said, "Again I say, thank you, Dr. Mensua." Sam nodded and smiled.

Basusu started to speak, but Bill held up his hand.

"Got one more thing to say. This one's real important." All eyes were on him.

Taking a deep breath, he announced, "Be it known unto all men present and absent, born and unborn, known and unknown, that Base and his family are free from this time forth. Let the same be written and signed by William Jordan . . . and be sure Bobby and Tim get a copy of it." With that, Bill Jordan shuffled back to his chair and sat down to enjoy the rest of the evening.

Chati caught her breath and stood with her husband. Basusu nodded and beamed proudly. All the years of turmoil from being ripped from his family in Africa to escaping to the North and finally facing Mr. Jordan signaled the end of one phase of his life and the beginning of another. He squeezed Chati and lightly kissed her forehead.

Joan and Sally rejoiced and enjoyed a cup of coffee together, shared as friends. Joan caught her husband's eye and mouthed, "That was wonderful." Bill blinked back tears and smiled in response.

The Jordans and Mensuas expressed their happiness among each other; and Sam, Greg, and Joe thanked Mr. Jordan, each informing him how their lives and careers were coming along. Jennie and Mary were especially elated and chattered merrily as friends without any limitations.

Suddenly, Jennie remembered the piano in the corner of the room. It was covered with several sheets and seldom played. Excusing herself from Mary, she wandered into the kitchen and approached Cathy, who was pouring herself a glass of tea. She offered a glass to Jennie, who declined.

"Miss Cathy, may I play the piano please?" she whispered in Cathy's ear.

"Certainly, Jennie. I wasn't aware that you can play," she replied.

"I've taught myself some," Jennie said nonchalantly. Approaching the piano, Jennie carefully laid back the sheets, uncovered the keys, and tested a few. Everyone looked to see where the source of music came from.

Jennie mounted the stool and like a steady flowing stream went through a few harmonies. Everyone, especially Mr. and Mrs. Jordan, was in awe of the melodic composition that filled the air. Totally consumed with her music, Jennie never once paused to acknowledge the "oohs" and "aahs" from her audience. Then she stopped playing and tilted her head, her eyes closed as if in deep contemplation. Her fingers began to move, and as was fitting, Jennie played "Amazing Grace."

The music played into the wee hours of the morning, celebrating a dream come true.

The End